CW00552652

THE BEACH HOUSE

NINA MANNING

Boldwood

First published in Great Britain in 2023 by Boldwood Books Ltd.

Copyright © Nina Manning, 2023

Cover Design by Head Design Ltd

Cover Photography: Shutterstock

A CIP catalogue record for this book is available from the British Library.

Paperback ISBN 978-1-80426-568-0

Large Print ISBN 978-1-80426-569-7

Hardback ISBN 978-1-80426-570-3

Ebook ISBN 978-1-80426-567-3

Kindle ISBN 978-1-80426-566-6

Audio CD ISBN 978-1-80426-574-1

MP3 CD ISBN 978-1-80426-575-8

Digital audio download ISBN 978-1-80426-573-4

Boldwood Books Ltd
23 Bowerdean Street
London SW6 3TN
www.boldwoodbooks.com

For Sarah, Geraldine and Sue. The best booky gals. I love ya x

PROLOGUE

The Beach House sits on a cliff overlooking the sea. A sanctuary, a retreat. Somewhere to come to escape the endless madness and feel secure. You can walk around the house, feel the space that surrounds you, yet also feel safe within its walls. The Beach House is a holiday home, but a home, nonetheless. But under the floorboards and between each brick, secrets linger. They cling to the curtains and are soaked deep within the fabric of every sofa and mattress. They echo in the hallway and corridors. People come and go; visitors, family, unaware of what went on, of the secrets that are tightly contained between the walls.

The Beach House has seen so much already and just when it thinks it can't take any more, four women arrive, each one of them harbouring secrets that could harm the other ones. But the old house can do nothing, except sit back and watch, as it always does.

1

NICOLE

She had used the word *slut*. Who said *slut* these days? Not anyone Nicole knew and certainly not a woman on their own podcast for goodness' sake. She didn't feel like herself recently, in fact she would say she had been out of sorts for a while now. She couldn't put a date on it, but if she had to – and if she was going to be really honest – it all began when she had been about eight, this feeling of uncertainty. A notion that she had forgotten to do something. That feeling you get as an adult when you leave the house in a rush and you aren't sure if you have your phone or if you turned off the iron. She had tried to suffocate it, to pretend it wasn't there, or that maybe it was part of her personality, who she was.

She knew she shouldn't have said it.

Slut.

The word hurt her heart. It was harsh; brutal. But it had just slipped out.

Audrey had been sitting opposite her, looking as pristine and glorious as the beginning of a spring day as they recorded another episode of their hit podcast show *Laying It Bare*. What had been a typical Instagram live for them quickly dissolved into a disaster. And because the podcast was being recorded live (whose idea that had been, she had no clue – it had seemed like an absolute perfect opportunity to really 'lay it bare'), they couldn't edit it out. Well, Nicole had insisted, and it was her studio, her podcast, her money. To remove it now would cause a stir, it would look like they had made a mistake, and Nicole didn't want anyone to see that she had made a mistake. That was unthinkable. Better to keep it in and forget the whole thing. People would move past it soon enough, and then the next episode would be out. Nicole had already got great ideas for that one, which would make everyone roar with laughter, the nasty little word would be long forgotten.

She hadn't meant it, not in the way it came out anyway. But how could she explain that to the listeners? She couldn't, because she could barely even explain it to herself.

'Just look at the comments,' Gram her boyfriend had said to her over dinner the night the podcast went live. 'You need to accept that what you've done could have catastrophic consequences for the business.'

The weeks had passed, and the figures were in. Followers lost on socials and the podcast ratings were down on the months even prior to the 'slut comment'. What was happening? Matt, the sound engineer, had tried to explain it to her, but she couldn't concentrate. She was always half somewhere else, in that place where she went to shake off the feeling that she had left something behind. She had launched into the *Laying It Bare* podcast without any thought, planning or preparation. She and her co-host Audrey had met a few years ago, when Nicole had leased the building and installed the pods to let out for recordings. Audrey was her secret weapon; ex-supermodel and all-round bloody superwoman. But now everything was in ruins. By using that word, she had undone everything that the podcast represented. She had taken it too far, crossed the invisible moral line.

As well as Audrey, there were two others on Nicole's small team – Margo and Paisley – and they were all different in many ways. There was surely not one thing that bound the four of them except The Studio, which Nicole knew they all loved, and it had quickly become an important part of each of their lives, none more so than Nicole's. She needed it in a way that was purely personal to her. She was sure the same was for Paisley, the studio receptionist, who dealt with the everyday admin, checking in the pod users and anything else in between. Paisley had a quiet dedication to her job that was unlike anything Nicole had witnessed in the twenty years she had been working. Nicole knew that Paisley would be looking for a pay rise soon, a promotion of sorts. But behind that pretty little demeanour Nicole knew there was a woman who would stop at nothing to get where she wanted to be; she was the type of person who was ready to step in someone else's shoes without hesitation. Margo, introverted yet able to turn her hand to any task, was Nicole's personal assistant. Then there was Audrey, a star in her own right. Nicole couldn't deny Audrey was the only thing holding the podcast together. Audrey had a huge following on social media, and the show's fans came to listen to her. Nicole was a mere nobody in comparison.

And now things were starting to go wrong... Nicole felt she had done the right thing by taking on premises just outside of central London and she figured people would travel for great-quality audio studios where they could record adverts, podcasts or audiobooks. Perhaps she should have thought that part through more. They did come, but not in the masses that Nicole had expected them to. And as she started to think about it, which she had been a lot recently, she realised that *Laying It Bare* was not an original name for a podcast and what were they talking about was not very original.

They weren't covering any subjects that hadn't been talked about a thousand times already.

Nicole adjusted her headphones, the thoughts of what was to come, where she was headed with her colleagues creeping into her consciousness. She knew they would be wrapping up soon and Audrey would open her phone and begin her usual post-show tweets and other social stuff. Things that made no sense to Nicole. She could manage the odd tweet at an absolute push if she really had to, but Instagram, TikTok, she kept well away from it. She knew she needed to be seen to make this thing work, but Nicole had tried to remain as anonymous as possible for a long time. She didn't like to flaunt herself around on the social channels. She knew she could be found if someone really wanted to find her.

Nicole often thought back to this time last year when her life was up in the air and she had no idea what was going to fall next and cause more damage. Luckily, nothing did, and instead, out of the blue, she was invited onto a local news channel to speak on a feature about mental decluttering. During the interview, she happened to mention her Instagram handle, and the next thing she knew, Audrey Westwood had got in touch and asked if she wanted to collaborate. Twelve months later, here they were. No conversation was off the table. Menopause, mental health, sex, drugs. Honesty was what drew the listeners in. But it still wasn't enough.

Audrey was chatting away opposite her, some anecdote about a modelling contract that had taken a sour turn.

'I was the only woman in the room. I would say there were about twenty men.'

Nicole was sure she had heard this story before. But she nodded along, played her part, began to think of the right question to ask next. Audrey was lining her up with some good fodder here; this next episode could be a hit if she got it just right. She needed to try to steer this conversation towards something that would grasp the attention of the listeners enough that they wanted to share it and talk about it with others.

'At what point did you begin to feel uncomfortable, nervous?' Nicole leant forwards, hoping that the sudden drop in the tone of her voice would make her sound intrigued, add some depth and drama to the content. She already knew what Audrey's response would be.

'I wasn't nervous. Or scared. Not once. This is my job; this is what I do. I parade around in front of lots of people. I don't feel intimidated by men. I've felt more intimidated being in a room alone with Naomi Campbell than I have in a room with multiple males.'

Audrey flapped her hand around as she spoke.

'I knew what I looked like that day,' Audrey continued. 'I was a sex object. That was the whole purpose of the photo shoot. I was selling underwear that would turn men on enough that they would buy it for their wives or partners.'

Audrey was settled into the expensive chair that Nicole had sourced for the podcast. Non-squeak, yet you could sink down into them. Nicole had a well-earned nap in one once. If the whole business failed, those chairs were coming with her.

Audrey carried on, setting the scene, labelling each of the male journalists in that room with a characteristic, a tic or something they were wearing.

'By the end of that session, I was giving them tips on how to woo the significant other in their life. We talked dinner dates and the importance of an egalitarian relationship, where the woman feels respected and not just seen as the person who does all the housework, cooking and cleaning. It was magic.'

'And did they all seem to take on your advice?' Nicole kept the conversation going, liking the way it was headed.

'I would say fifty per cent of them seemed to have a lightbulb moment. It was like, "Oh, so if I cook and clean after myself, my relationship might be a bit easier?" They were genuinely surprised.'

'And the other fifty per cent?'

'Either they already knew and were set, or they didn't care and had no intention of changing.'

Nicole felt a wave of relief. This was pretty good content; this was something women of all ages could relate to. She could count on Audrey to keep their head above water.

They were sinking and she didn't know how to save them. Things ticked over. But the reality was, these days, things needed to explode if they were going to succeed. Something like a podcast with Audrey Westwood should have been a total hit. Gram had said he was behind her, but she knew that he too saw her as a failure. Perhaps that was why he had suddenly become very distant. More so than he had been for the last few years. They'd had their problems. The baby conversation being the main source of resentment between them; he wanted children and she didn't like to think about it. But these last few months, she had felt him slipping away.

'And that I'm afraid is all we have time for this week on *Laying It Bare*. Please do join us again next time when we will be speaking to a sleep expert. So anyone with any insomnia issues, do get in touch via email at the usual address or through any of our social channels with your questions. And remember that rating the podcast is the best way to help us get heard by more listeners. Thanks again!' Audrey wrapped up as she always did. Nicole was fine with that. Let Audrey have her moment.

Audrey slipped off her headphones, pushed her chair back and crossed her legs, long limbs that were the very essence of who she was.

Nicole clocked a white Gucci suitcase against the wall and then looked at Audrey.

'The size of it!' she said.

Audrey shrugged. 'Well, I thought to myself, if I must.' Audrey rolled her eyes dramatically as she made what must have been the fiftieth joke about not coming on the last-minute working holiday that Nicole had organised.

Nicole had only known Audrey for just under a year and this was to be their first holiday away together. Albeit the trip was primarily to brainstorm ideas, what better way to get to know someone than on holiday? Then a tingle crept up her back and her neck, making her shudder as she thought about the reality of being there with her colleagues and the significance of the date that was fast approaching. It was going to be okay, she assured herself. But she had barely slept last night. She was feeling fragile, as though she needed an extra layer on.

'Bit chilly, isn't it, with that air con?' Audrey, who must have seen Nicole's involuntary shiver, picked up the white remote control and pointed it at the slim machine on the ceiling. The temperature of the room immediately rose. Nicole smiled at Audrey for her perceptiveness.

'Another great show, you two.' Matt walked across the room from his mixing desk in the corner.

Audrey smiled excessively.

'Always eager to please,' she said with a wink and a shimmy of her shoulders. Audrey could flirt for England; men and women alike, they all just seemed to melt at her words, the way Matt did every time. His face flushed slightly, but his eyes twinkled. It amazed Nicole how one woman could elicit different kinds of uncontrollable behaviours in people. She didn't class it as a skill, as such, it was just something innate that people like Audrey were born with. She was a people magnet. Nicole had witnessed it hundreds of times in the last year or so since she had known Audrey. The handful of times she had seen Gram change his entire persona when Audrey graced him with some of her finest lines had unsettled her. But she had smiled through it; an inane grin that told Audrey and everyone else in the vicinity that she was secure in her relationship, that she found Audrey's comments cute but entirely unthreatening.

'I'm all set for the girls' weekend,' Audrey said to Matt, gesturing to the suitcase again.

Matt followed her gaze and raised his eyebrows comically.

'Got a body in there?' he said.

'Only everything I need for this one.' Audrey ran her hands over the top half of her curves, and Matt shook his head, his face flushing beetroot.

Nicole felt herself deflate. Audrey always looked on the bright side, always ready to turn any situation into fun. Nicole had made it clear to Audrey that things were teetering, that she needed to get back in control. She had made it clear there was a real purpose to this trip and so she had made a last-minute decision for them to all retreat to her family holiday home in Dorset, The Beach House. She didn't want to shell out on accommodation for them all – the accounts wouldn't stretch to a Holiday Inn down the road in their current state – yet she needed them all in the same place for several days to make any dent in the problem. She would have been there anyway this weekend, more so than any weekend, and so here she was, killing two birds with one stone.

The Beach House had always had a hold on Nicole. It had been the holiday home that she had spent so many days, months and years of her life in, and despite the memories that crippled her daily, like an abused child who always returned to their primary caregiver, Nicole would always go back there to seek sanctuary. For solace. She would find it, but she had to take the other emotions that came with it. And in the next few hours, she would be home again. She only hoped this time, the old place would be kind to her.

Because she had a job to do, and that wasn't just trying to save The Studio.

Nicole looked over at Audrey again as she continued to embarrass Matt without a care. Her visit home wasn't just business; it was also personal.

2

MARGO

Margo hated packing to go away. She laid her clothes on the bed and shook her head in dismay at the dismal ensembles. She wasn't a shopper. Not like Nicole or Paisley, and certainly not like Audrey. Oh Lord, Audrey. How was Margo going to survive three days and nights under the same roof as a supermodel? Margo scoped Audrey's social media accounts regularly; the woman was a goddess, there were no two ways about it. Every piece of clothing she wore looked brand new and immaculate, and everything always fitted her curves perfectly.

Margo had thought about a little shopping spree prior to the trip but had run out of time. Her work always came before any other normal activity that other people enjoyed. Margo worked hard, but she also loved working. It was, you could say, her life. Which was why this trip away that Nicole had organised hadn't brought her out in hives. Normally, the very thought of socialising made Margo jittery, but she knew it was time to brainstorm ideas for the podcast and the business, as Margo was also fully aware of how much trouble The Studio was in. And if The Studio wasn't there, then Margo was out of a job, and if she was out of a job, then what else did she really have? Working at The Studio suited her entire personality. Jobs were like romantic partners: you only ever got a couple of chances at finding 'the one'. And her position at The Studio, was her true love. She would do everything she could to keep it afloat.

She wasn't thrilled about the weekend away, because it was still out of her comfort zone and there would be times when she would have to stop talking about work and look as though she were relaxing and enjoying a glass of wine, but stranger things had happened, Margo thought to herself as she piled her conservative wardrobe into a suitcase that hadn't seen daylight for over six years. That was the last time she had been on a holiday. And she hadn't even left the country. Things had got worse with her dad. He needed her now all the time. Work was the one thing she had that not only kept her sane but helped pay for the carers. She hadn't meant to let home life and work consume her and it wasn't that Nicole was high maintenance, but she had said on more than one occasion that she simply couldn't live without her, and so when the texts came through late at night, asking her to engage with something on social media, of course, Margo would answer them. She had been Nicole's personal assistant for a year, but she still hadn't worked out why Nicole was so averse to being on Instagram and why she only hung around behind the brand of The Studio.

Margo peered out of the window to assess the weather. Should she pack another jumper? Should she put on a thicker cardigan for the journey? Her attention was drawn to a parked car a little way along the street, and she thought she noticed a sudden movement from the person sitting in the driver's seat. They had pulled the visor down, though, so she couldn't see their face. Margo felt her gut tighten. She knew what date had been and gone and her eyes had been on the road outside her house for the last few days. It was just typical that Nicole needed her at a time when she really needed to be here, keeping an eye on the house and making sure it and her father were safe. She had been expecting a knock on the door any day now.

Suddenly, a shout and a loud smash sent Margo running for the door and hurtling down the stairs.

'What happened?' she cried, her voice high and stretched. 'What the hell, Dad?' She stood at the entrance to the kitchen and looked at her eighty-three-year-old father standing amongst the debris of a smashed cup and saucer. He eyed her for a second, then bent to pick it up. Margo leapt forwards.

'No!' she screamed, and her father almost fell back against the work surface.

'Shit,' Margo yelped and lifted her foot up and saw she had stepped in a piece of china; a thin slither had wedged itself in her foot. She pulled it out and winced at the pain. She should really wash and dress that, but she would be late. At least it was her left foot, which wouldn't be doing any work in her automatic car.

'Honestly, Dad. Siobhan will be here soon – can you please not touch anything until then?'

Margo's dad looked on with bewilderment.

'Eric!' Margo tried again, loud enough that it brought her dad back into the room from wherever he had just been in his mind. 'I need you to just sit down and wait until Siobhan gets here, then she will look after you. Do you think you can do that?' Margo took her dad's arm and escorted him around the broken crockery and into the dining room.

'Here, sit down, I'll make you a cup of tea.' Margo felt the familiar swell of guilt rising through her body whenever she got cross with her father. It was, of course, the onset of dementia, but she had yet to fully address it. She just didn't have the time. She brought in help occasionally and made sure he was comfortable but leaving him alone in the day was getting more and more dangerous. She needed to employ someone full-time, but the cost of that was just too much for her to take on right now, and with The Studio in financial jeopardy, she couldn't just ask Nicole for a pay rise, even though she had been there a year now, and she was overdue her promised twelve-month pay rise.

She began preparing a pot of tea for her dad and whilst the kettle boiled, she swept up the debris from the kitchen floor, making sure she got in all the corners in case her dad walked in with bare feet.

She carried the tea with a milk jug and a bowl of sugar to the dining room, where her father was still sitting, tapping his right fingers on the table and staring out of the window. Margo always left the curtains open here, as it looked out onto the main street, meaning Eric could have a view out into the world from his seat here as well as from his spot in the living room which looked out over the small, unkempt garden, even though he rarely looked out of the window in there because he was usually glued to the TV.

Margo went to the window and strained to look up and down the road. She couldn't see Siobhan's car anywhere. It was almost two, and Siobhan was usually early by at least five minutes. Margo needed to leave as soon as she arrived. It was almost a three-hour drive to Nicole's beach house, and she had wanted to give herself plenty of time to arrive. Dinner was at seven and Margo liked to have time to acclimatise when she arrived somewhere new.

Her armpits began to prickle with sweat. Was Siobhan going to turn up? Had she been delayed, or couldn't make it any more, meaning Margo would have to stay behind? A part of her wondered if she would be thankful not to have to go this weekend; if the absence of a carer for her father was all she needed to get out of having to be sociable with the likes of Audrey; if she could just stay here where it was safe, where she could keep a personal eye on her dad and not leave him vulnerable. Margo's stomach dropped again at the thought of leaving her father. But she needed to think about finishing packing if she was going to make it at all today. She cursed herself for not investing in some outfits and for not making the time to shop properly.

She raced back upstairs, finished throwing a few last essentials in and then dragged her suitcase downstairs. She glanced a look at herself in the mirror. Jeans, a nice top and boots. The go-to standard outfit she had been rocking for almost twenty years. She thought about the look she used to wear. It wasn't such a long time ago, was it? She used to take so many more risks with what she wore. Now it was all about feeling comfortable. Safe. It was all about just blending in to bring some confidence. And to not attract too much attention. But despite the clothes she wore to give her that feeling, she felt anything but confident. Putting her trust in Siobhan had taken a lot.

Finally, the doorbell rang, and Margo breathed a little easier. She swung the door open, but there, in the place where she had expected to see Siobhan, was someone else. A tall woman who looked Spanish or Italian, her hair scraped back in what was seemingly the signature carer low bun and wearing a uniform from the caring agency that she had hired Siobhan from several weeks ago.

'Hello, I'm Clarissa.' She smiled and flashed brilliant white teeth. There was a hint of a European accent there, one that had been lost over time.

'You're not Siobhan,' Margo said flatly, her stomach churning as she mulled over all the issues this woman's presence now raised. She would have to go through her father's routine and show her where everything was in the house. Should she even choose to let her in? She hadn't been given any notice from the agency. She had a good mind to call them, but she was running late.

'I'm sorry about that.' Clarissa looked a little perturbed by Margo's directness, and the smile was almost lost for a second before she brought it back. 'Siobhan is ill and so I was asked to step in. I am very familiar with last-minute jobs, so I am sure—'

'But you don't know my father,' Margo interrupted, 'and just now, he had an accident with the tea, and I'm due to leave any minute – I don't have time to show you everything.' Margo heard the strain in her voice. She took a deep breath. 'This is bad management. I will be speaking with the agency.'

Clarissa stood even taller than she had been, as though she had just taken in a huge breath.

'I can assure you this is normal practice for our agency. If your usual carer is unavailable, we always send someone else to replace them. We pride ourselves on this.' Clarissa looked happy with herself as she said this and because Margo was unfamiliar with caring agencies, she had only been using the service for a month and not because she had wanted to, she felt she had no choice. Her father couldn't be left alone. She couldn't be here every day and night to watch over him. And if she didn't go soon, she was going to be late. If she didn't show up to this meeting, retreat, whatever this was supposed to be, she could be fired. Nicole might let her go because she could barely afford to keep the business afloat as it was.

She stood back so that Clarissa could come into the house.

'Dad's through there,' Margo said, gesturing to the dining room before peering out along the street. The car was still parked on the kerb with someone inside. Did people have nothing better to do than sit in their cars, making others feel unsettled? She closed the door and followed behind Clarissa and watched as the woman fell into her role immediately, asking if Eric needed more hot water for his pot and trying to engage him in conversation about his day so far. It all seemed perfectly fine, but Margo couldn't shake the annoyance. It wasn't convenient to just send someone else. It was a deviation she didn't need right now. But she also needed to be on the work trip. She just needed to get on the road now and hope that she would start to mellow out into the right frame of mind for a weekend away. Margo took a second to assess her emotions, where they were stemming from, why there was a muddle in her mind. She always conjured up her mother's words when she felt this way: '*Untangle that knot of nerves.*' She glanced out of the window again and then back at Clarissa through her doorway of the dining room. She was a professional; she was going to look after her dad in the same way that Siobhan did.

But that was not what was bothering her. She looked at the car again, at the figure in the driver's seat slightly visible but not enough to decipher their features. She felt her gut swirl. Were her instincts right? Should she just go on outside and approach the car? She felt her gut wrench at what might happen whilst she was away. Margo broke her gaze away from the window, her mind was made up. She had to take the chance, she had to go to work.

Margo went into the dining room, gave her father an awkward hug, which was not reciprocated and then smiled uneasily at Clarissa. Margo scribbled her number down on a Post-it note along with the address of The Beach House and stuck it on the bureau in the corner of the dining room next to the window.

Then she backed out of the door, carrying her suitcase and placing it in the boot of her car. She sat in the driver's seat and looked back at the house. She could see Clarissa moving about through the dining-room window. Margo took a deep breath and tried to think like someone who could drive away and forget about things; out of sight out of mind. But that was never going to be Margo. There was too much at stake here. What was she thinking going away on such a whim? She hadn't been able to say no to Nicole. She tried to look back along the street to see if the person was still in the car, but her view was restricted.

Margo swiped at the satnav to tap in the postcode for The Beach House. Three hours and fifteen minutes from Putney. She hoped she wouldn't catch the school run or workers leaving early. As she pulled away, thoughts of her father and the potential danger she was leaving him in were replaced by a memory from a few weeks ago at The Studio's first birthday party. What she had seen haunted her dreams as much as the worries about her father. Margo worked pretty closely with Nicole most days, but this long weekend was going to be something else; she was going to be with Nicole twenty-four seven for three nights and that made the thing she had witnessed even harder to bear. How could she look Nicole in the eye knowing what she knew? And for the next three hours, that was all that would be playing over and over in her mind.

3

PAISLEY

The app was open on Paisley's phone. She had closed the map once she had arrived at The Beach House, and there it was, open on her screen. The damn app, always there, taunting her, reminding her of her failings. Oh well, she thought, she may as well use it one last time before she stepped over the threshold. For once she was there, inside The Beach House, things were going to change. She would never need to use gambling apps again. She had run out of options. All but one remained.

Even though Paisley knew what the word *addict* meant, she would still never attribute it to herself. God no. She knew she was in trouble; she knew she needed to stop, but she wasn't an addict. Addicts were those people who showed up to groups in cold stark village halls on a Tuesday night, drank insipid tea and took turns to monologue about their sad little journeys. No, Paisley had thought a lot about this, and she had decided that was not her. She was just a young woman who opened an app on her phone and spent some money from time to time. Well, that 'time to time' had been every day, and now she'd maxed out. She didn't have bailiffs banging down her door, but soon the loans would need to be paid off.

She pressed the button for one more spin, she held her breath and closed her eyes. This would be the one, this would be the spin that would bring her the win that she needed to get herself sorted. She was somewhere new, she was by the sea, her luck would surely change this time, she had been on a losing streak for far too long. This was how it was supposed to be, in her car, in a beautiful part of the country, a positive future ahead of her. She would open her eyes, see the stunning surroundings again, and then look down at her win. It was meant to be this way.

She opened her eyes, and instead of looking at the surroundings first, her eyes fell straight to her smartphone, to the app, and to the news that made her want to rip herself out of her skin. She let out a guttural primal scream. No tears came, just a slow release of rage. She stayed still for a little while, the tears didn't come, they never did, so she had to wait for the echo of the scream to subside in her head, then she could take a deep breath and move on.

Several minutes later, Paisley was still sitting in her car. To a passer-by, the scene would look perfectly innocent, as though nothing had happened to her. Paisley was adept at hiding her emotions, the lack of tears helped. Teaching yourself not to cry from a very young age was a skill not many could perfect. But that first humiliating sports day as a five-year-old girl had brought a tsunami of tears that made it seem as though the entire school were laughing at her. In hindsight, she knew it was just the bullies, but it was enough to make her wipe away those tears and learn how to stop them coming any time she felt frustrated, humiliated or just plain old desperate. The sting in her eyes would be fierce but she would manage to stop the flow.

She stared at The Beach House, a white building with a grey

slated roof and a long, steep driveway, surrounded by a clear aura of cloudless blue. Paisley couldn't work out where the sky ended and where the sea began. How did someone get so lucky to have a house like this in their family? How did Nicole get so lucky? Nicole had told them all about how the house had been bought by her parents in the eighties. She'd holidayed here as a child, and over the years her parents had done it up until they split. Nicole, her mother and her stepfather came here for occasional weekends and Christmases, and now Nicole used it for her own leisure. When she organised the working weekend, it was obvious this was where it would take place. Paisley supposed it suited Nicole perfectly because everything did. That was exactly what Nicole was about. Paisley felt that familiar surge of rage. Nicole, at the age of thirty-three, had managed to cement such an ideal life. Her own business, a nice pad in London with her boyfriend, Gram, and now Paisley was finally seeing The Beach House with her own eyes, the place she had heard mentioned occasionally when Nicole was on a call presumably to her mum, or Gram. It had always seemed like an enigma; *The Beach House*, words that she'd heard in whispered phone calls and hushed conversations. Apart from Nicole, Paisley didn't know anyone rich enough to own a house this size and not live in it permanently. Paisley swallowed down the anger and left it alone where it would fester in the pit of her stomach with all the other discarded emotions.

Three nights did feel like a rather long time to be shacked up in a house on the edge of nowhere with three other women she didn't know particularly well. Well, she did know them, but only in the professional sense based on the odd after-work drink. And then, of course, there had been the party six weeks ago. Paisley could never forget that. She had seen a side of some of her colleagues that she'd never seen before. That night changed everything.

But still, a holiday away was how you really got to know someone, wasn't it? Paisley guessed this was the reason for the get-together in the first place. Aside from the fact that they did have an inordinate amount of work-related issues to bash out – there was never enough time at The Studio to truly socialise because people kept coming and going and there was always so much happening with recordings. Plus Paisley spent a lot of time talking very quietly so as not to disturb anyone.

Paisley stepped out of the car, the sea breeze swept across her cheeks and she felt a sudden rush of dizziness and her stomach churned. She took three long, deep breaths and stood up straight, looking up at the building in front of her. There were no other cars there, so she was the first to arrive. But that was how she had wanted it. It was important for her to get her bearings. Paisley always liked to be the first to arrive for anything, but to be here first at Nicole's felt even more important on this occasion. She felt as though she needed to familiarise herself, set her roots down before anyone else arrived.

The Beach House sat upon a hill. A path ran past it and continued along the cliff face before disappearing from Paisley's view from the bottom of the driveway. She glanced to the left where a cluster of trees ran parallel to the house. From where Paisley stood, the sun caught her eye through a gap in the foliage and for a second she was sure she saw someone, a woman. She blinked firmly a few times and lifted her hand to block the sun, but there was no one there. Paisley watched the space for a minute, enjoying the smattering of heat. She saw that the garden was raised above the house at the back and a bench was situated just to the side: the perfect little suntrap. Paisley thought she would get herself settled and sit out with one of the herbal teas that she had brought with her and, despite the coastal breeze, make the most of the afternoon sun. She had brought quite a few extra food items with her, even though she had heard Nicole had hired in a chef for the weekend.

She liked to be prepared. And despite feeling a little out of sorts, Paisley was prepared. For everything that this weekend was about to bring.

Nicole had told everyone the code for the lockbox so that whoever arrived first could let themselves in. Paisley felt a swell of empowerment as she found the lockbox on the side of the house by the bins, and typed in the code. The box flipped open and she took out the key and felt the warmth of the metal against the flat of her palm. She looked around again at how secluded she was here; there was a glimpse of another house to the right but that was it. A flutter of panic and joy muddled together in the pit of her stomach; anything could happen here and no one would know. She looked down to the right where she could see a glimpse of the beach and spotted a lone walker. She looked up at the path that ran along the cliff and then down to her right where a rustic steep path led down to the sand and Paisley wondered if she would venture down there at all.

Paisley watched the walker on the beach. She looked for longer as she realised she was waiting to see a dog run up alongside them, but none appeared. The walker was alone.

She pushed the key into the door and stepped inside. The scent of fresh wood and newness was all around her, as though the place had been painted recently. She dropped her bag in the hallway and bathed in the expanse of light. Just off the hallway was an open-plan communal area with a gleaming white kitchen complete with a large island. A swell of excitement and desire swelled in her belly. She began the exploration. Nicole had mentioned that she occupied the room on the second floor with a sea view, and Paisley wanted to see which one it was before everyone else arrived. She walked through into the kitchen-diner first, which boasted large modern grey sofas and a coffee table next to floor-to-ceiling windows with a magnificent sea view. As well as the large island in the middle of the kitchen area, there was also a long wooden dining table that would easily seat twelve. It was the perfect family entertaining space.

Paisley thought about Nicole, who didn't have her own family. It was something she didn't really speak about. This huge beach house all to herself, yet no little ones to fill all the little nooks and crannies. Paisley wondered how much Nicole thought about the lack of tiny bare feet slapping against the cold hard tiles of this room. How was it possible to own such a huge house, to have it handed down to you, and only live in it occasionally? Paisley knew that whilst there was still time for Nicole to become a mother, it was not really on her agenda. It would never be on Nicole's agenda. Paisley closed her eyes and for a second, she could almost hear the sound of children's laughter echoing around the vast sparse room. She smiled softly to herself and opened her eyes. She listened to the screech of a seagull that had landed in the garden on a hexagon-shaped summer house, and she suddenly felt very at home.

Downstairs and off the hallway to her left was a utility room, a further a study and a small bedroom. Paisley took herself upstairs with her bag and looked into each of the other four bedrooms, all lightly decorated, each with their own individual style. She stood in one with its king-sized bed made up with crisp white sheets and plump pillows that stood upright against the headboard, like something straight out of a boutique hotel. A light sandy-coloured throw was spread neatly across the end of the bed for those chilly evenings. Paisley imagined herself sat in the chair by the window, drinking a warm beverage and watching the sunrise. This would do nicely, she thought to herself.

She found Nicole's room next door. It was decorated the same, but two floral cushions were on the bed. The bedside table was adorned with scented candles, a new-looking hardback notepad and a pot of hair ties – arranged neatly by the housekeeping staff,

no doubt. Paisley walked over to the wardrobe, clicked it opened
and drank in the expensive fabrics that hung in front of her. Something for every season and weather. Nicole was tall and slim, and
nothing in that wardrobe would have fit Paisley who was only five-
foot-five, and a half. The half was very important.

There was also a dressing table that caught Paisley's eye. Pots of
creams and ornate bottles of perfumes that Paisley knew cost a
small fortune were all lined up in neat rows, and a small vase of
pink and purple flowers sat on the corner of the table. Paisley bent
down and pulled open the top drawer. Inside were more toiletries
and make-up products all arranged neatly in small, acrylic, lidless
receptacles. Paisley perused the colours and brands for a moment
before finally plunging her hand in and picking out a small black
tube. She popped the lid off, sniffed the lipstick, and applied a little.
It smelt expensive and felt like silk on her lips. She put the lid back
on and slipped the tube inside her jeans pocket. Paisley scanned the
other items in the draw, her attention caught by a mix of gold and
blue in the corner of the drawer. Paisley was drawn to it like a
magpie.

Paisley heard the sound of a car door slamming and quickly
closed the drawer and ran out of the room. Surely no one had
arrived yet? Paisley went back to the room next door where she had
left her bag. This was her room, she decided. She peered out of the
window expecting to see Margo or Nicole. Another car was now
parked next to Paisleys at the bottom of the drive. Paisley waited to
hear the sound of the door opening as one of the others arrived but
heard nothing. She distracted herself with unpacking. Paisley
always unpacked when she arrived anywhere, even if it was just for
one night because unpacking was the best. She liked to feel as if she
belonged somewhere, even if it was just for a day or two. And it was
important that Paisley felt as if she belonged here.

She often still had flashbacks to the bullying she'd endured at school. She heard the cruel chants as though it were yesterday and not over fifteen years ago when she was a thirteen-year-old girl in secondary school trying to fit in, but failing every single time. She felt the cold shiver run down her spine and the sick feeling in her gut again. She wasn't going to let those thoughts ruin what was to come, what her future now held for her. Despite the setback in the car with the gambling app, there were still great things ahead, and she was almost certain that after this weekend she wouldn't ever need to use it ever again.

Paisley was pretty sure that the three other women who would be joining her here shortly had no idea what lay underneath the veil she wore for work. This was going to be a chance for them all to see a glimpse of who they all really were, and but until then, Paisley needed to make sure she kept up the same demeanour she had at work. Professional, kind, patient. And boy, was Paisley patient. She had waited so very long for her life to fall into place. When Nicole mentioned them all coming to The Beach House, Paisley felt her heart soar. Of course, this was the exact location. This was where it was all supposed to happen. For once, Paisley was going to take the spotlight. Audrey was in her late forties and had lived quite a life already through the nineties. She always had a tale to tell. And Paisley at almost twenty years her junior, felt she had barely lived. Audrey was always the life and soul. She had witnessed just how Audrey could be after a few drinks, like at The Studio's first birthday party. It was shocking the way she had paraded around and had draped herself over Gram right in front of Nicole. Paisley had seen the look on Nicole's face; that was a look of a woman who did not trust the two people she was supposed to trust the most.

There was a loud knocking, which must have been whoever had pulled up in the car moments ago. It couldn't be one of the girls already – they hadn't even clocked in on the WhatsApp group yet and all three had said they wouldn't be there until at least three or four o'clock. Paisley had made the effort to get to The Beach House by one so that she would have the place to herself for a few hours, and felt a surge of annoyance that might now not be the case. She padded down the wooden staircase back into the large hallway, glancing to her left as she did and seeing that view through the huge window. She shook her head in disbelief at just how spectacular it was.

She pulled the door open and was greeted by a young man, with a strong jaw line and a shaved head. He wore a faded black T-shirt and a serious expression, which he tried to wipe away when he saw Paisley.

'Hi, I'm Oli.' He didn't hold his hand out, as he was laden down with bags.

'Hi,' Paisley said, staring straight at him, struck by the green of his eyes.

'I'm the chef.'

'Oh, right, the chef.' Paisley took a step to the side. This was the chef who Nicole had hired. Did he come from a modelling agency? Or maybe they just sent the good-looking ones to tend to the groups of women.

Oli walked through, brushing Paisley's arm, and headed straight for the kitchen.

'You've been here before?' Paisley asked as she held on to the door handle.

'No, never, but don't worry, I'm good at finding my way around places.' Oli laid his bags down on the kitchen island.

'Oh, nice.' But Paisley was just glad because she didn't fancy trying to help him find where things were when she had no inclination to do anything right now but relax. She turned to close the door, and as she did she caught a glimpse of someone at the end of the driveway. For a second, she thought it might be one of the other girls arriving early after all. But it wasn't. It was a woman, wearing a bright yellow raincoat. She was standing still and staring along the driveway and up at the house. Paisley realised it was the same splash of yellow that had caught her eye earlier in the trees next to the house when she had first stepped out of the car. She had thought she had seen the face of a woman and now perhaps she had been right. The woman must have been on her way down and was now passing The Beach House. Paisley lifted her arm and waved at the woman, who looked like she was in her fifties, but the wave was not reciprocated. Instead, she just stared at Paisley for another moment and then turned and walked away.

'That was fucking weird,' Paisley muttered. She lived in a pretty vibrant village just outside Winchester and would often find herself saying hello four or five times to people as she walked her neighbour's dog. Paisley didn't have her own dog because she felt it wasn't fair as she lived alone and worked a lot, but when her neighbour injured her leg and couldn't walk her new puppy, Chips, every day, Paisley stepped in and did a morning and evening walk at a field a five-minute drive away. She found she loved the social life that came with walking a dog. Everyone always stopped and chatted and wanted to pet Chips the cockapoo. In the end, it was easier to let people think that Chips was hers. It wasn't lying, Paisley told herself, because she found people often believed what they wanted to believe. They would look at a situation and see what they thought was the truth. And that was fine with Paisley. She wasn't about to berate someone for something that looked so obvious on the surface. Paisley was only borrowing Chips and it felt good. Like the lipstick in her pocket.

As Paisley closed the front door, the image of the woman's stern face still imprinted in her mind, thoughts of whom she might be began to formulate. Was she a friend of the family? Perhaps she lived in the house along the way. She walked into the kitchen area and saw that Oli was now wearing a black chef's jacket and blue-

and-white butcher-striped apron whilst pulling out pots and pans and laying ingredients out across the counter. Paisley was half tempted to ask Oli what was on the menu, but she did enjoy a surprise, besides, her stomach was still gurgling. She decided to make herself a mint tea and sit out on the bench with her coat on and enjoy some peace and quiet. Then she thought she would feel a bit more sociable. And Oli had a nice face. She could keep him company whilst he cooked until the others arrived. She smiled at Oli as she made her way to the kettle, filled it up with water and flicked it on.

'Why don't I make us a nice cup of tea?' Oli smiled back. Then she took herself upstairs to grab something warm for sitting outside. She pulled the lipstick out of her pocket, looked at it again, and smiled before opening her toiletry bag and slipping it inside a small pocket. Her hands then grazed across a slim cardboard box with the word's *Pregnancy test* on them. The test she wanted to save and do tomorrow morning. She looked at it for a moment, smiled again to herself and then zipped the bag shut.

4

AUDREY

By the time Audrey had set off for The Beach House, it was gone 3 p.m. and the heavy London traffic was already building up with people leaving work and school runs. She had got stuck at The Studio helping Matt with the edit of the podcast they had just recorded and then had to peg it into town to grab a few last-minute essentials. It wasn't like Audrey to be so disorganised but she had been a little preoccupied the last few days. This time away was the perfect opportunity to relax despite the work-focused agenda that Nicole had put in place. How she wished she could just tell Nicole that it wasn't worth her time worrying about that any more. She wanted to tell her to just kick back and relax; that it would be the right thing to do, that it would be the one thing that would actually help Nicole with all the problems in her life. But Audrey couldn't. She had to stay quiet. It was going to be tough for Audrey because she usually said whatever came into her head, and she wondered if, after a few drinks, she would be able to hold it all in. So the only way to get through this weekend, pretending to Nicole that she was on board, was to lead by example. She would start drinking tonight, Thirsty Thursday! and continue for the rest of the weekend, hoping that Nicole would follow suit. Nicole was always riled up about something, and her concerns about The Studio were no exception. Nicole had been particularly ratty since the night of the party and it hadn't gone unnoticed by anyone, especially Audrey. Audrey hated the secrecy and the lies. She wanted it all to be over. But she had to be patient. Audrey was selfishly looking forward to a long weekend away and had no intentions of taking care of anyone but herself, but when Gram had messaged, saying that he and Nicole had said goodbye on bad terms, she knew she had a job to step up to. But she was sure she could manage it. Make sure Nicole was fed and watered, or rather wined? Easy. Audrey was as maternal as could be, she just hoped the wining and dining wouldn't turn to Nicole whining, because then Audrey would have to begin the lying. And she was a very bad liar.

Audrey hadn't seen the property in person, but she had seen where it was on a map. It was remote. Audrey could handle that; she had been feeling slightly anxious recently, but she put that down to the perimenopause. The thought that there would be no shops or lots of people made Audrey feel a little strange, like a coil in her stomach was winding up tightly before springing open really quickly, only to start winding back up again. At least there would be plenty of alcohol to numb the sensations.

Audrey truly loved the city and she loved the podcast. She had wanted it to work from the start. She had sought out Nicole so she could work with her because she thought she had found in her a feminist sister. Audrey had grown up with three brothers and a father who believed a woman's place was in the kitchen and the bedroom. So, it was no wonder Audrey moved out and ran away to London when she was seventeen. She was fortunate enough to bump into Frank, who became a sort of mentor/manager for a while. He built up her portfolio over the course of a year, found her some cheap digs in a basement flat and got her her first modelling job when she was eighteen. Her own mother never tried to contact her again. She occasionally heard from her brothers and she found out her father had died last year. But she had not been moved by the news, nor did she attend the funeral.

Audrey was the biggest supporter of women's rights, feminism and equality for women that she knew. It was the very essence of who she was. Of what she did. However, recently, Audrey, who was always so full of confidence and knew how to say anything, suddenly felt as though she were not able to speak some days. She had definitely noticed some of her confidence dwindling these last few months. It had started after an incident with a fan who had found out where she lived and had taken to standing at the end of the driveway and looking up at the house. Eventually, Audrey had to employ some temporary security until the thing died down. But ever since, where she had once been unstoppable, it was like someone was applying the brakes without having informed her.

It hadn't helped that the perimenopause had begun soon after, and she could feel herself changing physically as well as mentally. She'd had several bouts of anxiety recently and Audrey had never suffered with her mental health; it was just something she was fortunate enough never to have experienced. So, despite embracing the glamorous lifestyle in her youth, inhaling and swallowed everything that had been handed to her (she had never become an addict but she'd had her fair share), it had taken a while to figure out that the stilted feeling, where she would sometimes forget what she was trying to say, coupled with feeling panicky in shops and when she was around a lot of people that had been happening more and more, was not normal. The lack of confidence and fear of being followed had then conveniently teamed up with dry eyes, insomnia and sudden aching joints. Audrey was convinced she was going to go on being fertile and youthful forever. Most of the women she knew her own age had begun going through this years ago. If

Audrey had experienced any hints of being perimenopausal, she had just ignored them; she was still a working mother to three children at the end of the day, and most days were hot sweats and worries dealing with Casper (fifteen), Ellie (thirteen) and Milo (eight). Life was busy and her husband, Julian, a financial solicitor with his own practice, was a hard grafter so much of the childcare issues fell to her. She had never wanted help; she didn't want to be one of those famous women who paid nannies to look after her kids. She had been there for each and every one of them, and she was there whenever any of them needed her. The two elder ones were pretty self-sufficient now and little Milo had after-school activities, which meant Julian could pick him up. Julian had planned a lovely weekend with Milo, which made Audrey feel content knowing she could come away for a few days and not have to think about parenting, which as much as she loved it with every fibre of her body, was still the hardest gig she had ever landed.

She physically exhaled as she pulled up at The Beach House after a long drive. She was ready to eat and needed to have a large glass of wine immediately. Audrey had organised a hamper of gourmet food delights and flowers to be delivered to the house ahead of her arrival; she always thought it good etiquette to turn up at someone's house for dinner with a good bottle or two of wine, so a hamper seemed only fitting for a long weekend. Audrey was understated but classy. She didn't like to throw her wealth in the face of others, but she did like nice things, and if she was going to relax this weekend, she wanted to do it with a decent bottle of red and some gourmet snacks. Nicole was hiring a chef, but Audrey liked to feel surrounded by things that made her feel comfortable. A home away from home.

There were three other cars at the bottom of the little path that led up to the house and none of them were Nicole's. She opened the boot of her shiny black Range Rover and pulled out the Gucci suitcase and matching carry bag. She scooped up her handbag from the passenger seat on the way and headed up the path to the front door and knocked loudly. She looked around at the view, hearing the sounds of the seagulls and imagined herself waking up tomorrow morning without the bedlam of Milo banging and screeching about the place, Ellie coming into the kitchen and demanding food for her and her three mates who had stayed the night before after she had just cleaned up everyone else's breakfast, or Casper mithering her over a lost hoodie that he must wear to football training. Julian could worry about it all tomorrow; she was going to try to make the most of this time away. She felt her body begin to relax a little. The thought of that bottle of red was keeping her going, and as she turned to the door, it was opened by a young man in a chef's jacket and apron with a lopsided smile and sparkling eyes. Well, well, Audrey thought to herself, and suddenly the weekend had begun.

* * *

'So where did she actually find him, that's what I want to know.' Audrey was on her second glass of wine and sidling up to Margo on the sofa, watching Oli intently. Oli carried on with a professional manner as though he hadn't noticed a forty-seven-year-old ex-supermodel ogling over him. Audrey knew perfectly well that Oli was aware that she was looking at him. It was in the way his eyes subtly flickered over to her without actually ever looking at her; a clever technique many men had yet to master and instead would just openly ogle at her.

'He had put his card through the door. He's local, I think.' Margo shifted as she spoke, and it became obvious to Audrey that she was slightly too close to Margo and probably invading her personal space. Audrey was aware how socially awkward Margo was and occasionally liked to tease her about it, but not today. She was tired. In fact, she would go so far as to say she was physically and mentally drained. She had been giving so much of herself away recently that she had really begun to feel the weight of the last few months crashing down on her; she needed to shake them away. Somehow, she knew she was going to get inordinately drunk that evening even before she had taken the last sip of her second glass of wine.

The sound of steps outside and a clinking of a key entering a lock echoed around the open-plan kitchen-diner. Audrey watched Margo shoot up and head for the door.

'Ooo, that will be Nicole.' Audrey was unsteady on her feet and late with the announcement as Paisley was already down the stairs and hovering uncertainly in the hallway. Audrey was filled with a mixture of relief and happiness and terror at seeing her friend as Nicole stepped through the doorway. This was it, the long weekend had officially begun.

'It's chilly out there now,' Nicole said, shutting the door. Audrey watched as Nicole clicked not just one lock but three, including the main mortice lock. Margo was hanging up Nicole's coat, and Audrey felt that pang of annoyance at the way Margo was like Nicole's shadow sometimes. It was unnerving how close Margo kept herself to her boss.

'So glad you could make it,' Nicole quipped, keeping the joke running that Audrey had indeed not wanted to come. 'You seem to be settling in okay.' Nicole's eyes twinkled as she smiled.

'Yes, I am, this place is stunning. Such exceptional views and the decor is to die for' – Audrey leant in closer to Nicole, her red wine breath hot on her colleague's cheek – 'and the extra embellishments you had brought in have not gone unnoticed.' Audrey did a slight turn towards Oli and raised her eyebrows cheekily.

Nicole laughed. 'Only the best for you, my darling. I knew you would not be disappointed.'

'I'm going to pour you a very large glass of red wine, darling,' Audrey called over her shoulder as she sauntered towards the kitchen.

Nicole smiled and turned to Oli. 'Hello. It's nice to finally meet you. It all smells wonderful. What is on the menu for tonight?' Nicole edged closer to the island where Oli had been in full flow, but now had his eyes firmly on Nicole.

'A spring tomato gazpacho, followed by silver mullet with grilled spring onions, confit tomatoes and sauce vierge, finished off with an elderflower panna cotta and strawberry soup topped with strawberry meringues and cream.' Oli looked back down as though he had barely said anything and continued with his prep.

'Holy shit!' Audrey squealed. 'I'm at the fucking Ritz!'

Audrey handed Nicole a large glass of red. Nicole took a large gulp. 'How are you, Margo, was the drive here, okay?'

'Yes, I ended up setting off later than I had hoped, but it was fine. How about you? Did you get held up?'

Nicole swallowed hard and looked down and to the side. Audrey noted the stress etched across Nicole's face. She thought back to the emergency text she had received from Gram about their argument. His final text had read:

Keep her sweet.

After which, she had begun drinking. Audrey was a hoot at the best of times, but with alcohol inside her, she was the life and soul of the party.

The Studio's first birthday party had been when she and Gram had begun planning it all. She just wished she could tell Nicole what was coming was all for the best and that, in the long run, she would see that too.

5

THE PARTY

The champagne glasses stood lined up like soldiers, ready to be filled. The caterers had just arrived with the canapés and the karaoke was all set up in one of the pods. It was time to celebrate The Studio's first birthday. Everyone had groaned at the notion of a karaoke session, but Nicole knew that once the booze was flowing nicely, everyone would be fighting for the microphone to perform their best Freddie Mercury or Madonna. She had seen it hundreds of times before. It was the classic way of trying to shame the culture when, deep down, everyone had an inner performer just dying to get out. Under normal circumstances, Nicole would be so excited to see what state everyone was going to get into, but tonight, she just wasn't feeling it. She and Gram had argued again before they came out, but agreed to put on a face for the evening.

She was interested to know what Audrey would be wearing tonight. She had seen Gram do a double take too many times when Audrey was in the room. Nicole felt her gut twist thinking about the two of them.

Nicole didn't have to wait long, as just then, Audrey entered the room, and everyone's eyes were on her. She was squeezed into a tight red dress that could have been a second skin the way it clung to her curves, not a lump or roll in sight.

'All right, chick?' Audrey mouthed across the room as her eyes landed on Nicole first.

Despite Nicole's resentment of Audrey's ability to look impeccable whatever the occasion, Nicole couldn't help but feel a swell of warmth at Audrey's signature greeting to her. She had rarely heard her use it with any other women and that was the Audrey effect: she was able to make anyone feel special and Nicole was no different. Was it neediness? Wanting, no, needing to feel special? *'Only-child syndrome,'* came Gram's words. Why did that man think he could reduce everything about her to the fact that she had no siblings? Yes, Nicole was old enough to understand that she had a series of needs that would likely never be satisfied due to the untimely departure of her father when she was eight years old – he had upped and left just after the Queen's speech on Christmas Day. At the time, Nicole had thought it strange, and a strong stirring had begun in the pit of her stomach – the Christmas dinner she had devoured half an hour before gurgling its complaints. Perhaps he was going to the pub. Some people did that, she thought, although never her parents; they were strictly dinner-at-eight-in-fancy-restaurant types, with maybe a martini at the bar before. After kissing her briefly on her head and closing the front door behind him, she watched as her dad walked to the car, suitcase in hand, threw it in the boot and then drove slowly away. Her mother had been knitting and had not looked up through the entire episode, and Nicole had thought that maybe she had missed it. Did she know where her father had gone?

It turned out fifteen miles away to a divorcee called Shirley. *Childless.* That was the word that stuck out when Nicole's mother had explained it all to her on Boxing Day over cold cuts of meat and red jelly that made her mouth fill with saliva but not in the way the

Christmas dinner had triggered the day before. This saliva made her want to go and throw up in the toilet. Take That's 'Never Forget' played in the background; the soundtrack to the band splitting now held more significance to her own sad little life than she had ever expected or wished for.

'Congratulations!' Kate, the intern who had been with them for three weeks, screeched in Nicole's ear, tearing her from her memories, forcing her to turn and transform her gaze into a full-blown grin. The smile of someone who was ecstatic to be celebrating one year of a successful business. Not someone who had looked at the figures with her accountant a week earlier and cringed at the flailing numbers. Numbers that she had queried in case they were, in fact, a joke. Her accountant's sullen face assured her that they were not. And since then, she had been dreading this night, because having to keep pretending was becoming such a drag. She felt putting on a front had become the fabric of her very existence, and she wished she could shake off that cloak. She wanted to come clean, to tell everyone that things weren't so great. That *she* wasn't doing so great. But Margo had done such an impeccable job of organising the party, and so Nicole couldn't bring herself to cancel at the last minute. So she shook off her frustration – frustration that had evolved from a rash decision to pour money into a business that Gram had insisted wouldn't make her a penny – and donned a smile for the party she was hosting for her friends, family, colleagues and acquaintances.

'Thank you.' Nicole's cheeks already ached from forcing a smile onto her face that really didn't want to be there.

'Oh my God! This party is rad – Margo did such an awesome job, and everything looks amazing.'

Nicole wished the youth of today would not use so many poor adjectives. Next Kate would be saying *literally* in the most unliteral context.

'I mean she literally did it all herself.' Kate gestured to the balloon display.

Oh, there it was, Nicole thought. 'Uh-huh,' she said. 'Not all – that was bought,' Nicole said dryly.

Kate was sweet; a nineteen-year-old girl with braces and a bright pink highlights. Nicole hadn't managed to get close to her though, despite Kate's perpetual look of hope when she found herself alone in a room with Nicole, as if she might impart some life-changing business model that would see her through the rest of her life. So here, in Kate's last week, Nicole felt so awkward next to her, a slither of regret for what could have been that felt so raw and familiar inching its way up her chest, that she had to turn away, mutter an excuse and head for the drinks. She was sure Kate would be reporting back to all her friends post-internship that her boss was nice, but vague and distant.

'Darling, you are excellent.' Audrey's voice was in Nicole's ear. Where had she come from? She had been over the other side of the room seconds ago. 'I am glad I found you. Here, let's have a little toast, just us before the rabble gets here.' Audrey poured them both a glass of rosé. 'Something light to begin the proceedings.'

Nicole found that smile and brought it to the edges of her lips as best as she could and clinked her glass with Audrey.

'To us, to you and to me,' Audrey said. 'I know I am fabulous and I am the nuts holding this thing together,' Audrey exclaimed, the comment masquerading as sarcasm, but Nicole knew she was speaking the truth. Audrey was the star of the show. People came to listen to her. 'But you, my friend, are spectacular in your own right. You have done something amazing, and I think The Studio is going to explode next year.'

Nicole knew that Audrey was alluding that maybe things had not been so hot on the finance front, and Nicole felt a rash of hot anger explode through her. Audrey acknowledged the comment with a tight smile and a firm nod of her head.

'Oh look, there's Suki.' Audrey shimmied away, but not before planting a firm kiss on Nicole's cheek, leaving her emotionally stranded between rage and rapture.

Nicole looked about the room, which was now filling up with more guests. She smelt the familiar scent of aftershave and the warm notes of a voice that had soothed and reassured her so many times. 'Looks like it's going to be a riot. How many did Margo extend that guest list to in the end?' A warm hand touched her arm.

'I want to say two hundred.'

'Two hundred? Can we fit two hundred in the building?' Gram looked around.

'I don't think two hundred will actually show up.' Nicole looked at her boyfriend. 'Will they?'

'We'll have to see, we'll have to see.' He headed to the bar, where she could bet he was making a request for his favourite drink, a southern comfort on the rocks, and watched as the bartender poured one for him. Nicole couldn't stand the stuff. The sweet smell of the liquor made Nicole wretch, but it had been his signature drink since she had known him. At least when he got drunk it was a predictable state. He would become slurry but usually remain steady.

As the guests filed in, the sense of unease felt tight in Nicole's chest, as if she couldn't quite breathe. It all felt wrong; celebrating when there was really not much to celebrate.

6

NICOLE

Nicole thought about the The Beach House and how the building always appeared to be looking down at her, condescending, as though it couldn't quite believe that she had returned again. That she kept returning.

Her mind was like a washing machine on the final spin. The Beach House made people fall to their knees with appreciation. She could see it now in the three women she was in the room with; they all saw its majestic beauty. It was exactly the sort of place people craved. With the madness of life always catching up on you, everyone wished for a beach house, an escape. Nicole was lucky enough to have one. She knew that. But she was also unlucky enough to be carrying the dark memories that the bricks, mortar and wood had absorbed over the years. Each trip back, she was greeted by the squawk of the gulls, the thrash of the waves, the fresh sea breeze. Yet every creak of a floorboard or squeak of a door nudged a memory loose from within its walls, and then, for the entire trip, Nicole would wrestle with the past, trying to keep it at bay: far enough away so she could rest and recuperate, yet close enough that she would be reminded of what she had done so she would never really get too comfortable, never really enjoy herself enough. But she had plenty to occupy her mind when she was here this time. So maybe, just maybe the old place would keep its whispers to a minimum.

The energy at The Beach House this evening was different. Her colleague and employees were all out of their comfort zone, she could tell. She could sense it. And that had been the one of the deciding reasons to bring the women here, away from London, away from their usual haunts. It was good for people to step out of the norm. You might see a side to them you hadn't seen before. Catch them unawares.

This was the first time she had allowed visitors into The Beach House when she wasn't present. The lockbox was there for her and her mother and her stepfather, John, but even they had become less frequent with their visits recently. Nicole was both surprised and relieved by the noise and smells coming from the communal area. Margo had been as attentive as usual on arrival, taking her coat and hanging it up for her. A small gesture that wasn't necessary but had the hallmark of Margo all over it, but she could see how uncomfortable it was for Margo. Being here was probably the most difficult for her out of the three.

Nicole clocked the chef she had booked, her gaze lingering on him for a few moments before she approached him to ask him about dinner. He had a nice look about him. Audrey would be pleased with that. Then she checked herself. Why was she concerning herself with Audrey's wants and needs? Oli was here for her convenience, it just so happened that he was a little bit easy on the eye.

As she was thinking of Audrey, the woman herself appeared. And suddenly her friend's arms were tangled around her, the familiar smell of Chanel No. 5 overpowering her own fragrance, and as she pulled her head back to speak, the tang of alcohol on her breath followed.

'Looks as though dinner is nearly ready, I'll round up the troops.'

Nicole patted her arm. Clearly, there was already a lot of alcohol coursing through Audrey's veins, so maybe she wouldn't notice if she was a little off with her, if she wasn't her usual relaxed self around her co-host. Nicole could hardly be called touchy-feely at the best of times, but still, she was holding back tonight, not offering what she would usually give of herself, which was never one hundred per cent – no one ever got one hundred per cent of Nicole.

* * *

Thankfully, dinner was a triumph. Nicole had been worried. She had never used a chef before at the house but when she found his card pushed though the letter box on her last trip here, she was glad she had kept it for this occasion. It was exactly what Nicole needed after that hideous journey here, and the thought that she didn't need to worry about feeding anyone for the next three days was a weight off. Everyone seemed relaxed and full and content, which was what she had wanted. There needed to be a certain degree of calm and order to the weekend. It was a very important time and Nicole wanted them to all be as relaxed as they could possibly be.

It was now getting on for 9 p.m. and she was tired. She had left London much later than she had wanted to, the brief conversation she'd instigated with Gram before she left having evolved into so much more and ended in shouting and sobbing from Nicole's end as she stormed out to the car and sped off. Her phone had beeped several times in her bag on the passenger seat and when Nicole stopped at a petrol station to refill the car and have a toilet break, she checked the messages. Some were from the girls, all telling her they were there and loving The Beach House already. But the majority were from Gram. They began as a continuation of their argument but by the fifth one, he hadn't so much as apologised but had calmed to the point where he was hinting at some sort of neutral ground and that it was important that 'they talked'.

Enjoy your weekend. I will speak to you when you get home.

Nicole hoped that after his last message she wouldn't hear from him all weekend because in some ways, she *did* want to enjoy this weekend.

Nicole drank her wine and looked up at Margo. Margo was looking at her expectantly. Had she just said something? God, she had been miles away, stuck in that bloody kitchen rehashing out the same rubbish she and Gram had been regurgitating for years. It was truly exhausting. She needed to just surrender herself this weekend.

Relax. She took a deep breath, let it out and took another long sip of wine.

'I'm sorry, I was miles away then, Margo, what did you say?' Nicole looked across the detritus of a dinner well enjoyed, empty glasses and plates on the table, to Margo who was sporting red cheeks. Nicole had put the log fire on just before dinner and now, with the heat of all the cooking and the fire, coupled with several glasses of wine, everyone was looking a little flushed.

'I said, it will be good to start bashing out some new ideas this evening.'

Nicole clocked Audrey shooting Margo a look, one that could have been perceived as a warning. But Audrey wasn't that way with Margo. Nicole knew Audrey found Margo a little annoying, but she still appreciated she was a grafter. Nicole would need to have a quiet word with Margo, let her know that she wanted the ideas to flow naturally.

'Yes, we'll crack on after breakfast tomorrow. We're all tired from travelling. I think a good walk across the cliffs will blow away some cobwebs and get some of the grey matter ticking over again. What do you say?' Nicole knew that walking was not Audrey's favourite pastime. She fancied taking the long route.

Margo brought the enthusiasm for everyone; her eager face only matched a close second by Paisley's. Audrey looked unimpressed and was starting to show signs of someone who was not going to make it past nine thirty at the rate she had been knocking back the wine that came after the champagne that had come after the wine she had already drunk before Nicole's arrival, according to the almost empty bottle of red on the counter as she walked in. Nicole had been impressed but not surprised by Audrey's extravagant hamper gift. It was thoughtful. After all, that was the very essence of Audrey, the woman she had come to admire this last year. But she would be sure not to open any of it and take it home to devour alone.

'Sounds good to me – a good walk is exactly what I need. I feel so stiff at the moment – I really need to stretch my legs out,' Paisley said, looking like an excited teenager; even though she was twenty-nine, she still had such a girlish look. Nicole had to try so hard to keep that youthful exuberance that Paisley reeked of.

Nicole caught herself. What was this new emotion she had coursing through her? It was anger. A fierce rage that was trying to take her body hostage. But she wouldn't let it, because she needed to stay in control this weekend.

'You and your family must have loved walking here when you were a kid,' Paisley said sweetly.

'I...' Nicole began, wondering how to slot into the conversation that her father had walked out on them when she was eight and that it was just her and her mother until John had come into the picture.

'We did,' Nicole said easily, surprising herself. This weekend was not about dredging up the past, although there was enough of that all around her; you wouldn't need an excavation to dig up what had been haunting her for most of her life.

'It's such a delightful spot. You must love coming back here?' Paisley said again, a persistent brightness to her voice.

Nicole paused this time, unsure how to play it.

'I do love it,' Nicole said eventually, because there was so much to love about The Beach House.

'So was it your mum who got the place looking like this then? It's so modern,' Paisley added, looking around.

Nicole nodded. It had been her mother; her way of enticing her daughter to spend more time here. And it had worked. She had managed to paint over the cracks and the dirty marks. But Nicole knew what lay beneath. The old house had witnessed so much that it was engrained into the wood and bricks. Nothing would ever rid the place of that. Nicole felt it had earned its right to hold on to those memories.

Nicole glanced around the table and her eyes found Margo's. They locked for longer than a second before Nicole looked away. Nicole thought it strange that Margo was looking at her with such intensity because, usually, she was unable to hold eye contact. Maybe the wine had softened her edges this evening. Although Nicole hadn't seen her drink too much. Or had she not been paying enough attention? She had felt something in that look, but then Nicole couldn't deny the fact that she had spent most of the dinner mulling over the argument she'd had with Gram. Had she been able to keep the pained expression from her face this evening?

Nicole's attention back in the room, she realised Paisley had said something to Audrey and Audrey was laughing uncontrollably. Margo was stacking the plates, beginning to clear the table, when Oli appeared between her and Margo.

'I'll do that. You sit down.'

Nicole realised she had barely said a word to their chef this evening, but Margo carried on stacking.

'No, honestly. I don't mind, I'd rather be doing something, so let me help.'

'Okay, well don't tell my boss.' Oli looked over at Nicole and flashed her a smile. Nicole felt a flutter in her stomach, which quickly rose to her chest, and she found herself looking for a ring on Oli's finger. There wasn't one. Why did she feel a sense of relief at that discovery? Was it this place, The Beach House? Maybe it was the pull of the place, the old feelings that it managed to stir up inside her. She was experiencing and feeling things that were not entirely appropriate. Oli seemed and looked younger than her. Things hadn't been great between her and Gram recently, that was a given. Maybe this was the bit of light relief she needed to help her through the weekend. With Oli in such close proximity, Nicole began to feel hotter than before. She needed some air. She picked up the empty wine and champagne bottles from the kitchen counter and popped them into an empty cardboard box, ready to step outside with them.

'Hey.' Oli's hand was on her arm. 'I'll do that, honestly, you don't need to bother yourself, I can do this.'

Nicole looked down at her arm where Oli's hand was gently resting there. He looked down too and then swiped it away. Nicole tried to soften the expression that she realised might have hardened over dinner. As she did, she found that Oli was returning her gaze with a look that was explorative and, to Nicole – who had not been in a situation that required her to flirt or respond to flirtatious

behaviour for a long time – seemed suggestive. She turned away
and picked up the box.

'Honestly, I've got this.' She took the box and headed for the
back door.

The decor of The Beach House had changed considerably over
the years; it was almost as if her mum had tried to wipe away the
years of pain and heartache the place had brought. But it had
brought equal amounts of joy and had been the sanctuary her and
her mother had needed after her father left them. But apart from
the way her mum had decorated the place, some things remained.
The back door was the same, and Nicole felt a joyful familiarity in
the way it squeaked. She balanced the box in one hand and flicked
the key with the other. She pulled down the handle and edged the
door an inch. She felt her body shudder from the rush of nostalgia
as the door sang out its familiar three chords that always reminded
her of the chords from Queen's 'We Will Rock You'. She had never
spoken about the sound of the squeaking door and how it made her
feel, not even to Doctor Sanderson. Still, after all these years, she
was held captive by every quirk of her childhood holiday home.

She stepped outside into the cool night air, but flinched when
something flew past her face. A bat. Only a bat. A scrap of a
memory from when she was very young surfaced in her mind. An
erected tent; a campfire; sitting under the stars toasting marshmallows; and the bats. So many bats she couldn't believe it. She had
begun to shriek – she had after all been a little kid and occasionally
that was what little kids did, especially when they were fuelled by
sugary marshmallows and a cocktail of fear and elation.

'Oh, shut up, Nicole, for the love of God.'

Her father had stood up and walked back to The Beach House.
Nicole sat still for a while, not knowing what to do. She had probably only been about five or six. Eventually, the fire began to fade
and the wind began to chill around her. She went back into the

house. Her father was sitting at the kitchen table – it was still open plan, even back then – a glass of whisky in front of him with one hand clasped around it, the other pressed against the side of his head as his elbow supported it on the table.

'You'd better just go on up to bed,' her father said. Nicole had remembered that her duvet and favourite teddies were still out there. She had looked out of the window at the dark night and scuttled off to her bedroom and crawled under a thin blanket. She had looked in on her mother on the way and saw an open bottle of pills next to her bed and her mother lying on her back, head tilted to one side, mouth slightly open and softly snoring. The open bottle of pills and her mother sleeping was a combination she had become used to seeing back then and a signature part of her childhood. Thank goodness her mother had come through it. She had John now. And Nicole always thought she had been given her own second chance when she met Gram. Maybe she was wrong.

'Boo!' came Audrey's voice behind her, and Nicole spun around, the box which was still in her hand wobbled and one of the empty wine bottles toppled out and smashed on the ground around their feet.

'Shit, sorry.' Audrey stooped to pick up pieces of broken glass. 'I was being a twat.'

'Stop.' Nicole grabbed hold of Audrey with her free hand. She hadn't meant to squeeze it so hard, but Audrey didn't notice. 'You're drunk, it's dark. I'll come back out with a dustpan and brush and torch in a minute.'

Audrey stood back up. She pulled out a packet of cigarettes, knocked one out, lit it and took a long drag. The smell of cigarette smoke wafted straight over to Nicole; the scent was so intoxicating. No one really smoked any more, it was all vapes, but Audrey was old school, and the smell of a cigarette took Nicole right back to her teenage years. A hazy memory began to form and she shook it away.

She did not want to think about that. She never came here to think about that, yet it was inevitable that these memories would catch her unawares here, where she was always vulnerable.

Audrey inhaled deeply, lifted her head and then blew the smoke up in the air in such a theatrical way that she was reminded of a film star.

Audrey caught Nicole watching her. 'God, I love a fag,' she said after the exhale. 'I have a few drinks and that's it, I'm a smoker again. Never get properly addicted though.' She took another inhale and looked at Nicole. 'Can you believe with everything I have been though and experienced in my life, I didn't even come out of it with an addiction?'

'There's still time,' Nicole heard herself say.

'Sorry, I know you probably think badly of me, and it's not in keeping with your beautiful beach manor.' Audrey waved her hand and cigarette around. The smoke coming close to Nicole again, titillating her senses, fuelling the memories.

Nicole shook her head. 'It's not a manor, and I don't think badly of you.' But even as she said it, Nicole thought back to that afternoon and the argument with Gram and how Audrey's name had rung loudly in the air between them and then continued to echo in the room long after either of them had stopped speaking. She looked at her friend, a woman who had been her companion for over a year now. A woman with whom she had spent a lot of time recently. A lot of that time had been at hers and Gram's house in London. Nicole hadn't wanted to see Audrey how everyone saw her, as a threat, as a predator towards men.

Audrey took a few last long puffs of her cigarette whilst she raved about the dinner and then stubbed it out of the wall and popped it in an empty plant pot. 'I'll bin those before I leave, I promise.' She sent an air kiss Nicole's way and went back inside the house. 'I'll get the dustpan and brush if you like?' Audrey called over her shoulder.

'No, it's fine, I'll do it,' Nicole said as she realised she was still holding the box of empty wine bottles. She stepped across the smashed glass and lifted the bin lid.

Crack.

Nicole spun around. The bin lid slammed down hard where she had let go of it. The sound startled her as much as the initial cracking sound she had just heard. The security light was on, but beyond where the light stretched to was a blanket of darkness that could be hiding anything. Or anyone.

No, Nicole scolded herself and lifted the bin lid. She was being jumpy. She had been here enough times over the years, but she still felt that edginess as soon as the sun went down. She threw in the box then put the wine and champagne bottles in the small glass bin. Then she turned and was face to face with Oli.

'Shit!' Nicole screamed. She hadn't seen or heard him come outside.

'Sorry, sorry.' Oli put one hand out in surrender in a way Nicole thought felt a little dramatic. It was she who was jumpy tonight. It was she whose frayed nerves hadn't been calmed by the alcohol that she'd consumed that evening. She was the one who was hanging by a thread with images from the past and the present running through her head, unable to calm any of them.

'It's fine,' she said. The aggravation was clear in her tone.

'Audrey said you needed this.' He held out the dustpan and brush with the other hand.

'Thanks.' Nicole went to take it and Oli seemed to change his mind.

'What am I thinking?' He bent down with the dustpan and brush and began to clear up the mess.

Nicole didn't protest this time. It wasn't her fault she had dropped the bottle and Oli was here as a paid help.

'Thanks,' she said, watching him. 'Did you have to come far for this gig?'

Oli stood up with the glass in the pan. He lifted the lid to the glass bin and dropped it in, then he turned to Nicole.

'I'm just down in Kimmeridge.' Oli leant his weight on one foot. 'Do you spend a lot of time here?'

'Not really. I try to, but I am so busy with work that I usually save it for special occasions.' Nicole stopped herself. She really didn't need to explain anything to this guy, even though he had an alluring manner about him and eyes that seemed to make her forget what it was she thinking or talking about for a few seconds. There hadn't been many men who had done that to her over the years, and a strong sudden memory gripped her. As much as The Beach House was a beautiful escape from the manic city life, the tendrils of the past would always reach out and grip her just tightly enough to remind her of what she had done, what she was responsible for.

'Shall we get back in? It's a bit chilly out here.' Oli held his arm out for Nicole to pass. She smiled at him and headed to the back door. Oli was back at the bin, shutting the lid. Nicole took one last look around at the darkness surrounding the building. The winter nights would soon be drawing in. Most might want to lock the doors to keep out the ghosts, but although Nicole religiously double-bolted each night, the worst night terrors were already inside with her. Now, in order to keep herself safe, Nicole knew she must keep her friends close and her enemies even closer.

7

MARGO

The kitchen was gleaming, Oli having cleaned up and already left for the night by the time a freshly showered Margo sauntered downstairs to make herself a cup of hot chocolate before bed. She was a little woozy from the two glasses of wine at dinner that she now wished she hadn't drunk, and even though she indulged in every course that was on offer, plus coffee and petits fours, her body was still craving something else.

Margo was glad that Nicole hadn't brought in a London chef that would need to stay. She wasn't sure she would have felt comfortable with a strange man staying in the house all weekend. Three nights was a long time to be anywhere with anyone she wasn't entirely comfortable with and she was already trying very hard with the three other women. You had to put a lot of trust in others in a situation like this. It had taken Margo quite some talking to herself to even get here, to leave her dad, to put a stop to the cata-strophising, especially after she had spent far too long watching a parked car in her road and wondering if the person inside was going to arrive on her doorstep.

And then there was the sleeping. Like anyone, Margo was at her most vulnerable at night. Watching a lot of scary movies when she was a kid didn't help. Not a sensible move, she now knew. She hoped she would sleep well tonight; if she'd arrived earlier, she could have taken a long walk along the Jurassic Coast and inhaled some of the negative ions. It was probably in *Psychologies Magazine*, that Margo read about negative ions, the invisible molecules that our bodies absorb in abundance in places like beaches and that are reported to produce biochemical reactions that ease stress, and if there was one thing that Margo needed now, it was to de-stress. She had so much on her mind, including her main reason for being here: she needed to protect Nicole. She had a strong almost maternal-like urge to make sure her employer – someone she considered a friend – was okay. Then there was her father. She had received one text from Clarissa, which had been too short and abrupt for Margo's liking. She needed details; she needed to know how much her father had eaten, whether he had done any activities, if he had spoken much, whether he'd asked after her? But Margo had texted three more times since the one singular text and had heard nothing back. She was trying very hard not to just get in the car and head back home to check on everything. She needed to put her faith in the agency, but she had seen some horror stories on TV documentaries where elderly men and women had been treated appallingly by their caregivers. It was abuse. There were no two ways about it. And now all she could think about was her father in a situation where she couldn't help him. She would ring the agency tomorrow morning and try to get some feedback. She couldn't just leave. Her job hung in the balance and she needed it now more than ever. She *and* Dad needed it more than ever: even though Eric was slowly slipping away from her in his mind, she still had to do everything to protect him.

The kitchen was softly lit with the under-cabinet lights in the

kitchen, creating a cosy feel that reminded her of when she would
come downstairs in the dead of night as a child to fetch a glass of
water; it always felt like forbidden territory. It was funny how
certain feelings followed her into her adulthood no matter how
much she had grown and her life had changed. This was Nicole's
house and of course she was allowed to walk about in the middle of
the night if it suited her, yet there was still something so exciting
about it. She had heard the bath running in the en suite of Nicole's
room and the snores coming from Audrey's room. It was getting on
for 10.30 p.m. and so far it had felt like a really long day and they
had only made it through a couple of hours: and had to get through
until Sunday morning. She shouldn't be counting down the days;
this was the perfect opportunity to just live in the moment. She
thought about Nicole relaxing in the bath upstairs. Her boss had
looked tense over dinner. Margo thought she knew Nicole pretty
well, and she knew the trouble The Studio was in. In fact, she knew
more than she had let on to Nicole: she had seen and heard
enough. Quiet conversations between Gram and Nicole occurring
just as Margo happened to be outside a room. Nicole's messages to
Gram left unattended for long enough to sneak a glance. Nicole
silently weeping in the toilets as Margo stood outside the door and
listened to the soft gasps and sniffs.

Margo opened a cupboard and it squeaked.

'Oh!' came a voice from the darkness on the other side of the
room.

Margo had jumped, but in the low light, she hoped that Paisley
had not caught it. Why was Paisley even sat in the dark for goodness' sake?

'I didn't see you there,' Margo said softly; she felt the dark and
the quietness of the house required her to keep her voice low.

She strained to look over to the corner of the room, where the
light and heat of the log burner was slowly petering off and Paisley

sat, face illuminated by her phone. Suddenly an image from weeks ago at the party flashed back into her mind and Margo felt her stomach turn. Suddenly the idea of a hot chocolate repulsed her.

But Margo wasn't the sort of person who let others get inside her skin, so she made herself a hot chocolate and whilst she had intended to sit quietly in the low light and listen to the house as it cooled down – she always enjoyed the creaks and groans of an old house in the evening – now she would chat with Paisley. She felt she had made enough conversation in the few hours she had been here, but she had been told by insensitive colleagues that she could come across from time to time as someone who was unaware of certain social etiquettes. Margo didn't know how to rectify that. But she knew if she wanted to get on in life, if she wanted to feel part of the gang – the clique bunch at The Studio, the Nicoles, and the Audreys of this world – then she needed to adapt to her environment. Learn how to read people and situations better.

Despite her inability to fully understand and keep up with the office chatter, Margo knew there were some things that didn't need explaining. Some things were presented to her exactly as they were. Once again, her mind travelled back in time to The Studio's first birthday party. There were so many drunk people and yet Margo had been sober, able to see what had been going on in front of her without any doubt in her mind.

Margo took her hot chocolate and made her way over to the fire and sat in a chair opposite Paisley. Paisley glanced up from her phone, her eyes settling on Margo's mug. Should she have offered one to Paisley, or even just made her one without asking? Just for show. She didn't feel comfortable around any of these women, but she felt the least comfortable around Paisley and she knew she was going to have to force herself to socialise with her over the weekend. Paisley was a lot younger than her and on another level when it came to socialisation – the sort of socialisation that Margo strived to get right but didn't always succeed.

Margo sipped her hot chocolate. Paisley shifted in her seat, her finger tapping away on the screen. The atmosphere had an icy edge to it. Paisley spent an inordinate amount of time on her phone, and Margo didn't know how to get on board with that. Margo cleared her throat and blew on the hot liquid. She cleared her throat again, this time as a prelude to a conversation starter. Paisley glanced up at Margo and then let out a sigh. Margo's whole body shrunk backwards, the words that had been forming in her throat swallowed down with the hot liquid.

The crash that came next reverberated around the entire room.

'What the fuck?' Paisley shouted crudely and leapt up as Margo jumped, spilling some of the hot chocolate in her lap (fortunately missing the sofa); she still felt the impact of Paisley's choice of expletives harder than the burn that was creeping along her inner thigh. Margo had never enjoyed swearing but it was one thing she had become accustomed to listening to during her time at The Studio.

Margo presumed the sound had come from outside, and so she stood up, careful to avoid any further spillage as she set down her mug on the coffee table. She followed Paisley to the front door.

'Was it the front or back?' Paisley looked at Margo.

'We were sat closer to the back door – I think it came from there,' Margo said and Paisley let out a slight huff as she walked back through the house.

Margo ducked into the utility room and found a torch hanging from the wall. She waved it at Paisley, expecting some sort of congratulatory expression, but Paisley's face remained taut. Was she scared? Perhaps Paisley had also watched scary movies as a kid. Maybe they did have some common ground between them, but Margo refused to think about what that could be now.

Margo flicked the torch on, moved to the door and unlocked it. She glanced back at Paisley, checking to see if she was still following. Paisley gave her a firm nod accompanied by a small nudge, which Margo didn't react to but instead swung open the door in one swift movement. This seemed to alarm Paisley, who took a few quick steps backwards. Margo stepped outside and the security light flicked on, illuminating the back step and the cause of the ruckus.

'Bins?' Paisley said, peering over Margo's shoulder but staying firmly on the threshold.

'Looks like it – probably an animal. Wild cat, maybe?' Margo stepped forward to assess the two wheelie bins that were now facing downwards, their lids open, spilling the one rubbish bag Oli had put out earlier and the recycling bin with cardboard had fallen onto the open bin of wine bottles. She bent down and began lifting the bins and placing the rubbish back in.

'Do you think it was a cat? What if it was something bigger? A bear or something.'

Margo snorted. 'No bears in Dorset last time I checked,' Margo said.

'How can you be sure, Margo? Animals are migrating and evolving all the time.' Paisley hugged herself and looked around cautiously.

Margo turned and looked at Paisley this time. She didn't say anything, just observed the way Paisley was standing there in her loungewear and fluffy slippers, clutching her smartphone and she felt a surge of annoyance at this woman. They had only been together a few hours and in that time, Paisley had eye rolled with her mouth agog, talked with her mouth full on three occasions, and said, 'Oh my God, that's hilarious,' without even cracking a smile, proving that whatever had been said that was supposed to be 'hilarious' had barely titillated her. It was a pet peeve of Margo's. All the time they had been working together, Paisley's traits had been shown in sepia but were now revealed in full Technicolor.

Now Paisley was standing behind Margo, snapping photos on her iPhone.

'What are you doing?' Margo asked, trying to remain calm. She was trying her best to remain a likeable person on this trip, not to be too aggravating. She had to remain amiable for Nicole. She was only here for Nicole. She needed to make it through the weekend. Whilst her mind swirled with unsavoury thoughts about her co-workers, she needed to stay focused. '*Eyes on the prize, Margo,*' her mother had always told her when she was alive. They were the words she heeded the most in life.

'I'm taking photos in case we need to show someone.'

'Who?'

'A wildlife expert. They might need to see the evidence.'

'What evidence? A bin has been knocked down.' Margo shut the lid and turned round to face Paisley. 'All done, I'd like to finish my hot chocolate now.' Margo pushed past Paisley into the utility room and washed her hands. When she came out, Paisley was still standing by the open door, looking redundant.

'Okay, we're done. You can, you know, carry on doing whatever it was you were doing.'

Paisley let out a loud sigh. What had she been doing when Margo had stumbled upon her? Paisley was always on her phone during working hours, so, of course, she would be on it just as much if not more in her spare time. But technically this was a working holiday. Margo had wanted to continue relaxing in the sitting room, but she didn't fancy facing awkward silences with Paisley. Part of her wanted to peer over at Paisley's phone. She was sure she wouldn't be surprised by what she saw on there. She knew exactly what Paisley was up to with her phone and what she was trying to hide from everyone; she had witnessed it first-hand at The Studio, and she was sure the same was going on here. It was all Margo could do to hold it in and not go running to Nicole and spill everything to her boss, to let her know the secret Paisley was hiding. But Margo had to wait. It could push Nicole over the edge. She could get angry and end up firing her. And right now, Margo needed her job more.

8

PAISLEY

The sun streamed through the window at a silly hour because Paisley had forgotten to fully draw the curtains before she went to bed. She had fallen asleep with the notebook next to her bed. Shocked that she had forgotten, she went to push it under her pillow, but before she did, she glanced at the open page:

I think about you and us a lot. I know that's wrong. I know what happened was wrong. I want to tell the world but I also want it to remain our secret forever.

Paisley shut the book and shoved it back under the pillow. It was time. She grabbed the slim box from her wash bag on the way, and once she was sitting on the toilet, she ripped open the box. She pulled out the stick held it under her and peed. This wasn't the first time she had done this. Paisley was adept at peeing on a stick, a seasoned user of home-pregnancy test kits. So far she had invested — Well, she didn't like to think about what she had spent on ovulation kits and pregnancy tests. It was taking far too long to become pregnant. She was now twenty-nine and she was worried she had left it too late. Women's ovaries were shrivelling up and men's sperm count was dwindling all the time, or so she had read. She was behind in the race; she was going to lose, just like she had lost at school. All those sports days were rigged anyway, but for people like Paisley, they only served as occasions to humiliate her more. To show her weaknesses. This could not be another weakness; she needed to be a fertile woman, to create life, to give life. She had brought more loss with the gambling apps; enough in less than three years than could take the rest of her working life to pay off. A baby would fix everything.

She stopped peeing, and without looking, placed the stick on a piece of toilet roll on the side of the bath. She stripped off and stepped into the shower. If it was bad news, she was sure she wouldn't want to face the day, so this way she would just need to plaster a smile across her face and she would be ready. No one would know any different. This morning would be the same as any morning that she'd had to face people knowing her womb was an empty vessel, incapable of creating life. She was incapable. Of anything. But to the outside world, she showed a thriving side.

She showered quickly but thoroughly, then wrapped herself in a towel and considered getting dressed and drying her hair before she checked the stick, but the recommended three-minute wait had long passed and she feared something might go wrong if she left it any longer. If it was positive, maybe she would miss the line, it might be faint and could be fading as she stood there dripping from the shower. She began to catastrophise and soon her head was swimming with thoughts, everything except the one thing she needed to focus on.

After pulling the towel tighter and securing it by tucking one end inside, she bent down, water from her hair dripping onto the floor, and picked up the pregnancy stick. She turned it over and emitted a sound that was unfamiliar even to herself, something she had never heard come from her own mouth before. Then the emotions came. But they were different to anything she had felt previously because this time it was going to be different, this time she wasn't just Paisley Smart, loser of everything. She was now a mother.

She rushed over to the bed, retrieved the notebook from under her pillow and opened it, casting her eyes over the previous entries.

There are so many memories I have of us. So many. When I think of cold nights, I automatically associate them with warm hands. Your warm hands. That's what I think of when I think of you. When I think of us, I like to go back to the day I met you. That's my favourite memory. I turn it over and over in my mind, reliving it, trying to feel every sensation that I felt that day I met you for the first time. It's a wicked game but as soon as I have grasped the feeling, the very core of the emotion being together in that room the very first time, it has gone. I am left then, all alone, grappling for a feeling, for a sensation, for anything I can hold on to. If I try to conjure it back, it won't come. I must wait and be patient for the next time. And so I wait, as I always did, for that one moment that I can hold and cherish again. Until the next time. Until the next time.

Paisley closed the notebook and put it safely back in her bag where she was sure it would be safe from prying eyes. Then a large smile erupted over her face and her whole body tingled. She was a going to be a mother.

9

AUDREY

Audrey woke with a smile on her face, as though she were in a Disney movie. She had slept solidly for eight hours. No one had been lying next to her snoring all night, nor was she up half the night worrying about the antics of her two eldest kids – she simply texted Julian before she went to bed to ask if they were home and safe and he replied that they were. Nor had Milo come in at the crack of dawn, insisting she make him breakfast. So all in all, she felt pretty good. Except for the thing.

Audrey's stomach dropped suddenly, the smile and the happy feeling evaporating. Damn it, why was life so complicated? Why did there have to be so many peaks and troughs? Audrey would pay good money to have a period of calm where nothing big came along and disturbed her psyche. It was either some huge cost for the house, a worry with one of the kids, or some rift with a family member. Or something work related. Or in this case, friend related. Audrey had had a lot of work-related complications over the years, and even though she was practically retired as a model – she still got asked to do the odd campaign or host a charity event – now the podcast was more or less her life. She was living and breathing that show because everything that was part of her life, automatically became part of the podcast if it was broadcastable, and if it featured her kids or her husband, she would just ask their permission first. Audrey had sought Nicole out; she was the founding member of *Laying It Bare*, even though Nicole played a huge part in the entire process now.

Audrey went to check her phone to see if there were any messages from her kids or husband, which she was sure there would be, but when she flicked the screen to life, episode twelve of series two of *Laying It Bare* was still open on Spotify. She had gone to listen to it last night before she went to bed, but she must have passed out before she pressed play. Why was she punishing herself this way? She didn't need to keep hearing the damn sentence to know that it had thrown a massive spanner in the works. She was trying not to feel anger at Nicole, because she knew what the business meant to her, what the podcast meant to her. But for the love of God! Why on earth use the word *slut* and in the context of women who have one-night stands and then still broadcast the damn episode? And now Nicole had to read comments on her own personal social media accounts that had nothing to do with the comment; it was simply an excuse for people to crawl out of the woodwork and do their worst on Audrey. She had heard it all before; it was nothing new to her, but she couldn't help but feel a surge of anger at Nicole. Nicole who was messing everything up with her throwaway comments. They could have got away with it, what with it being a live broadcast on Instagram, so why post the podcast unedited? Audrey knew a few things about the world of media and one thing was that people never really forget. They always take any opportunity to drag up the past. 'Do you remember when...?' The fact that Audrey had been instrumental in the split of a famous actor and his wife twenty years ago was not wasted on this bunch of vultures who had been waiting in the sidelines all this time, ready to pounce; to start scavenging on the last morsels of a story that they knew was so old and rotten but they knew would probably poison them anyway.

Why had Nicole been so adamant not to edit out that sentence? The Studio was heading for the trash anyway, and now the podcast wouldn't be far behind. Then what would that mean for a forty-seven-year-old ex-supermodel who had little else to offer except aesthetics? More anti-ageing adverts, maybe the odd invite on morning TV to discuss something relevant to a career that was so far in the past she could barely recognise it herself any more. What she needed was a rebrand. This podcast was supposed to be it, the beginning. There could have been presenting jobs, maybe the odd bit of acting after this. But Nicole had managed to put a stop to that. And now, Audrey was finding it difficult to play dumb to Nicole's actions, but she was very good at plastering on a fake smile to appease everyone around her. She wanted to enjoy this weekend. There was very little she could do now anyway, here at The Beach House except be the very best friend and co-host she could to Nicole. Just maybe they could salvage a little of the podcast and suggest they go out on a high.

Audrey picked up the recording where she had left off last night. To be fair, Audrey liked to listen to all the episodes once they were out. It was the professional perfectionist in her, she would listen and then learn from every place she went a bit too overboard or where she found herself talking over Nicole, or where her laugh sounded a little too piercing. These were all the things to consider, and she could only improve if she too became the listener. But she had over-listened to this particular episode, heard aspects to her voice that had grated on her because of the repetitiveness. Now she had begun to hate herself as well as Nicole amongst all this. It was all over the social channels. And, of course, Nicole with her head in the sand was aware but refused to acknowledge it. She had made the choice not to interact on social media, and so it was left to Audrey to pick up all the flack. People were talking about that comment. Still. People could keep listening to this episode, keep sharing it, bringing new listeners and fanning the flames. Things didn't just calm down that quickly when it came to topics like this. It was women's rights stuff; it was the antithesis of feminism at its absolute core.

Audrey found Nicole's decision not to be on social media very peculiar. She was a modern woman in her thirties, who hosted a podcast and ran a recording studio but did not have a single social media account, apart from the official The Studio account, which was run by Matt and Paisley. Audrey had tried to have it out with her on more than one occasion but Nicole became so defensive every time. And in the end, Audrey had just accepted that it was Nicole's prerogative.

Audrey pressed play on the podcast and skipped back thirty seconds. She heard her own voice first.

'*I mean we all went out and got drunk when we were younger, didn't we? We all made those errors of judgement that we regretted in the morning – I mean what was a good night out without the walk of shame the next day?*' Audrey flinched at her own high-pitched laughter that came through the small speaker on her phone. '*I think one-night stands are okay for women – they are for men, so why do women get so much flack?*'

Then Nicole's voice came next. And what Audrey had come to realise now, having listened to every podcast episode – sometimes more than once – was that Nicole's voice was calm, almost neutral. There was no pitch to it, no wobble or waver, and certainly no ridiculous laugh afterwards that would cut through glass the way Audrey's could.

'*I think, regardless, women will always be seen as a slut if you have a one-night stand.*'

Audrey heard her own voice on the podcast again. She cast her memory back to when they were recording the episode and whilst Nicole had been speaking, Audrey had been thinking of the next thing she had wanted to say, so she barely remembered Nicole's comment. Although the word *slut* had rung loudly round the studio and she noted at the time that even Matt's eyebrows had shot up an inch when he had barely flinched in the history of the podcast, despite some of the more risqué content they had used in past shows. During that recording, she'd had some facts and figures in front of her, a recent study on men and women between eighteen and thirty-one about relationships, and she had begun to read them out. The conversation had been quickly steered away from one-night stands, and not even on purpose. Maybe this was why there was such an uproar; it had been such a throwaway, careless comment that it made Nicole look bad. Perhaps it was her cold delivery that sounded almost calculated, rather than the opinion. Perhaps if she'd heard what she'd said in the manner in which she had said it, she would consider rephrasing it, putting out an apology or even just explaining herself. But Audrey knew that this was the reason Nicole chose to be off social media; she didn't want her life to be ruled by the scrutiny of her words. The world was full of opinionated people, mainly a lot of women, who were their main target audience. The world was changing. There was so much now that you couldn't say, there was so much that could be misconstrued, that could go viral within an hour and have half of the world discussing it. Nicole knew she could be categorised as anything by anyone within a second. What was the other option?

Audrey had quizzed her about her lack of online presence. 'I make a show, I put my art out there into the world,' was Nicole's comment the first time. Audrey had thought it bold that Nicole had referred to a podcast as art, but she then realised she was doing exactly what Nicole was trying to avoid: judging. But it was a strange dichotomy that Audrey was trying to fathom. The tools and platforms were there to expose your every word to potentially millions of people daily, but to do that was to expose yourself ready for attack. How could the exposure come without the latter?

Audrey rose from the bed and looked at the beautiful day forming behind the cracks in the shutters. She had only been awake for a matter of minutes, but she had processed so much in that time.

But talking to Nicole about the comment was way down on her list because to do so would rile her up, and right now, Audrey needed to keep Nicole in her good books. Just for a few more days.

* * *

Audrey was surprised to find Oli in the kitchen. Although it didn't bother her that she had come down only wearing a black chemise with an aqua-green-and-orange kimono; it didn't quite cover everything up top and Audrey was fully aware there was some cleavage on show, but she had spent most of her late teens and twenties walking around in underwear, and she was aware of the effect it had. Even after two decades, it still gave her a little thrill that her body was able to elicit certain responses even now. With the damage that Nicole had caused with her comment, she needed to revel in the notion that she was still wanted.

She walked up to the island where Oli was already busy prepping what looked to be a delicious and healthy breakfast. Audrey was thrilled that this was her life for the next few days and imagined herself living here for longer. It had been a while since she had been looked after this way. She had allowed herself to get too bogged down with family life and had forgotten about herself. She was not sure why she and Julian hadn't invested in a second home in the UK before. They had a property in Portugal and two in

London and they spent time in the Cotswolds at Soho Farmhouse. But she was past thinking about investing in more properties now; she'd had her time and fun with that. The trouble was, Audrey could get bored very quickly.

'Morning.' Oli placed a freshly squeezed green juice in front of her.

'Wow, now that is what I call service.' She picked it up and took a sip through the metal straw. It had a hint of apple sweetness and mint, with an aftertaste of cucumber and kale. 'Mmmm, it's amazing. I need this after all that food last night. I think I'm going home a stone heavier.'

'You must still have a good metabolism – you look great,' Oli said casually as though he hadn't just paid her a very personal compliment. Audrey smiled to herself as she sipped her juice.

'No one else up yet?' she asked.

'You're the first,' he said, keeping his eyes focused on the smoked salmon slices he was separating.

As if conjuring someone with his words, Audrey heard footsteps and turned to see Margo coming through into the kitchen. She was wearing jeans and a T-shirt. Impressive, Audrey thought, the woman had managed to get herself up and put together this early. But that was Margo. Always so keen. What was that sensation through her body? Some sort of slight rage, jealousy, maybe? Something had annoyed her about seeing Margo up and dressed so early. She lifted one finger to the neck of her kimono and pulled it across to meet the other side, suddenly feeling resentful that Margo had reset the dress code for this morning when Audrey wanted to kick back and relax for another hour or two.

She rarely spoke to Margo, but this 'slut' incident needed to blow over quickly and Margo might be the one to help. She did know her social media. She was also good at her job as a marketeer, and she was certain she would be able to come up with some sort of spin to make things better. She could even write something on Nicole's behalf. Make it sound as if the whole thing was not meant to be serious, that perhaps she was joking. Audrey loved their show like one of her own children. She didn't want to lose it.

'Morning, Margo,' Audrey said as Margo sat down at the island.

'Good morning, Audrey.' Margo began to slide about a little in her seat, trying to find a comfortable position. Audrey had the height, so bar stools had never been a problem; she could simply lift a leg and she was on. It always amused her how others experienced difficulties.

Oli was on the other side of the kitchen, searching for something in the fridge.

'Breakfast is looking at bit tasty.' Audrey leant into Margo. Margo forced a smile.

They both looked at Oli for a moment, Audrey with longing and wonder. What would it be like to be with someone fifteen years younger than her?

'We—'

'I need—'

Both women started speaking at the same time, then they looked at one another. Margo gave a lopsided smile and Audrey laughed.

'I think we're both going to say the same, aren't we?' Audrey said to Margo.

Margo nodded. 'I wanted to speak to you yesterday when we arrived, but then Nicole got here and then it was dinner, then the wine—'

'Yes, I get it.' Audrey cut Margo off before she relayed the entire evening up until the point when they went to bed. 'I wondered if you might be able to use some of your magic to create a bit of an angle on the whole "slut" thing, or maybe you could distract the followers, get them looking at something else for a while, until the whole thing really dies down, or disappears altogether. I mean, I can't have that sort of responsibility on my shoulders, and Nicole, she seems quite low already, wouldn't you say? This could really tip her over the edge. I mean I have no clue what is the best thing to write, no clue whatsoever. You're the expert on this.'

Audrey leant back in her seat. Oli was back at the island. She lowered her voice to an almost whisper.

'Sorry to bombard you first thing in the morning, but I just really think anything would help. I know we're here to brainstorm ideas about The Studio, but in the short term, can we not just get something out ASAP? You know I'm just the brawn in this gig. You, Margo, are the brains.'

Audrey saw Margo shift again in her seat but Audrey was clearly saying all the right things. Margo, like anyone, thrived on praise, but it was much more than that. Margo lived for it.

'I... I just feel as though she is going through a lot,' Margo finally spoke, 'and I'd need to run anything like this past her first.'

Audrey tilted her head to one side. 'What do you mean?' She sipped her green juice through the straw.

'She seems, very distracted at the moment. Wouldn't you say? Haven't you noticed?'

Margo played with a teaspoon on the counter, turning it over between her fingers. She felt a tinge of annoyance at Margo's act; if she were at home, she might ask one of the kids to stop doing it.

'Okay,' Audrey said, feeling uneasy.

'I think this house holds a lot of memories.'

Audrey was intrigued. 'I know that. Then why did she bring us here?'

'Don't get me wrong, she comes here all the time, I just think she finds it difficult. Sometimes. Maybe. I don't know.'

Okay, thought Audrey. *Time to wrap this up.* Wherever Margo was going with this, it was on a one-way street to nowhere. Audrey was well aware of Nicole's father leaving when she was a little girl. Quite frankly, it was nothing new. Half the girls in her school had dads who were gone by the time they were ten. And half of those had their own kids by the time they were in their late teens. Whatever worries Margo was holding on to for Nicole's sake, she could own those worries; Audrey didn't need more shit to deal with this weekend. She had plans to get very drunk and relax before she returned home to her manic home life. As much as she loved the bones of those kids and Julian, she missed jetting off for days at a time for a glamorous photo shoot, getting pampered in five-star hotels and coming home relaxed and rebooted, ready to be the best mum and wife for a few months until it was time to fly off again.

It had been almost a year since Audrey had been away without her kids and husband. Margo didn't know how lucky she was that she didn't have those sorts of responsibilities and that she could just up and go whenever she wanted.

'So, that's the plan then? You're going to find a spin for slut-gate, and we can try to salvage some of this train wreck of a podcast, and before madam knows it, it will all be a thing of the past.' Audrey nodded towards the hallway. 'What's Matt saying about it all?'

'Do you mean the comment?' Margo asked sheepishly.

'*Slut*. She called women who have one-night stands sluts.' Audrey's voice rose ever so slightly. As did Oli's eyebrows.

'He texted last night. He says it still looks really bad,' Margo said softly.

'It does look bad. It's so not what the podcast represents, and I can't believe I hadn't even clocked it the first time, when she actually said it live – I was so busy thinking about what I was saying next, it went past me.'

'Breakfast will be served at nine, ladies. Is that okay?' Audrey looked up at Oli and how his twinkly eyes were trying not to focus too much on Audrey, who had managed to let the kimono slip again; this time, it was hanging from her shoulder as well.

'Sounds wonderful, Oli. I'll go and get a shower.' Audrey slipped off the stool. 'We'll carry on this conversation after breakfast, Margo,' Audrey added with slight authority.

Margo nodded.

Audrey picked up her green juice and headed back upstairs to her bedroom.

The bedroom that Audrey had taken was on the second floor, opposite Nicole's. She had just reached the top of the stairs when Paisley's bedroom door opened, and she practically skipped out of the room. She was wearing a white-and-green spring floral dress that was pinched in just under her breasts and came down to her knees. Audrey thought she looked like a 1950s housewife; all she needed to do was pin that long dark hair up into a bouffant and she was there.

'Morning,' Audrey said, making her way across the landing to greet Paisley. They kissed each other on each cheek, a different kind of greeting altogether from the one she gave Margo downstairs in the kitchen. Audrey tried to imagine that if she had leant in to kiss Margo, she would have probably curled into a ball.

'Morning, Audrey. My goodness, you look spectacular this morning.'

Audrey smirked. 'Well, I like to make an effort at night, even if it's just me, you know.'

'I do. I do,' Paisley said. Audrey had presumed if you had been single for as long as Paisley, you would just opt for an old T-shirt for bed, but maybe it was something she did.

Audrey considered Paisley for a moment. There was something different about her this morning; she was wearing a very natural make-up look and she seemed to be physically glowing.

Paisley began to move past her and towards the stairs. 'I'll see you downstairs then?'

'Okay!' Audrey sang, pulling herself out her thoughts, and watched Paisley make her way down the stairs, leaning over the balcony and following her as she went into the living area. She heard Paisley greeting Oli and Margo, and then she heard a sound from the bedroom behind her. A soft sob from Nicole's room.

Audrey crept on her tiptoes until she was just outside Nicole's door, which was ajar. Audrey wasn't sure why she didn't just walk straight in, ask Nicole what the matter was and try to comfort her. But it was something in the way that Nicole was sitting on her bed, her back to Audrey as she faced the window. She was hunched over, her shoulders shaking. The occasional sob was released. Audrey recognised it as the sort of crying she herself had experienced a few times in her life. Once when her grandfather died, and once when she'd miscarried before she became pregnant with Ellie, her rainbow baby. It appeared to Audrey, even with Nicole's back to her, that this was a deep guttural cry, the sort of cry that accompanied a true sadness, a burden that Nicole was carrying heavily. Margo had been right; there was something that was upsetting Nicole and instead of noticing last night, the way Margo had, Audrey had got drunk and it had managed to pass her by. Margo had been cagey downstairs just now, she was sure of it. She could have said more. Why didn't she just get her to spit out whatever she thought was wrong with Nicole? She must have had her thoughts. Audrey began to back away, trying not to put her full weight on the floorboards, which she knew were old and could let out a creak at any moment.

But before she could take more than a few paces, she heard an almighty shriek from downstairs. Immediately, she knew it was Paisley – Margo would not let out a noise like that. Audrey looked over the banister, as she was still on the side closest to Nicole's bedroom. She saw out of the corner of her eye that Nicole had come out of her room. She was wearing sunglasses. *Good call*, Audrey thought to herself. She immediately felt guilt at being so close to Nicole's room. Did Nicole sense that maybe Audrey had seen or heard her just now? It didn't matter now as Paisley's distress call had them both hurrying down the stairs.

10

THE PARTY

Nicole had brought in the most amazing caterers and Margo couldn't help but shove canapé after canapé into her mouth when no one was looking. She realised after the fifth canapé that Nicole had spotted her. She thought quickly about what to do, and in the end she just laughed and so did Nicole.

'There will be nothing left for the guests,' Nicole quipped. The smile still lingered on her face.

'I know, I'm sorry.'

'Don't be – I'm joking. You ordered loads,' Nicole said and Margo watched as Nicole began to look around the room anxiously as more and more guests began to trickle through the door into the large foyer where the drinks and canapés were laid out. Margo could sense Nicole's anxiety and she wondered if it was because she was inviting so many people into the studios to drink alcohol with only a few meagre canapés to line their stomachs. They would need to be shovelling in as many a minute as Margo had been to compete with the wine, beer and a misty green cocktails that were being handed to each guest as they arrived – and that was before they'd even brought out the champagne for the toasts.

The Studio stretched across the whole of the top floor with eighteen separate rooms in total, many of which had been made into 'pods' where clients hired them out by the hour to record anything from a podcast to an advert. The rest of the rooms consisted of a large conference room, where Nicole was hosting the karaoke tonight; a large office, Nicole's; a storage room and a few still-empty rooms. Nicole was still deciding what to do with those, as there seemed to be enough of the pods to go around for the time being. Nicole had anticipated a surge, but they rarely filled half the available suites throughout the week. But the thought of all these clients, associates and friends of Nicole's, all just wandering around the huge building, with access to every room, when they'd had a few drinks made Margo feel uncomfortable. She was on edge, which was maybe why she was panic eating. Margo was usually so regimented with her three meals a day; breakfast like a king, lunch like a prince, supper like a pauper. It was likely that Nicole was feeling the same as her and that the nerves were skyrocketing at the thought of so many people. She knew by now that she and Nicole shared a few traits – she could see it in her mannerisms from time to time. She felt special having that slight connection to Nicole, even though Nicole herself maybe wasn't aware of it. It made Margo feel better about herself; most of the time she felt she was alone with her weird thoughts.

* * *

By nine o'clock, The Studio was buzzing. That was a word Margo hadn't ever used before, but it felt as though it described the place perfectly. There was a permanent noise that sounded like a large bee was in the room, and Margo wished she could put in some earplugs but then she wouldn't be able to hear anything that was going on. And tonight she wanted to be the eyes and ears of the place because well, it was a crazy thing Nicole was doing, inviting so many people into one building. Margo knew that anything could happen and whilst it was down to Paisley to deal with the health and safety, Margo was also fully trained in that department and she knew that Paisley was going to be far more interested in drinking and socialising than taking care of people's welfare.

But that was fine with Margo. She was never much of a socialiser anyway; always more of an observer.

She liked to listen to conversations that were happening around her. She found them fascinating. It was her favourite pastime because then she didn't have to interact. Because no one expected a response from her, because no one thought she was listening. It was easy to listen to conversations that were happening at The Studio because the place was like a rabbit warren. There were several adjoining doors on the one side of the floor and sound travelled particularly well there. Margo could be stood just inside the doorway of one room and she would hear what was going on in the next room or out in the corridor without having to strain her ears at all. Except for the pods, which were all soundproofed.

Margo stood in the foyer and smiled as she watched the happy faces of all the people who had arrived. They were all already knocking back the cocktails, some were drinking beer and soon the champagne would be out once Nicole made her speech. The caterers were doing a fine job of circulating with the canapés, but Margo had had her fill.

It didn't take long for the guests to begin spreading themselves out around the whole of the top floor. Some who hadn't been inside and seen the pods yet were particularly interested in getting a look at those and pose for some photos with a set of headphones on, pretending to adjust buttons on the mixing desk in the main edit suite – a room that was so full of technology Margo was sure it had set Nicole back quite a bit, it was certainly the most extravagant part of The Studio. She started to feel nervous, poised ready to tell people to mind their drinks.

Margo tried her best to keep her eye on everyone and everything that was going on. Even though it wasn't a job that had been assigned to her, she felt a sense of responsibility because she was the only one who drank so little; if something, went wrong, if something was stolen, with all these drunk people about, who would be able to give an accurate account of what had happened? Margo cherished her job at The Studio, and she wanted to make sure that the beautiful space she worked in stayed just so.

But just as she had anticipated, before too long, the guests had spread to every corner of the top floor, and it was now impossible to keep track of everything. So she decided to keep moving between the main rooms in the centre of the space. That way she felt she had the best opportunity to see people coming and going, even if she couldn't see what they were up to most of the time.

Margo was fully prepared for an incident that might need putting in the accident book, or she might need to remind the odd person to rein it in a little. By 10 p.m., she could hear the voice of her colleague Audrey getting louder. She kept her sights on Audrey for a little while, shadowing her wherever she went, but Audrey was too drunk to notice. There was plenty of other action going on around her and she was aware of people moving between every room but, for some reason, Margo kept close to her colleague for a little longer.

11

NICOLE

Paisley was standing in the kitchen with Margo and Oli next to her. Nicole could smell it before she had even made it down the stairs. Dog faeces.

She arrived next to the small group who were standing holding their noses. Paisley looked at Nicole and then back at the mess and began to wretch. She pushed past Nicole and into the hallway, towards the toilet. Nicole was secretly hoping that Paisley wasn't about to throw up on the floor and would make it to the pan on time.

'What happened?' Nicole asked wearily. She felt so tired; the crying had taken it out of her.

'I was in the bathroom,' Margo said.

'I was putting some stuff in the bin outside,' Oli said. 'Paisley said she was in the toilet, but I didn't see.'

Nicole looked at the front door which was wide open. 'Why is the door open?' she asked.

'I had been to my car to grab something, but I was sure I closed it on the way back in,' Oli said. He sounded sorry and desperate all at once.

Nicole looked at him. 'It's okay. No one is in trouble here.'

'I guess the dog just came in, took a shit and left,' Oli said, shaking his head in bewilderment.

'Why would you say it was a dog that came in? Did you see it?' Nicole looked around for any other packages.

'Well, I didn't, but it's obviously from a dog.'

Nicole nodded.

'I think Paisley almost stood in it,' Oli said and almost laughed. Nicole looked at him a little too sternly and he turned back to the island and retrieved a roll of kitchen paper. 'I've got this.'

Nicole snatched the paper out of his hands. 'Don't be daft, you're the chef – I don't want you touching animal poo and then cooking our food. Go on, scoot.' Nicole waved Oli away with her other hand. He looked perturbed and it hadn't escaped Nicole's notice. She was well aware that so far on this trip she had not been the best version of herself. Margo had been observing her last night over dinner. She had bumped into Audrey on the landing and she must have heard her crying, or at least silently questioned why she was wearing sunglasses at nine in the morning. Now she was losing patience with the chef who was only trying to help. But this was Nicole's issue; this was her house and if anyone had to clean up the shit, it was going to be her. She held her breath, scooped up the majority with wads of tissue, and placed it in a bin bag that Audrey had thoughtfully laid out next to her. She filled a bucket with disinfectant and hot water and thoroughly mopped the area, then she removed the mop head and took that and the bin bag outside. Once outside, she closed the back door behind her. She could do with two minutes alone. She had felt Oli's, Audrey's and Margo's eyes burning into her.

The smell was potent in her nostrils and she thought she might vomit. Of course, there was every possibility that a stray dog or even a local dog had just wondered in and taken a dump in the middle of her kitchen floor, then scarpered before anyone saw it. Or – and this was what Nicole felt sicker than the actual stench of faeces – maybe it had been put there. Because the circumstances felt too familiar, too uniform. She had been here before experiencing childish pranks like these. And for it to be happening this weekend of all the weekends. Nicole had not anticipated anything like this, but of course it was always a possibility. The need to be here with her work colleagues to save her business had overruled the date: 28 October tomorrow. It didn't matter how long she stayed away, the ghosts just didn't want to rest. There were some things that didn't want to stay hidden; they wanted to keep rising and reminding Nicole of what she had been responsible for. Perhaps she had been too hasty to come away, but Nicole had her plans, her reasons for needing to be here, but now it seemed that the past wanted to intercept.

12

MARGO

The dialling tone rang out until eventually Margo hung up. She checked her messages again for the fifth time that morning: no missed calls and no personal emails. It was Friday and she had begun to realise that no one works on a Friday any more. Perhaps the office was closed early for the weekend. Clarissa, her father's carer, was not answering her mobile either and Margo was feeling irate about the whole situation. Maybe she should get in the car and drive home after all, just check everything was okay. No, her brain was overloaded with decision-making enough as it is, like trying to decide what to wear for the mini hike Nicole had planned. Something about getting the grey matter working, Nicole had said. Margo hoped it would be a good distraction from her dad back at home without her.

Breakfast had been a bit hit-and-miss. After the dog poo incident, there was a lingering scent of disinfectant, but beneath that Margo could still smell the faeces under the artificial cleaner. She was sensitive to smells and was thankful that the bedsheets had been washed without a strong-smelling fabric softener and so she had slept fairly soundly last night. Although it had taken her a while to drop off, as once the house was quiet, her thoughts became loud. She knew she had some work to do trying to rectify Nicole's comment. Of course, she knew that Nicole was in a bit of trouble over it – she was Nicole's assistant and handled most of the marketing for the studios and for the *Laying It Bare* podcast after all – but that was the least of her worries. The comment had caused far more of a stir than Nicole or Audrey could ever had conceived. But whilst six weeks ago, Margo would have been worrying about how to fix situations like this, now she had other things to manage. Like the secrets and lies of others. She was now the keeper of information that she had not requested nor desired to know. Since The Studio's one-year anniversary party, she was faced with a dilemma that she couldn't have foreseen. Not in a million years. She had almost blurted it out to Audrey earlier because she thought Audrey had been talking to her about the same thing. But, of course, Audrey was referring to the 'slut' comment. Nothing more. Margo knew how these things worked; this would consume the listeners for some time, and there was no denying it was going to influence the listener ratings. Margo wasn't sure how long that could affect the podcast for, but eventually, they would win their listeners back. It was a popular show, headed by Audrey Westwood, for goodness' sake. She was a popular figure with a huge social following. Nicole had taken the decision not to use social media, of course, and so she hid away from it. It was a good decision as far as Margo was concerned. The knock-on effect that the backlash over these sorts of events had on someone's mental health could be catastrophic, and Nicole already appeared fragile enough. Not that that was something new; Nicole had always seemed delicate for as long as Margo had known her. What was it that was bothering her? Margo wondered, and was it anything that she might be able to help with? Was it do with the information she knew? Margo prayed that it wasn't. She wasn't a liar, but she also didn't feel she had the vocabulary to explain what she had seen. Margo had tried hard to unsee the event from The Studio party, but it was no good. Sometimes, it woke her up in a panic. She wasn't sure she would be the right person to speak to Nicole about this. She thought about where they were, surrounded by cliffs and fierce drops and the vast deep ocean. Should she be keeping a special eye on her? Margo wondered. She had caught Nicole's eye yesterday, but Nicole had pulled her gaze away. Margo wasn't very good at saying things with her eyes anyway. She could barely say what she needed to with her voice.

Perhaps Nicole was just disappointed in her, for not stepping up and dealing with the 'slut' comment quicker, which was why they were all here. Margo knew that The Beach House had some history, something that rattled Nicole, but she was never quite sure exactly what. She'd heard snippets of conversations between Nicole and her mother and Gram, the tones and words of which suggesting the complexity of Nicole's relationship with her childhood family holiday home. But it had never been revealed to her and Margo had certainly never probed for more information. But now Margo was here, she could sense it. She selfishly hoped it was only The Beach House itself that was causing Nicole's solemn mood and not anything Margo had done. And was certainly nothing to do with what she knew had happened at the party.

Margo's phone rang and she saw Clarissa's name flash up. She answered as quickly as possible.

'Hello, hello,' she said almost panting out the words. She walked to the front door hoping for the best reception.

'Hi... you... just... happy... inside... today...' came the broken words from the other end of the line.

'Clarissa, I can't hear you, you're breaking up. Can you move somewhere with better reception?' Margo knew there was every possibility it was her own reception here at The Beach House.

'Just... true... in... we... night...'

'Clarissa!' Margo called. 'I'll try calling you back.' Margo hung up and hit redial. The phone rang out to a generic answer message.

Margo tried to call back and again, but she just got the answerphone.

She sat down on a chair in the hallway feeling defeated. She would try and call back on the walk. She was early, she knew. She had arrived at breakfast for eight because she thought that was a reasonable hour to arrive, not too early, not too late, but she had only found Audrey there, still scantily clad, Oli's eyes poring all over her. Then after breakfast, everyone disappeared, and Margo hadn't seen or heard anyone since. She didn't want to appear rude and start calling for people or knocking on doors, so she stayed where she was in the hallway, with her phone clenched tightly in her hand in case Clarissa called back again. At least she was there. Her voice had sounded fairly neutral. Margo was always aware of the pitch of people's voices. If there was a hint of a highness she was wary, her defences were up. People usually spoke with a high voice when they were unsure about things. They thought they were soothing but it sounded like alarm bells to Margo.

Margo crossed and uncrossed her legs until her bottom began to ache from sitting. She walked to the window in the hallway on the opposite side of the door. It was a very spacious hallway – it was the first thing Margo had noticed when she arrived – about the size of her dining room and kitchen combined. Through the window she saw just a smattering of clouds against a perfect blue sky. A beautiful autumn day. If there was an emergency with her father, then Clarissa would have found a way to contact her about it, and from the smattering of words she could hear, there didn't seem to be anything to be alarmed about.

She walked across the hallway to the front door and opened it to appreciate the day even more and to breathe in some sea air.

She could see Oli at the end of the driveway next to the path

that led down to the sea. He was with a woman, in a bright yellow
cagoule. The woman seemed to be wound up; she was shouting
and gesticulating and then pointing up at the house. Oli wasn't
reacting. He looked like he was trying to walk away, but the woman
had grabbed hold of his bicep and was trying to pull him back, but
Oli was obviously stronger and yanked himself out of her grip and
walked back up the drive, his head down, focusing hard on the
ground beneath him. Before he could see Margo standing in the
doorway, she closed the door so it was ajar and then hurried back to
her seat. She really wasn't the sort of person to involve herself in
other people's business, and whatever Oli had or hadn't said to that
woman to make her act that way was not Margo's affair. This was
one of those everyone-knows-everyone areas, with only a smattering of houses here along the cliff she would have presumed the
locals would have been welcoming. She imagined it was something
as trivial as Oli dropping some rubbish and the woman getting riled
up about protecting the area. Oli seemed an amiable chap; she
wasn't sure what he could possibly have done that would have
upset anyone. He certainly seemed to be on his best behaviour here
in The Beach House.

Margo looked down at her lap and began fiddling with her
phone as she heard Oli come in through the door. She looked up
and gave an awkward smile because she felt terribly guilty for
having spied on him.

Oli looked a little harassed, as though the incident with the
woman had shaken him, and it took all of Margo's strength not to
ask him what had happened. She also knew it was common practice to ask if he was okay, but she wasn't sure how that conversation
would go beyond that one question. He might nod and say he was
fine and what was she supposed to say after that? No, it was better
to stay quiet. She could always mention it casually to Nicole later.
Ask her if she knew who the woman in the yellow cagoule was.

Oli went straight to the kitchen area and began pulling things out of the fridge, presumably to prepare for lunch. Margo was still so full of a hearty breakfast she couldn't really think about eating just yet. What she needed was a long walk to burn off some energy.

She made her way into the communal area. Oli nodded at her and then his concentration was back on his work; he was very diligent. Margo had been standing in the hallway for some time, so it felt good to stretch her legs whilst she waited for the others. Who knew how long they would be. She walked to the other side of the room so she was facing away from the island. In front of her was a cabinet, a solid wood number that Margo had admired from afar last night, observing all the trinkets that adorned the surface. She was aware of Oli behind her, chopping and then moving around the kitchen space, and she cleared her throat, a tic she had inherited from her father when she was feeling uncomfortable. There were only a few items on the cabinet and Margo looked at each of them in turn again. First a spiral-shaped statue that upon closer inspection Margo decided was supposed to represent a wave. Next, two heavy books on top of one another. The top one was called *Ocean Views*. Margo made a mental note to check it out later after the walk. The final token piece was an ashtray. Large and oval and made from thick glass. Margo envisaged it slipping from her hands and smashing onto the wooden floor. She decided not to pick it up. Then she spotted there was something tucked underneath it. Margo bent to take a closer look and could make out a sheet of folded newspaper. It looked entirely out of place amongst the symmetry of the three trinkets. Margo glanced behind her. Oli was gone. She slipped the paper out from under the ashtray, her heart beating twice as fast as she envisaged the ashtray falling to the ground and smashing into a thousand pieces. But the paper slid out easily. She looked behind her again; she was still alone in the room. She quickly and carefully unfolded the paper. On the open side was

an advert for a chairlift. She flipped it over. At the top of the page
was the name of the newspaper, *Dorset Herald*. The date was Saturday, 22 May 2004. Margo's eyes fell on the headline.

Locals pay tribute to teacher

Margo gulped and greedily took in as much of the story as she
could, aware that someone could come into the room at any
moment. Yet the piece of the paper was just here where anyone
could see it. The man, Andrew, a thirty-five-year-old teacher from
the area, had been suffering with his mental health at the time of
his suicide. Margo felt her heart thump harder. The word suicide
always gave her the shivers. She hurriedly took in a few more words
about Andrew's family, about how he left behind a wife, Claire, and
how he'd been a great asset in the local community, launching an
allotment which grew vegetables that were then given to a local
food bank. Margo felt she had got the gist of the feature and folded
it back up and carefully returned it to under the ashtray. She turned
around as Oli appeared in the kitchen again; his head was down, he
was looking at his phone as he wandered back into the kitchen. He
glanced up at her and Margo flashed him an awkward smile and
hurried back into the hallway and stood looking up expectantly at
the stairs.

The article was playing over in her mind. Andrew Best, local
man. Nicole must know him. He had died here on the cliffs near
The Beach House and an article about it was stuffed under an
ashtray in the living area. Margo had been sitting in the corner just
next to the cabinet last night. She had clocked each piece on the top
but hadn't noticed anything under the ashtray. She would have
remembered seeing it. She had memorised a lot of what was in the
house already, so it could only have been put there after she had
gone to bed or today. But why would Nicole hoard away an article

like that? Margo presumed that Nicole knew this Andrew. Margo did a quick sum; the article was over eighteen years old. Nicole was thirty-three, so she would have just been a teenager at the time of his death. As Margo continued to think about the connection between Andrew Best and Nicole, she heard someone making their way downstairs. It was Nicole. Her relief was palpable as she let out a loud, thankful sigh. Nicole was dressed smartly in light jeans that stopped at her ankles and a white-and-black striped T-shirt. She was pulling on a chunky bold blue cardy as she approached Margo.

'Sorry, have you been waiting?' she asked her.

'No, just doing some things on my phone,' Margo lied.

Nicole turned and called up the stairs. 'Guys, are you ready to go?' Nicole pulled on a beanie hat and a purple ankle-length puffer jacket.

There was silence for a moment, then the sound of two doors closing one after another and the animated sound of Paisley's voice blending with Audrey's deeper velvety tones. Margo liked listening to the muffled sound of people's voices from afar. She found it soothing. She much preferred it to listening to people talking near to her.

Audrey and Paisley both arrived in the hallway looking as glam and chic as they could ever be, and Margo realised she had let out a small sigh.

'All right, Margo?' Audrey asked in a way that was pushing passive aggressive. But Margo knew she had irritated her this morning, and they still had much to talk about.

'Sure,' Margo chirped, knowing that would deter any further questioning.

'That breakfast was something else, Nicole. Can I take your chef home with me? I need him to teach me things,' Audrey said in that way she had that made the unsexiest things sound sensual. Margo found it mildly annoying and had come up with a way to turn it around so it was a game, where she would try to guess when Audrey was going to make one of her playful remarks and she usually got it spot on.

'Right then. If we're all geared up, let's go!' Nicole led the way to the front door. Margo wondered if the woman she had seen getting cross with Oli earlier would still be there and if she might have something to say to any of them. Oli was behind the island, busy chopping a red cabbage.

As Margo was the last out of the door, it was up to her to close it. She happened to take one last glance into the kitchen just as the door was almost closed, and in that last split second, she watched as Oli took the chef's knife he had been holding and stabbed it firmly into the wooden chopping board.

13

PAISLEY

The fresh sea air on her face was exactly what she had needed. The house had become stuffy over breakfast and the stench of dog shit had remained in her nostrils for far longer than she would have liked. She wondered if this was the beginning of morning sickness. She had read every article and eBook on pregnancy; Paisley imagined she would be the sort of woman who had a textbook pregnancy. She was five weeks gone. She was positive about that. It was easy to be that sure when you knew exactly when you conceived. Paisley tried to ignore the patterns of doubt in her mind, that she hadn't gone about this in the traditional way. But she would love this baby more than it would ever know. It was the gift that she had been waiting so long for. She knew she would receive mixed responses from her friends and family because she hadn't really known the father very long at all and because of the way it happened. But if this was the way it had to be, then so be it. She would choose this over no baby any day. Not everyone could go out and meet Prince bloody Charming and pop out several sprogs. Paisley thought about Audrey with her three perfect kids and the doting husband. She then thought about Nicole: no children, but she had everything. The perfect partner, the perfect job, house, holiday home and car, and yet, she didn't want to bring a kid into this world.

Paisley had thought about telling the girls this evening – a little Friday-night surprise news to get the conversation going over dinner. She would see how she felt later. This walk she knew was going to take it right out of her. She had been so tired recently; she had presumed it had been from the stress of the waiting, the stress of trying to conceive. Would it be inappropriate to mention it over dinner? She wasn't sure if she was ready to share the news yet. It was big for her; her life had been pretty unfulfilled and mundane to date. It was the sort of news she had been desperate to share for so long that she was nervous, and rightly so. There would be questions, and Paisley wasn't sure if she was ready to answer them just yet; it was a pretty delicate situation. Paisley knew she really should wait. She needed backup. She needed a scan, confirmation from a doctor, but most of all she needed the support of one person who would help her to answer those questions.

The other three women had walked a few feet ahead of her already. She pulled her phone out of her pocket and checked it for messages. She had sent a text this morning, right after she had done the test. The father of her child needed to know. But somehow she knew that everything was going to be okay, that he was going to be happy and embrace it as much as she had. He did want children, after all, that she knew for sure. She wanted him here with her. She needed him here. Now she was pregnant, she was sure he would want her to relax, even if it was just for the sake of the baby. She could quit her job, let him take care of her.

She checked ahead of her again; the girls were deep in conversation. She quickly bashed out a second message.

Hello. It's me again. I hope you received my last text about the pregnancy. I know it might seem a bit of a shock because it happened so fast, but believe me, I am shocked too. But I think this is the best thing that could have happened. I really think this could be the making of us. I have it all planned out, we just need to sit down and have a conversation. But you must not worry, I will be here for you. I know you will be here for me too – you are such a kind and generous man. And your son or daughter is going to love you with all of their heart. It's finally happened, you're finally a father. I know how busy you are today, but text or call as soon as you can. All my love, Paisley.

Paisley slipped the phone into her coat pocket as a small smile played across her lips. It was true that women feel joy at this little secret that they keep inside themselves, and that was exactly how Paisley felt, a great sense of pride that she was carrying and growing a human and no one except her, well her and the father, knew. In a way, she wanted to keep it to herself for a little while longer. It felt like the most amazing achievement anyone could imagine or hope to experience. Nothing could beat this feeling she was experiencing. She was truly on cloud nine.

There was a slight chill in the air today, even though the sun was bright. Paisley had put on a chunky sweater under her coat, which she thought looked cute. She had always prided herself on the way she dressed, but as she walked she began to think about when she would begin to show and when she would actually tell people. That brought her back to her original train of thought about when she ought to be telling people, especially those she worked with, because soon she would have to say something. Of course there would be people who would not take the news well. But in a funny way, she was looking forward to them finding out more than anyone else.

14

AUDREY

The walk was hard because Audrey had not drunk enough liquid before she left the house. In fact, she had drunk very little after the green juice Oli gave her this morning and now she was regretting it. She thought about the vat of red wine, champagne and then more wine she'd drunk the night before and her mouth filled with saliva. She stopped and leant over to take a few deep breaths. Paisley happened to be walking right behind her. 'Oh my God, Audrey, are you okay?' Paisley caught up to her and looked as though she were ready to launch into first-aid mode. She had been so keen to get her certificate when she began working at The Studio and made it a point of reference as often as she could.

'I'm fine, Paisley. Just a little too much wine last night.'

Audrey thought about last night and who else had been drinking and if they had drunk to the extent she had. She wasn't worried about it though. She wasn't a bad drunk; she was always able to style out any episode, even when she had been photographed falling out of a restaurant or late-night bar in London, back in the day when journalists liked to pap celebs looking their absolute worst so they could sell a few more tabloids.

Maybe that still happened, she knew it wasn't very 'of the time', but sometimes Audrey longed for the good old days of climbing into a taxi absolutely trolleyed and the journos getting the most perfect image of her with her mouth wide open, probably shouting some sort of profanity. It would always make her laugh.

Perhaps her dicky tummy and slight panicky feeling were also spurred on by stress. Nicole was worried about the financial state of The Studio in general, but Audrey's priorities were with *Laying It Bare*. She needed to make the podcast work. She had such high hopes for it in the beginning, but now Nicole was so preoccupied with the whole business collapsing. And there was something else too. Margo was right: Nicole did seem off. Maybe it was The Beach House. What was worse was that without trying, Audrey had ended up in some sort of secret club with Margo over the 'slut' comment.

Even though she felt sick, Audrey knew she would be on it again as soon as they got back; a hair of the dog and a nap would see her right until dinner. She began thinking about Oli and whether he was any good at making a Bloody Mary.

Paisley was looking at her with curiosity.

'Are you sure you're okay, Audrey? You don't look at all well.'

Audrey pulled her shoulders back, puffed her chest out, pushed her sunglasses back along her nose and marched ahead of Paisley.

'Oh, believe me, love, I've survived worse than this.'

Audrey supposed she could tell Paisley all about the nineties and the drug-fuelled parties she'd attended, long before social media was able to record and publish every single move you made. But Paisley seemed so pristine, and Audrey was sure she seemed like the sort of girl who would be easily shocked. But they were the best times – hedonistic – and to this day filled her with an aching nostalgia when she thought about them. Not just because she'd been high as a kite, but because she had been free. She had no worries, no one to answer to. Everyone had worshipped her. She had been the main attraction at every party, in every room she walked in to. Now, she was just a bit tired and fed up. Which was why the podcast was so important to her, if she didn't have that to vent though, she was sure she would go mad. This was why it was crucial that they didn't piss off their listeners, that they were made to feel listened to. Audrey felt her gut tighten and her mouth fill with saliva again.

She slowed and then hung back, letting Paisley pass as they headed up the cliff path. The vast stretch of ocean was a sight to behold. The sun reflected on the water, and it twinkled like millions of diamonds were floating on top.

Paisley had her head bent down, looking at her phone. Was she not here to enjoy the walk?

Nicole and Margo walked almost in sync, and when Audrey reached them, she gave them both her best beaming smile, trying to ignore the churning gut.

'I say, do you think your chef has some vodka and tomato juice?' she asked.

'I love the way you refer to him as "my chef",' Nicole said.

'Well, he is, isn't he?'

'I suppose he is now.'

'So you'll use him again?' Audrey raised her eyebrows.

'I might.'

'Oh I say. Well, I'll be back when you are.' Audrey laughed, and she heard noises from both Nicole and Margo. Margo's was more of a grunt. Which she ignored.

'Are you happy with him? I mean it's got to be a bit weird inviting a stranger into your house. As hot as he is.' Audrey nudged Nicole. Nicole pushed her weight back into Audrey.

'It's fine... I mean he seems okay. He's very professional.'

'Do you think it was a bit weird about the dog poo thing? Do you think he, you know, knows something?'

'Oh my God, Audrey. You make it sound like an Agatha Christie novel. A dog strayed in and shat on the floor. Nothing more to think about here.'

'Right,' Audrey said, noting the strain in Nicole's reply, but it still seemed odd to her. A random dog, walking in and taking a dump and then leaving and no one saw a thing? She decided not to push it with Nicole. Her nerves were clearly frayed and this was supposed to be a break of sorts. Even though Nicole had seemed adamant that they would be discussing work whilst they were here, but with the amount of alcohol that was stashed around the place, Audrey was wondering if that was even going to happen at all.

'Anyway, he's far too professional – he's ignored all of my advances,' Audrey said so seriously that Nicole couldn't help laughing.

'Oh no, well, that just won't do, will it? I'm sure if you pick out something particularly alluring, you might be able to turn his eye.' Despite the banter, there was a flatness to Nicole's voice that made Audrey feel uneasy. But then again, she might just be paranoid from the hangover.

'Well. If I'm being honest, I would say it was *you* he was interested in.'

Nicole didn't speak, so Audrey continued.

'Yeah, I noticed it last night at dinner. I was sitting next to you, remember, and opposite the island where Oli was doing his thing, and yeah, I just noticed that he looked at you. Like more than a couple of times. He seemed almost, I don't know, like he was studying you.'

Nicole was frowning at this point. 'Well, don't forget you had had quite a lot to drink, and Paisley was sitting to my right, so he was probably staring at her.'

Audrey looked thoughtful for a moment.

'I was drunk, Nicole, fair enough, but he wasn't looking at

Paisley for Christ's sake. He was looking at you and that, my friend, I could see *with* the beer goggles on.'

Audrey noted how Nicole changed the subject pretty swiftly after that and began talking about the hike and how she had been doing this walk since she was a toddler. How her parents worried for her safety and attached a lead to her like a dog so she wouldn't topple off the cliff edge. She laughed fondly as she said so, but then Audrey noticed something lingering after she had laughed. It wasn't an expression or a word, more like a feeling, like melancholy.

They reached the top of the cliff and looked out at the view.

'Hey, what's this?' Audrey said, pointing to an old bunch of flowers that had been woven into the wire fence. They were sodden and brown, as if they'd been there for months.

Nicole was quiet for a second, then she turned and pointed to the bench that was behind them.

Audrey walked over to it.

'"For our beloved Andrew Best. Always in our hearts."' Audrey returned to the fence and looked questioningly at Nicole. 'Who was Andrew Best? Are you okay, Margo?' Audrey spun around to face Margo who had gasped.

'A man who lived around this area. He... he took his own life, right here.' Nicole pointed down past the bunch of flowers to where the cliff face was steep and rugged; towards the bottom, it spilled out into jagged rocks.

'Jesus Christ,' Audrey said quietly. 'And someone puts those flowers here?'

'His wife. Usually every year. On the anniversary.'

Audrey looked at the dead flowers; the anniversary must have been several months back.

'Wow. For how long? When did he, you know, die? How old was he?'

'Over eighteen years ago now. He was thirty-five.' Nicole looked suddenly into the distance.

Audrey clocked this. 'My God, did you know him?'

'Of course, I knew everyone around here back then. It's a very small community. Only about thirty people tops live in this stretch.'

'I'm sorry, Nicole,' Audrey said because she felt it was necessary.

Nicole shook her head. 'It's breathtaking up here, though, isn't it?' which signalled the end of the conversation.

Audrey nodded, because it really was. She had travelled around the world, visited some truly exotic locations and seen a few good views in her time, but this was up there with the best of them.

Paisley and Margo caught up and the four of them stood, silently admiring the view. The silence was interrupted by Paisley's phone ringing. She looked at it where she had been clutching it in her hand and a wide grin spread across her face.

'Oh, excuse me,' she said and walked a few feet away back down the cliff path.

Audrey was intrigued. Who could have been calling Paisley to have brought a smile like that to her face? She watched with interest as Paisley answered the phone with an expression of delight and excitement, pacing back and forth to the fence at the edge of the cliff face. She said a few words and then stopped, listening intently to the other person on the other end of the line. Almost immediately, she lost the excited energy and stopped pacing. She began talking again, still with plenty of animation, but when she stopped speaking for a second time, she looked obviously crestfallen; her energy had depleted, her shoulders practically hunched over. She walked to the fence, leant on it and held the phone away from her and stared at it disbelievingly. It looked to Audrey as though whoever was on the other end of the phone had hung up on her. Paisley glanced sheepishly across to where Audrey was standing with Margo and Nicole, who were pointing out things they could see on the horizon.

Audrey managed to style out staring at Paisley by continuing her gaze to the right, as though she were simply looking around and hadn't just been taking in the whole conversation whilst simultaneously trying to work out who Paisley could be talking to and what they had been saying to her. Whatever it was, it was not good; it had made Paisley's whole demeanour change from thrilled to despondent in a matter of seconds.

Audrey prepped herself for the return of Paisley, her face ready to assist her with her bad news.

Paisley seemed to be taking her time walking back, and she was still looking at her phone when she arrived next to the group. She had somehow morphed her expression into something that resembled a smile.

'It's a gorgeous view, isn't it?' Audrey turned her body back to the fence once she saw that Paisley did not want to engage.

She heard a mumbled response from Paisley.

'All right?' Nicole said; a generic sort of statement that really didn't require a response, but Audrey replied jovially nonetheless.

'Absolutely, this view is incredible.'

'I know,' Nicole said as she looked out across the water.

'Oh, that's the woman from earlier,' Margo suddenly blurted out and began waving her hand in the direction of a lone woman standing on the beach. She was wearing a bright yellow mac. Audrey scanned the empty beach for a sign of a dog or companion because the woman was standing very still and looking up at them. The beach, which was about fifty-foot below where they stood, was totally empty except for the woman. She was the only person there. That unnerved Audrey. She could handle groups of people all shouting and screaming her name, or even the odd person who would tentatively approach her and ask for a selfie or, back in the day, an autograph. But there was the other memory and it flooded back with such force that Audrey took a few steps back. The image of someone standing at the end of her driveway still haunted her to this day. It had been a one-off stalker, and they had gone once the injunction had been served. But Audrey had forgotten how much it had spooked her until the woman standing and staring in a very similar fashion dredged up all her anxieties. Audrey's skin prickled as the wind picked up. She couldn't help but let out a small moan as the memory gripped her.

No one looked at her. Paisley was still dealing with her phone dilemma, bashing out a text message, whilst Margo and Nicole looked on.

Suddenly, Nicole was away and stomping up the hill followed by a startled but compliant Margo. Audrey looked at Paisley to encourage her to walk on too and then glanced once more over the fence and then cliff edge, but the woman was gone.

15

THE PARTY

Paisley had arrived late to the party because she had been agonising over her outfit for the best part of three hours. She had already picked out what she wanted to wear days ago, but when it came to putting it on, she felt nothing about it looked right. So it was back to the drawing board, which resulted in arriving after nine to what was already a room full of very drunk people. Paisley had hoped to be on the same wavelength, but now she had some serious catching up to do. She didn't like being the only sober person in the room. There were a few cocktails lined up on a table in the foyer and so she grabbed one and downed it quickly without anyone noticing. She picked up a second one and took long swigs of it as she scanned the room.

She saw Matt immediately. He looked so suave in his suit jacket and white T-shirt underneath. It was a look on men that Paisley had come to love.

The alcohol had already begun to take over her body – whatever was in those cocktails was meant to relax the guests quickly. Paisley went to make a beeline for him. As did a woman with long legs and brown locks down to her lower back, who grabbed his arm, whispered something in his ear and he began to laugh.

Paisley took a step back, sipped her drink and then clocked Nicole with Gram. She wandered over to them. She felt both of their eyes on her immediately. The dress she was wearing ended at her butt cheeks and cupped them just enough so that the dress didn't ride up any more. It was a risqué choice for Paisley. She'd intended to go for something more demure, but she'd felt frumpy in the outfits she'd picked out for herself. And she had to admit, there was something about this dress that she made her feel quite special, and the number of looks she had received from men already in the few short minutes she had been here was astounding her. It made her think that maybe she should have been wearing something like this before now. Perhaps the attention she had been trying so desperately to attract from Matt all this time would have come more easily if she'd considered her outfit choices a little more carefully.

Nicole had said something kind about her dress and how lovely she looked. Paisley noted Gram's eyes lingered a little longer on her legs, then he looked up at her face and smiled.

'So glad you could come,' he said, and Paisley felt a stab of annoyance at his comment. Why wouldn't she come? She had worked at The Studio for the entire year so why wouldn't she be here to celebrate the anniversary? Gram had spoken to her as though she were someone he barely knew.

Paisley felt her stomach tighten with annoyance, and so she quickly excused herself to go to the ladies. She stared at herself in the mirror for a long time before she locked herself in a cubicle. She put the toilet seat down and took her phone out of her handbag. She opened the gambling app and felt the familiar mix of dread and excitement. Why was this her life? Why hadn't she met someone by now? She was almost thirty. She had been ready to have children years ago but what was it about her that scared men away in the end? Was it the talk of children? Had she been too full on? Paisley believed in honesty; what was the point in lying or hiding behind a veil? She wanted kids, she always had done. There was no two ways about it.

She spent the next five minutes spending £150 on cyber roulette. It was only the door to the toilets opening and the cackling sound of women falling into the other two cubicles that brought her back to the present. She didn't even feel the usual dismay she felt when she lost because she was slightly numb from the alcohol and the women were now shouting across her cubicle to one another. She slipped out, washed her hands and headed back to the party.

She knew that Nicole planned to do a speech at 10 p.m., and so she just needed to get to Matt.

She stepped out of the toilet and then heard him before she saw him: a loud long wholesome laugh that penetrated the room. It was strange, because in his working life at The Studio, Matt was a quiet soul. People saw him as studious, constantly working overtime as a sound engineer to ensure that deadlines were met. Wasn't it funny how people had various personalities, traits that would come out at different times, or for different people? He was a great sound engineer, and he was the nuts and bolts of the business; it really couldn't work without him. Quite often clients brought in their own sound engineer, but even many of them had chosen to use Matt on their future projects. And he worked on solo projects outside of The Studio too; he was very work-focused, which was what had drawn Paisley to him. Who wouldn't want to take a man like Matt home to meet their family?

She had been out one night after work with him a couple of weeks back, along with a married couple who had been recording a podcast. She hadn't been invited, but the conversation between Matt and the clients went on in reception where she was working, flowing between all of them, so much so that when they mentioned they would all head to the pub to keep chatting and would Paisley mind locking up, it made sense to her to wander round after them. There had been an initial element of surprise on their faces when she had entered the pub, but once the drinks began flowing, she and Matt were laughing about everything and anything, then when the couple left to go home, it had just been her and Matt, several drinks in. They suddenly began talking about more intimate things: ex partners, whether either of them dating (no), what they looked for in a relationship and the most important element to the conversation, whether either of them wanted kids. Yes, was Matt's answer. And Paisley's heart had soared. He walked her to an Uber and had leant down and kissed her gently on the lips. By the time she had opened her eyes, Matt was already walking away. She hadn't stopped thinking about that kiss, but there hadn't really been an opportunity to speak with him since. Paisley had become painfully shy around him and Matt was his usual jovial and professional self at work. But because he didn't say anything, neither did she.

The gambling had been a way to distract herself after a particularly bad break-up, and during those few weeks when they had worked together but barely spoken, Paisley still felt hope, that something might come from it again, if they only had the opportunity. Gambling was the only way she could get through as she waited it out. Tonight was going to be the night though. After tonight, everything was going to be different.

16

NICOLE

How was it even possible? Perhaps Nicole had mistaken her. Perhaps it was the bad memories coming back to haunt her because of where she was. Nicole knew there was no mistaking that look, that stance. And Margo had said she had seen the same woman earlier, which must mean that she was real; she had been here today and next to the house. Claire Best. Why was she here? She'd sold the house that she and Andrew lived in years back and, from what Nicole had heard, had moved to Devon. The word *revenge* rang through Nicole's mind like a foghorn, so painfully loud that it was impossible to ignore. Claire Best had never got over her husband's death. She had walked around the village like a ghost for years, tormenting Nicole and her family, before finally putting her house on the market and moving away.

After Margo had pointed out the woman, who she had instantly recognised as Claire, Nicole had rushed up the cliff face. There was still a way to go until they were at the top and then the path would flatten out, so they could walk for a good distance to take in the splendour of the cliff view, before the descent down to the beach and then back up again near to The Beach House. She slowed now so she could allow the others to catch up with her, and when they did, she smiled a broad, welcoming smile, as if everything was fine, as if she hadn't just seen a figure from her past. Nicole was aware of how tense she'd been last night. Coming back here this weekend had been a big deal. She had hoped that the old place would bring her some sanctuary, some time to reflect on her past decisions, and what the date meant to her. Whilst the presence of the other women would offer her some distraction. She didn't want to think too much about the secrets the old house was still clinging on to. But seeing Claire on the beach was a reminder that no matter how much time had passed, some people did not want to forget.

17

MARGO

Why did Margo feel as though she had said something terribly wrong? She had caught up with Nicole after she'd sped off up the hill when Margo had pointed out the woman on the beach. Nicole had been behaving unusually ever since they had arrived and it had been playing on Margo's mind. She knew she had postponed telling Nicole what she knew for too long now, but as each minute edged past, she was pushing herself away from speaking the truth because she could see how Nicole was growing more and more tense by the minute.

They arrived back at The Beach House after a full hour and a half of walking. They were never as far away from the house that they couldn't ever see it; it was always within view, they just walked along way down and then a long way up. They had to stop three times for Paisley to catch up because she was so engrossed in her phone and Margo was certain she had been crying at least once. The Beach House was filled with beautiful scents, a far cry from the hideous dog catastrophe that had occurred just before breakfast. Margo was still uncertain about what had happened, because she was sure Paisley had been in the room at the time, but Paisley was adamant she had been out of the room and had missed all of it.

The walk had done Margo some good though; she had so much pent-up frustration about her father and the caring agency not calling her back as well as the matter that was pressing hard on her conscience. She had managed to get through to Clarissa's phone and had left a long and detailed message, which had eased Margo's worries a little. One less thing to worry about now she could sense Audrey on her case. Margo just wanted to focus on moving forwards, finding a way of saving The Studio for Nicole and for the safety of her own job.

But Margo was thinking more and more about her role as marketing manager. Would she still have the position if Nicole ever found out what she knew. If Margo could just turn back time, she would have gone home after The Studio party and not agreed to be the one to lock up. Then she would be none the wiser, she would be totally free of all this baggage she had been carrying around for weeks.

Margo's phone rang loud and shrill as they all congregated in the hallway removing coats and boots.

'Bloody hell, Margo. Are you going deaf in your old age?' Audrey commented as Margo sheepishly took out her phone and swiped at it to answer; the number was barely a blur in her vision by the time she had got the phone to her ear.

'Hello,' Margo said, breathless from the walk and now from the anticipation and worry that her father would be on the other end, pleading for help because she had left him at the mercy of a complete stranger who was probably not even an agent carer but a psychopath who liked to mug off old men.

'Hello, Margo.' It was Clarissa with her slight accent. 'I am here with your father, we are doing okay, just so you know.'

'Ah, thank you, Clarissa.' Margo instantly felt relief flow through her veins. 'I really appreciate you getting in touch. I was getting a bit worried after our call didn't really connect earlier, and I called the agency and left a message on your—'

'Yes, as I say, we are well and your father he is very happy. He slept well last night and we have a busy morning today.'

Margo could almost feel herself begin to float as another weight began to leave her body. She could get through the next couple of days.

'That's great, Clarissa, thank you so much.'

'No problem at all, but I need to tell you that someone was here. We saw them walking around the house when we got back from our walk.'

Margo's stomach dropped and the weight she had felt drift away moments before was back and slamming down on her shoulders, making her hunch over so much she had to slump into the chair in the hallway. The group had dispersed into various areas of the house, so she was alone in the hallway as she braced herself to hear what she had been dreading hearing for a long time.

'It was a man. I told him to clear off, so he went.'

She almost laughed out her response. 'Oh, okay.'

'You are not worried? I thought I should call you. Check this was not a serious issue for you.'

'No, no, it's fine. As long as you didn't let him in,' Margo said.

'No, I waved him away, told him I am calling police. He ran away quick smart.'

'Well done. He's obviously a debt collector but looking for the people who lived in the house before us. You'd think they'd look at my old dad and realise he is not the sort of chap to be caught up with loans sharks at his age. Anyway, they don't seem to be getting the message, so I may well be calling the police when I get home,'

Margo said to reassure Clarissa, because she knew she was not calling the police when she got home or ever. But it seemed her sanctuary with just her and her father was up. It was time to face what was to come.

18

PAISLEY

Paisley had paced the bedroom like a trapped wild animal for over forty minutes. She knew that lunch was almost ready and that a call up the stairs or a knock on the door was imminent. She was riled up to the point that she thought she could very well scream at the top of her lungs if no one was in the house. Oh how she'd longed for a primal scream when they had reached the beach. She'd wanted to run at those waves and pour all her energy into them through one long, loud shriek. Now all she could do was pace and wait. Pace and wait. Wait for him to call.

He had said he would call her when she was somewhere where he could hear her properly. The waves and the wind had penetrated the mouthpiece and rattled down the connection. He had been in shock, she had heard that in his voice. A baby was what he wanted and now here she was, with child, and he was acting stunned. God, she had heard this about men, about how they sometimes retreat to their caves for the first few months of a woman's pregnancy. Never mind that was the time when the woman needed them the most, when her body was going through so many changes, and yes, come to think of it, Paisley had been feeling pretty sick recently but she had not connected the sickness with the pregnancy. How silly, she thought. Of course, it was that. But it was easy to see now she had the proof. Everything was easier once you had the facts. She could hear the movement of the house downstairs, the cackled laughter of Audrey.

Oh Audrey. How Paisley wanted to like that woman, but it was not possible to like someone who was so unlikeable. How could the woman who had everything still whine and moan on that podcast as though she had been dealt the worst card in the world? Paisley got that it was what made the show so appealing – to women over thirty mainly – but Paisley would have thought that by now, Audrey had everything she could ever want.

What Paisley needed was for him to call her back. It had been almost an hour since they'd had the broken conversation where he couldn't hear her and had told her he'd call her back. She'd text him twice to say she was back at The Beach House and she could see he'd read the first one. He was at work, she got that, but this was a monumental moment, and she expected a little more urgency on his part. After all, he'd done the urgent part the first time around no problem. That was why she was in this situation in the first place.

She felt the call of the gambling app on her phone, urging her to open it and play. But she fought it and went to her handbag instead and pulled out the notebook.

I am trying to remember the first time we laid eyes on one another. Because it's so funny, the way things have happened. I couldn't have imagined us together for a single second until we were. Until my whole world melted away and it was only you and I left in the universe. I think I might actually love you. Is that crazy? Despite the way this has happened, despite knowing what you did was wrong, I am in love with you. It's not just a silly infatuation, it is true love. My heart hurts thinking of you. I have to write it down because if I don't, then I feel like I will explode because I can't speak to anyone. Holding it in doesn't work because I find I can't concentrate and then, well, that's when people start to notice. I can't focus on a normal task for longer than a few minutes before my mind starts to wander and then I am somewhere else altogether. Somewhere with you. I know we have only been with each other a handful of times, but I need to tell you these things. For now, I will write them here. One day I hope and believe we will be together forever.

There was a light knocking on her door. It startled Paisley, and she stuffed the notepad back into her bag.

'Lunch,' she heard Audrey say on the other side of the door.

'Okay, just coming,' she said politely and then tried his phone once more only this time to be welcomed by the sound of his voice-mail message.

'*Hey, tell me something awesome,*' came his voice.

Paisley hung up.

* * *

The sight and smell of lunch brought a spark of joy, but he was within that spark. Paisley was imagining the two of them here together, with their own chef and their little brood of babies running around. She knew if she imagined it for hard enough, she would be living that life. She had imagined the baby for so long, and now it was here, she didn't need to dream any longer.

Paisley noticed there was champagne on the table in a large silver ice bucket. Oh Christ, things were going to get messy again, like last night. Audrey was basically going to have pickled insides by the time she left here on Sunday. This was not the place Paisley wanted or needed to be right now. She needed to receive a call back by five o'clock today; she was going to have to start making some demands.

Audrey glided into the room, having changed out the clothes for the hike into a green boiler suit coupled with loads of chunky jewellery, her hair piled into a messy bun on her head.

Paisley felt a swell of anger at the ease with which this woman seemed to breeze through life. Although she wasn't jealous of her age, Paisley did secretly hope she could look as good as Audrey did when she hit forty-seven. She thought about that age and realised she would have an eighteen-year-child by then. She wondered if there would be any siblings to go with him or her. It wasn't the most ideal situation to be in, with this much uncertainty. It certainly wasn't supposed to be this way. Paisley had hopes, to settle down and do things properly. The fact that there was a hint that her plan could easily spiral out of control was riling her up.

But she had a baby to think of now and she couldn't just keep getting angry when it suited her. The table was filling up with delicious delights that would nourish her foetus, so she decided to park the anger and frustration for the next hour and just sit and eat.

As she went to sit down, her phone rang out loudly and she grabbed it from the table, the name flashed on the front: *The Boy.* She had thought it cute at the time, something she had seen or heard on a TV programme. Now she swiped the phone off out of sight, embarrassed in case anyone saw.

'Hello?' she answered breathlessly, standing up from the table, no longer caring that she sounded sad and desperate.

'Are you alone?' came the voice.

'I will be,' Paisley began heading towards the back door.

'We need to talk.'

19

AUDREY

Lunch ended and Audrey felt happy and full, and plus she was topped up with alcohol again too. She felt Margo turn to her once Nicole had excused herself to go to the bathroom. Paisley had returned briefly and excused herself for a lie-down. She didn't look well at all.

'So, should we see how much social exposure our little "slut" comment has got now?' Audrey asked her colleague.

'I don't think so,' Margo said firmly. 'I can see she's stressed enough.'

'Oh come on.' Audrey opened the app on her phone. 'Let's just see for a moment.'

'I don't want to look,' Margo said, and Audrey heard a different tone to her voice than usual, one that suggested that Margo might actually be relaxing. As though she really didn't care either way.

'Well, I'm going in,' Audrey said, testing Margo, but Margo looked unperturbed.

Audrey glanced at Margo again and opened Instagram on the *Laying It Bare* page. She checked the comments for new ones and then looked at the messages. There were the usual DMs: women asking for tips from Audrey, could they come on the show, could they advertise this, would they like to work with this brand? And so on. But amongst all of those, Audrey happened upon an entirely different email, one that had already been looked at, as it wasn't showing up as unread. It was from a listener, but not the type that Audrey was used to reading about on the page.

They had addressed it to Nicole. Audrey scan-read it. Unable to believe what she was reading, she read it again. And then again.

Nicole arrived back at the table. Audrey had not heard her approach and quickly clicked her phone to black. She beamed up at Nicole, but her mind was on the message and what she was going to do about it. She found she couldn't really look at her for very long.

'What have I missed?' Nicole sat down, flicking her hair over her shoulder and picking up her wine glass.

'Nothing,' Audrey blurted and realised too late that she sounded like a guilty child.

Nicole rested her eyes on Audrey for a moment before picking up her phone, reading a message and then tutting loudly.

'Everything okay?' Audrey asked, moving her plate to one side. She should clear up really; the mum in her was telling her to get up but Audrey the model was demanding she stay put and be waited on.

Nicole looked at Audrey blankly for a second. Then she smiled. 'Er, yes.'

Nicole sounded disingenuous.

'Margo was telling us all that she could make a better soufflé than our lovely Oli made for our lunch just now,' Audrey said, forcing a hint of a laugh into her voice.

'Margo, I didn't know you were into cooking?' Nicole picked at a cracker and some leftover grapes.

'I... occasionally dabble,' Margo spoke softly.

'Well, I will look forward to sampling some delights in the future.'

Nicole took a long sip of wine, but not before Audrey clocked her face. Had she been crying? It wasn't just the red eyes that gave her away this time; she had a thin smudge of mascara that ran in a single trail down one cheek.

Audrey turned her attention to Oli, who was now clearing the table around them, silently removing crockery and empty serving dishes and cutlery. Audrey watched him to see if he would look at Nicole the way he had last night; Audrey had seen intrigue in his eyes when he spoke to her. To be honest, she was slightly perturbed that her own playful flirtatiousness had gone undetected by him, but she was glad he had shown a bit of interest in their host. It was high time that someone noticed Nicole, Audrey wanted that for her, she really did. Audrey needed Nicole to feel special. To feel wanted.

As Audrey looked at Nicole, the Instagram message was still fresh in her mind, as though she were still reading the words, but Nicole was either deep in thought or she was doing a very good job of pretending that Oli was not inches away from her face as he hovered around, collecting the empty glasses. Nicole had to be blind to not notice what was going on. Audrey could spot sexual tension between humans from a mile away; she was like one of those heat detectors that showed up the red spots on cameras where humans were hot. She could almost see the colours herself the way people seemed to light up around one another.

If only Nicole would play along, it would be so much more fun. The weekend needed an injection.

Audrey felt the urge for a cigarette. It would be an ideal time to slip away so that Oli could have a private moment with his boss, plus she needed an opportunity to look at the Instagram message again. She was completely bewildered and in shock; the only person she could speak to this about was Margo.

'Hey, Margo, fancy a breath of fresh air?' Audrey said and practically grabbed Margo by the arm and dragged her to the front door.

'What are you doing?' Margo hissed when Audrey had opened the door and they were stepping outside. They turned right to walk up to the raised garden where they could sit on the bench and Audrey would show Margo the message on Instagram when they both stopped and stared up at the side of the house.

'That doesn't look right,' Audrey said.

'It's not,' Margo said. 'Someone has thrown it at the house. Is it...?' Margo moved closer to the wall. She pushed her face closer to the brown blobs that were clinging to the cladding. 'Cow manure.'

'What? Surely not? Bloody hell, the cows around here have got some aim.' Audrey laughed. This must have happened whilst they were eating lunch. 'Do you think this has something to do with the poo from this morning?'

Margo already looked deep in thought. 'I don't know – it does seem odd though, doesn't it?'

'Yeah, like someone wants to make it known they see one of us here as shit,' Audrey said. Audrey thought back to the woman on the beach, the one who reminded her of her own local stalker. This couldn't be a backlash from the 'slut' comment, could it? She looked around tentatively, a slight panic rising in her chest. Was someone here for her?

'Hmmm,' Margo said. 'One of us? We're newbies round here. I've certainly never visited The Beach House before, have you?'

Audrey shook her head. 'First time for me.'

'Do you suppose then, someone could have it in for Nicole?'

'It is the biggest house around here, that's for sure. But what could Nicole and her parents have done to annoy anyone?'

Margo looked sheepish and Audrey glared at her.

'What do you know, Margo?'

'Nothing,' Margo answered.

Audrey took a deep breath. 'I don't think we should tell her about it though – it's literally too much shit for one day.' Audrey almost laughed.

'Well, I'm not climbing up there and wiping it off. Besides, the cladding will temporarily retain a tiny bit of moisture, there will still be marks left until they dry or it rains.'

'Well, you sound as if you know what you're talking about,' Audrey said suspiciously.

'It's common sense, that's all, Audrey.'

Audrey let out a sigh. She had been a little tough on Margo since they'd arrived, but it was harmless banter. Margo did tend to take some things literally.

'We have to get rid of this?' Audrey continued to examine the wall. She looked around for Margo, but she was already grabbing a hose and attaching it to a pipe on the outside wall. So much for a lovely relaxing weekend.

20

THE PARTY

Another cocktail was in Audrey's hand and she wasn't sure how it had happened. She certainly didn't remember putting it there, nor did she remember someone handing it to her. She had been at the party for less than two hours and already she was losing chunks of time. She decided to opt for a large glass of sparkling mineral water after this cocktail.

Nicole had been a bit off with her since she had arrived. They were usually all about the banter and the odd serious piss-take but this was a feeling, an energy that was dripping from Nicole, that lingered. She was hoping this evening was going to be an occasion where they could get back to their old selves.

Gram sidled up to her. She felt herself ease in his presence. He was a truly lovely man. A different breed altogether from her Julian. Julian had so many great qualities, but Audrey had felt relaxed with Gram from day one. They had so much in common; they laughed so much at everything, to the point she had witnessed the annoyance across Nicole's face as the two of them acted worse than a pair of kids. There was often alcohol involved, but even without booze, she and Gram were able to vibe. She had quickly become close to

Nicole, but the bond she had with Gram rivalled that. Not that she would ever admit it to anyone, definitely not to Nicole anyway. She and Gram didn't even have to say it either.

'Started off a bit too hard?' he asked her with that hint of sarcasm in his voice.

'I did, I'm afraid. I got a bit overexcited by the look of the cocktails and I think I've had at least three. Did you put this one in my hand by any chance?'

'Of course not. I would never condone such behaviour,' he said with a definite smirk and Audrey couldn't help but laugh.

'Oh God, it's going to be one of those nights, isn't it?'

'I'm afraid it is,' Gram said. 'I've had a shitter of a week.'

'Oh no.' Audrey took the final swig of the cocktail, placed it down and downing a glass of water almost in one.

'Yep.'

'Is it the usual?'

''fraid so. Am I so boring and predictable?'

'No, not at all. You know I am always here, I will always listen.'

'I know.'

'No Julian tonight?' Gram made a show of looking around for Audrey's husband.

'Big case,' she said.

'Snowed under,' Gram said understandingly.

'Yep, all-consuming as usual.'

'Oh dear. Well, someone will be coming out all the better for it. He's a good man.'

'He is.' Audrey looked around, feeling the swell of the crowds around her.

She looked back at Gram, who was smiling. He was the same height as her, which was a refreshing change. Usually anyone she made any sort of connection with would match her sense of humour but would only ever reach her shoulders, or vice versa. To have the whole package was an absolute treat. There were so many things about the two of them that matched that it filled Audrey up with love and affection.

'Shall we find a quiet place later?' Gram looked at her fondly.

'Absolutely.'

'Oh, hang on, Nic's about to do her speech – I'd better get over there.'

'Yep, you'd better or you'll be in trouble.' Audrey laughed. She watched Gram walk away.

A waiter arrived in front of her with a tray of champagne. Audrey took one and had a sip immediately. She watched Gram join Nicole, and she saw Nicole looked startled at first to see him, then her face softened just in time. Audrey released a silent sigh as she thought about how Nicole was still clueless as to what was around the corner for her. Audrey shuddered, allowing herself a tiny slither of glee. But for these few minutes, she would support her friend, keeping up the pretence, just as Nicole was, that everything with The Studio was okay.

21

NICOLE

Nicole scanned her eyes over the newspaper article. She couldn't remember the last time she bought a newspaper. In fact, Nicole or her family hadn't bought a newspaper since 2004. The twisted interpretations of the media and their effect on the minds of the masses was something that Nicole learned about long ago.

This newspaper article, dated May 2004, had been brought here. And with Claire Best lurking around The Beach House and the dog faeces in the kitchen, Nicole was certain she was behind this. How dare she! Nicole felt her chest and throat burn with anger. This was her house, she was here to relax – well part relax, part work – and she didn't need that Claire making trouble like she did last time.

Maybe it was a mistake to bring the girls here. Nicole hadn't anticipated this, Claire being here, the past being raked up, and the questions. Nicole had found it difficult to answer the questions on the walk earlier. There was so much more to say about that and yet Nicole would never be able to find the words. It was if the last eighteen years hadn't happened, and, yet at the same time, it only happened yesterday. Those moments lingered inside her all the time, yet they felt so far removed from her life, the way it was today, because she had made it so. Yet here was Claire walking around as if she was back here and this was her home again. It was completely bewildering.

Nicole told Oli she was popping out. He stopped what he was doing and looked at her in that inquisitive way that she had already noted, even though Audrey felt she needed to point it out.

'Okay, sure, have a good walk,' he said, and she felt him watching her the whole time as she walked out of the door.

Where was everybody? Paisley had disappeared just as they were sitting for lunch and now Margo and Audrey were both missing too. She had decided she needed to walk over to the Bests' old house to see if, by some miracle Claire had decided to buy it back again and that was why she was here. Stranger things had happened. Nicole and Audrey had interviewed a couple for the podcast who had been married for five years, divorced for three then re-married last year. People did weird stuff like that, and after what had happened to Andrew, it would not surprise her in the least if Claire was back here to rake up old memories.

Nicole pulled her thickest coat on, as the sun had decided not to show itself this afternoon after their morning walk, and stepped outside. She practically bumped into Audrey and then looked over her shoulder to see Margo looking shady again.

'It seems someone around here has something against you, Nicole,' Audrey pointed up at the house where the cladding had been hosed down yet several brown splats remained clinging to it. Nicole felt the familiar rage that she had experienced all those years ago run through her like wildfire. She needed to walk, to get away from the memories that were coming back.

Back in the day, after Andrew had gone off that cliff, Claire had completely lost her mind and similar incidents had begun to occur. Nicole would wake up in the morning and find bags of dog poo had

been put in the letter box. Her mother's tyres would be flat. School-
boy pranks, her stepfather had called them. And it did feel that way
at the time, and now these incidents felt very much the same. They
felt immature, a copycat of the previous incidents that had
happened all those years ago.

She shook her head at the mess on the cladding. It didn't worry
her too much. It would wash off.

'Do we need to call the police, Nicole?' Margo said in her most
serious voice, which made Nicole almost want to laugh.

'No, no, Margo, thank you, it's fine. It's just kids being silly.
Bored kids with nothing to do around here.'

Margo looked relieved at that. 'Oh good. That's good.'

'I'm just going to stretch my legs.'

'Again?' Audrey hooted. 'You're a sucker for punishment.'

Nicole gave a small wave, unable to bear the small talk or the
possibility that there would be more questions about Andrew, or
Claire or the cow pat on the cladding and how all of the three were
somehow all connected and Nicole had all the answers. The past
was always there.

As Nicole began to walk down the hill to Crest Wave, where
Andrew and Claire had lived, she began to wonder if she had
subconsciously brought her colleagues here at this time, knowing
that the real task she needed to tend to would put her out of her
depth and that she may not have time to consider saving The
Studio. The Beach House was always such a distraction to her, the
memories were always so fierce.

She made it down the hill in ten minutes and then followed a
small road that led right down to the beach where Crest Wave sat
proudly on the edge, looking out over the sea. It had always been
such a beautiful house when Claire and Andrew had lived there. It
wasn't much, just three small bedrooms, a sitting room and a large
country kitchen, but that was all they'd needed. Nicole approached

the house, and as though it was only yesterday, she opened the picket-fence gate and walked along the small path to the front door. The garden looked very well-tended but the exterior of the house looked weather-worn, something that she was sure she would not have been allowed to happen when Claire and Andrew lived here.

Nicole stood at the front door. She hadn't stood there for almost two decades. Even though she had passed the house from the main road, she had never found any reason to come down this small lane that also led to the beach when she'd always had her own route from The Beach House right outside the front door. But the memory came back to her, almost as if it were happening right that moment, and that the front door would open and Andrew would be standing there, looking at her.

The front door did open then, even though Nicole had not rung the bell or knocked.

'Can I help you?' A woman, maybe a decade older than Nicole, stood in cycling shorts and a dark football T-shirt. Nicole wouldn't have known which team it was. The woman's face was tinged pink, a film of sweat across her forehead. A dog appeared at her feet, sandy coloured and long haired. It let out a small bark and the woman shooed it away. Nicole tried to look past her, a part of her brain telling her that the hallway would still look the same after all this time. Bu it didn't. There was a small table, which held a notepad and a landline phone. It was pretty sparse-looking. Not like the bureau that used to sit proudly in the hallway, groaning under the weight of textbooks, letters, papers and magazines.

The woman moved to her left to gauge Nicole's attention, or to stop her prolonged glance into her home.

'I'm sorry, I didn't mean to intrude, it's just I live at the top, at The Beach House. Well, not all the time. It's our family holiday home.' Nicole watched as the woman crossed her arms and began to look bothered by Nicole's presence. 'I used to know the Bests when they lived here, and I recently saw Claire Best around here. A part of me convinced myself she had bought back Crest Wave.' Nicole looked up at the house and then back at the woman.

The woman uncrossed her arms, no longer seeing Nicole as a threat. 'No, 'fraid not, No one named Claire lives here, or if they do, I definitely needs to get my eyes tested.'

Nicole nodded.

'Right, well, I was just passing and thought I'd pop by just in case.'

The woman gave an awkward smile and looked glad the interaction was coming to an end. She went to close the door and at the same time, Nicole turned to walk to the gate.

'Hey, The Beach House, you say?'

Nicole turned back around. 'That's right,' she said, now regretting ever coming.

The woman narrowed her eyes. 'You're her, aren't you?'

'Sorry to bother you,' Nicole called and continued walking to the gate.

'You are, you're her. I heard all about you and Andrew Best's suicide.'

Nicole felt her skin prickle.

'I honestly don't think you should come here again.'

Nicole rushed to get out of the garden, pinching her skin as she tried to close it behind her without looking back at the door. She heard the door close and then hurried up the road.

Nicole felt the lunch and the champagne that she had just consumed swishing in her stomach and felt a sudden urge to be sick. Why did Nicole not know who now lived in the Bests' old house? Had she really segregated herself that much? It occurred to her that she had partially lived in this little hamlet all her life, and she remembered a time when her mother would greet people as they walked. Now Nicole didn't know anyone. Yet the story was still circulating, still being kept alive by people that she didn't even know.

Nicole didn't look up back. She just walked back up the hill to the main road that would take her back to The Beach House. When she reached the top of the hill, she felt her knees almost buckle. She leant over to catch her breath and the tears fell relentlessly until she was crying so hard she felt as though she couldn't breathe. It wasn't the first time she had cried since she had been here. There had been a lot of that over the years at The Beach House and plenty since she had arrived yesterday. It was part of the process, the grief that would always be a part of her.

'I heard all about you and Andrew Best's suicide.' Nicole heard the words of the woman again.

As if she had been the problem. As if *she* had been the reason Andrew Best had jumped to his death.

22

MARGO

The worry was ripening in the pit of her stomach. Margo sat alone in her bedroom mulling over everything. She could hear the movements of her colleagues in other parts of the house as well as Oli the chef preparing the evening meal. But underneath all of that noise, she could sense the growing unease in The Beach House. The presence of the woman at the end of the drive, the prank with the dog mess, and whilst she had assured herself and Paisley that the bins falling over were just an animal, she wasn't so sure any more. She knew that The Beach House had its own skeletons in the cupboard that dated back to when Nicole was a child here and she had heard the strain in her voice when she talked about the place. There was an element of mystery which had been confirmed by the eighteen-year-old newspaper article she had discovered under the ashtray. It was as if someone had wanted her to discover it there.

And now Margo had arrived with her own secrets and now she could feel The Beach House groaning under the weight of deception. How much longer could she keep holding on to what she knew, how much longer could she keep saying nothing to Nicole, and betraying her friend.

23

PAISLEY

He was coming. Those were the only words that Paisley could hear in her mind. Of course he was going to come. He had no choice but to come. Paisley needed him. More than she had ever thought she would need a man. She had been without one for so long. Years, in fact. There had been snippets of time where she had dated for a month or so and they had hinted at commitment, settling down, holidays, house, the whole thing. But no one ever stayed. This was the closest she had come to being with anyone and she really didn't want to mess this up. Tomorrow, he would be here, and then she could show him the pregnancy test and he would understand that this was real. He wouldn't need to be scared any more.

She suddenly felt hungry in a way that she hadn't the entire trip. She had missed lunch and had hid in her room, texting the same message over and again until finally she got the response she needed. She could hardly wait but she needed to refuel after the lack of food and the stress of today so she would be ready for tomorrow. Bright and fresh-faced. She knew once he saw her and truly understood there was life growing inside her, he would be totally on board.

Margo was chilling in the family room. Paisley found herself beaming at her, something she wouldn't normally feel inclined to do because, quite frankly, Margo annoyed her. Paisley always felt the way Margo tried to instil her authority into every situation, as though she were in a higher position than she was. Paisley didn't feel there were any differences between what she and Margo did in terms of the workload. Paisley's job was very stressful at times – she had to deal with people face to face on a daily basis – whilst Margo hid behind her screen most of the time. Paisley knew that social and marketing stuff was important, but she also knew that it was what Margo loved to do and what she thrived on.

'Hey,' Oli greeted her as she came into the dining area. Paisley eyed Oli for a moment. She rested her hand on her stomach the way she had seen so many women do, even though there was no bump there yet, but soon there would be.

'Dinner is in about an hour, is that okay?'

'Oh, yes, sure.' Paisley was disappointed, her hunger had grown since she had inhaled the scents of the cooking.

'But I do have these little amuse-bouche.' Oli pushed a small wooden board towards Paisley. 'It's a caramelised onion and anchovy tart.'

Paisley felt her heart sink. She wasn't entirely sure if she was able to eat anchovies. She hadn't researched the food groups well enough yet. But the smell was so tantalising.

'Do you have any bread?'

Oli smiled and nodded and swiftly sliced three pieces of bread and placed them in front of Paisley with a small ramekin of oil and balsamic vinegar.

'Yummy,' Paisley said. Although she had a hankering for salted butter, he had already gone out of his way enough already and she was past hungry so she accepted the oil and began eagerly dunking.

'Have you seen Nicole?' Oli asked as he swept away crumbs and wiped the island surface.

'Not since lunch.' Paisley looked around. 'But I'm sure she might be around somewhere.'

'So, maybe, if you're free later' – Oli wiped away the already clean surface with a dry cloth – 'we could pick up from where we left off yesterday,' he spoke quietly.

Paisley thought about yesterday. When she had just arrived, she and Oli had the whole place to themselves and she had made him a cup of tea. She had found him very easy to talk to and things evolved pretty quickly. They had an awful lot in common, it seemed.

'Yes, I think I would like that,' Paisley said giving in to a little flirtatious behaviour – she was after all on cloud nine.

Paisley stuffed the last few pieces of bread into her mouth and stood up and excused herself.

'I think I'll have a little lie down then, as I have another hour or so.'

Oli smiled. But didn't reply, he just continued working methodically.

Paisley began to think how much sweeter everything would be soon. Especially as *he* was now coming here, to The Beach House. She knew exactly what a big deal this was for him. It meant he was serious and she didn't need to worry.

Paisley began walking upstairs. When she reached the landing, she heard the door to the main bathroom slamming and banging; someone must have had a shower and left the window wide open. She had noticed that the wind had got up since they'd returned from their walk. Would it be a stormy night? In a way, Paisley imagined she would relish snuggling down and listening to the sound of the wind and rain crashing against the windows. Another part of her would be scared though, she knew that.

She walked into the bathroom and, indeed, the window was wide open, the wind blowing hard. She walked over and reached for the handle. As she did, she could see the road and walking along it was Nicole. She was hunched over as though she were completely out of breath, but when she went to stand, Paisley could see she wasn't just out of breath but very obviously distraught. Paisley caught herself as a small smile escaped across her face. Something was obviously bothering Nicole and somehow that pleased Paisley.

24

AUDREY

Audrey looked at the Instagram message. Again. She tried to gauge what it meant. She hadn't had time to talk to Margo about it yet, what with the cow pat and then everyone dispersing before dinner. It was clearly some crazed fool, fangirling a little too hard, and the best thing Audrey could do was delete it. Along with the hundreds of negative comments about the podcast.

She read it again.

Nicole, if you read this, please get in touch with me. I have some very important information surrounding Andrew Best and what happened on 28 October 2004. I think you would be interested to know more. Please DM me or call me.

And there was a mobile number. The girl's name was Jess. She didn't look very old, so it had to be a prank or, at the very least, a journalist. Audrey knew very little about the Andrew Best incident that Jess was referring to. It was now October and tomorrow was the twenty-eighth. Which meant the incident that Jess was referring to happened eighteen years ago tomorrow. What was the connection?

With the way that woman had stood on the beach and stared up at them, she began to wonder what the hell she had got herself into.

Audrey turned her attention to the comments still flooding in on the *Laying It Bare* pages and her own accounts.

My god, Audrey, you completely ignored Nicole's outrageous comment about one-night stands. I'm sure you've had plenty in your time so why not speak up for the women who enjoy a one-off session with a complete stranger?

And that was just one of the comments left on one of her social accounts. It was obvious that people were riled and looking to her to make a difference. They weren't just comments on her recent posts, but they were flooding her inbox. It was alarming. So many likes and ticks and follows over the years, but this was suddenly what truly mattered to her, this was what was making her heart pound and her stomach flip. Women who really cared and were fighting for their rights, for their voice in society. This was where Audrey felt she had a place these days, not parading down a catwalk, swaying her hips or pouting at a camera. No, she felt right at home right here, with women from all around the world reaching out to her.

Audrey had made the bad decision to begin sifting through the messages, perhaps with the notion to answer a few, but now she was facing them head-on, she thought maybe a little more reflection time would be a good idea and then she could create one of those annoying apology posts she had seen so many other women write. Why was it always women that were the ones who needed to apologise for their behaviour or for voicing something? Why did men seem to go around do exactly what they wanted and no one ever expected an apology or acknowledgement of their mistakes from them?

Audrey felt the messages come at her like a tidal wave. She sucked in air and tried to steady her breathing so she could find herself in the moment and not get swept away by it. This was not real, this was just people who had been triggered in some way, or were affected by what had been said. And that was the problem. People had too much to say and social platforms were a way to vent. And because Audrey was a part of that now, she had no choice but to deal with it.

Why hadn't she just opted for a life away from social media the way Nicole had? Then she wouldn't need to be dealing with this shit. She now had to face the comments because if she ignored them, then she too would be seen as a terrible person and there was already enough hate going around about the comment as it was. If Audrey didn't try to step in and say something, then things could get ugly. And there was too much at stake already.

Audrey could have scanned the messages all night but eventually, she was drawn back to the one message in the *Laying It Bare* inbox. She looked at the messages and saw there was now another one from a @JessGrace, the same person as before. She read it, then she dropped her phone onto the bed as one hand covered her mouth, the other on her heart.

25

THE PARTY

'I started The Studio one year ago today, and I am so proud of everything we have achieved in that time. There is still so much to do and so many avenues we wish to explore.' Nicole paused to look at Gram for a second, who squeezed her hand tightly in his and grinned back at her. They were doing well, showing her team and colleagues and their friends what a wonderful couple they were. 'We're both such creative people and we work so hard – this business is our baby.' Nicole paused again and looked down at her feet, she swallowed hard and took a deep breath. Gram moved his weight from one foot to another. The room was silent. 'We're all on different pathways, right? But ultimately we're all heading in the same direction with the same outcome: we just want to make a difference. I hope that by putting The Studio here and with so many of you wonderful people supporting us, we have managed to make a small difference to all of your lives, to the wider community and across the internet.' Nicole paused once more, this time for effect. 'Thank you all for coming, and here's to our first successful year in business.'

Nicole raised her glass. 'To The Studio.'

'To The Studio,' came a ripple of voices. And then cheers and clapping. People made their way over to Nicole and there was hugging. Nicole managed to squeeze her way out of the crowd of people as it once more dispersed amongst the many rooms.

A broad lady with purple hair that Nicole recognised as one of the team from the local Mercedes garage – they'd recorded two adverts and a jingle at The Studio – rushed over through the crowd, almost like a surge, and Nicole stepped back almost spilling her champagne.

'Oh God, sorry, love – I didn't mean to almost knock you over.'

'Don't worry, um...' Nicole searched her mental attic for the lady's name. This was one of the downsides of not being on any socials; she forgot people's names after they had left the building. There was no seeing them again on Facebook or having their name pop up on Twitter or Instagram.

'Pauline,' the woman said flatly.

'Yes, yes, Pauline, of course. How are you?' Nicole remembered the jingle vividly; she'd hummed it for a week after they'd left The Studio.

'I'm really good, thank you, Nicole.' Pauline moved closer so Nicole could smell a concoction of wine breath and a very potent perfume. 'You're such an inspiration, you young lot, always about the business, never about family these days. Do you have your own family, Nicole?'

Nicole frowned. 'Excuse me?' but her attention was now on the corner of the foyer where she had heard the sound of glass smashing. There was a loud cheer and Nicole watched as a few of the waiters stood around, clearly not sure what to do.

'Would you excuse me?' Nicole walked away, heat rising into her chest. She went past the mess, and into the kitchenette off the reception. She was looking for a dustpan and brush but found Audrey and Gram in there.

'Oh.' Nicole looked at them both, searching for some sort of answer although she wasn't sure what she was looking for.

'Hey.' Gram was leaning against the counter in the small room. Audrey had her back to Nicole when she came in the room but spun round when Gram spoke.

'Hey.' Nicole tried not to sound suspicious, but she was aching to know what the two of them were doing in here alone, in such close proximity, and then she saw it. The first aid kit from the wall was open and contents spilled over the counter. Audrey was holding a plaster that she looked to be struggling with.

Pauline's words were suddenly echoing through her mind again. She looked at Gram and how close he was to Audrey. Echoes of the conversations they'd had over the last five years about children seemed to fill the air around her. Conversations that ended with Gram walking way, deflated and beaten. Nicole was at Audrey's side in one stride; the broken glass was pushed to the back of her mind as she dug deep into her maternal soul and took the plaster from her friend.

'Come here.' She opened the wrapper and stepped back.

Audrey pointed to her foot. 'I forgot to break these in before I wore them.'

Nicole sucked air in through pursed lips at the red and sore-looking blister on Audrey's bare heel. Nicole bent down, pulled off the white strips and placed the plaster over the blister, then stood up and put her hand on Audrey's shoulder. 'Better?' she said softly.

'Much better.' Audrey leant in and kissed her friend on the cheek. Nicole glanced at Gram. He was smiling at her, with his eyes as well as his mouth. Nicole smiled back; doubts about her friend and boyfriend were ripe, and they had been following her around for a while now. At any other time, she would have accepted Gram's fond look as an appreciation of showing her softer side, allowing the maternal instincts to shine through. Gram wanted babies, and she didn't. Nicole would not make a good mother, she just wouldn't. This was why Nicole knew he was drawn to Audrey. She was the ultimate woman; Audrey oozed sex appeal, yet she could flip a switch in an instance and be the most loving, caring being. She was an earth mother, a goddess. She had everything. What did Nicole have? A failing business, an empty womb, space in hers and Gram's life that should have been filled with football matches and kids' play dates, birthday parties and family holidays. And here was Audrey, yet again, reminding Gram of what he was missing out on.

26

NICOLE

The smell of dinner welcomed Nicole as she entered The Beach House, but her appetite had well and truly gone. Thoughts and memories were racing through her head and there was no room for anything else let alone the concept of food.

Paisley was standing at the island whilst Oli was leant down on the counter; they looked to be deep in conversation. Alerted by Nicole's entrance, Paisley moved swiftly away and Oli stood to attention, grabbing a cloth and wiping the surface. Paisley smiled meekly and went to the sitting area, her phone clutched tightly in her hand.

Oli greeted Nicole as she approached the island. 'Dinner's nearly ready. Are you... okay?'

'I've been better,' Nicole admitted. Paisley wasn't far enough away for her to feel comfortable enough to start opening up to a relative stranger that she was feeling emotionally drained, that she could lie down for a week and still need longer. She spied the bottle of brandy on the kitchen counter; there was plenty of wine and champagne and gin around, but Nicole needed a hit of something, and fast.

She pointed to the bottle. 'Do you need all of that for cooking?'

Oli spun around. 'No, just a splash for the steak sauce.' Oli was already pulling out a crystal tumbler and pouring a double shot. He pushed it across the counter to Nicole as she perched on the stool as though they were in a bar.

'I feel like I'm in a western movie.' Nicole recognised there was humour to be found in the situation and that she needed to draw attention to it. Oli was not here to hear all her woes and she certainly wouldn't be sharing them with him either.

He stood on the other side of the island and asked again, 'Are you okay?'

This time, Nicole looked up into his eyes and felt a wave of emotions that she wasn't sure what to do with. Here was this beautiful young man with impeccable manners who also happened to be a brilliant chef, and then there was her, struggling with so many areas of her own life. It would be so easy to fall into the arms of another, to forget all her problems, to live in the moment for even just an hour.

But whilst Nicole felt a wave of desire for this man, there was something else that was sitting there along that passion. A strong will to pull this man to her, to just have him close to her, to mother him. It was confusing, this maternal desire and sensual lust, battling against one another, and so she tried to push all thoughts of Oli away. Yet there he was, right within reaching distance, in her own home.

'Nicole.' Oli spoke gently, his voice puncturing her messy thoughts. 'Can I get you anything else?'

Nicole shook her head. 'No, thanks, Oli. You've been truly amazing. All of this food, and you're so efficient, and really I have barely noticed you've been here.'

Except Nicole had noticed his every move; his presence was like a constant shadow that warmed her soul whenever he was near her.

But she was bewildered by the effect he was having on her, because Gram had been her world for so long. But she wasn't sure if there was anything left between them any more.

Her phone vibrated and alerted her to a text message with a light ping.

Nicole thought back over the day so far and how many times she had heard from Gram today. She was sure this was another message from him, talking at her as he had been all day. She had ignored the last few pings, but the worry that something might genuinely be going on was enough for her to flip her phone over and swipe open the message. Oli respectively stepped back and continued prepping on the other side of the island.

Nicole read the words over and over as though she couldn't believe what she was seeing.

I need to see you. Can I come to The Beach House tomorrow around dinner time?

It was a rhetorical question. Their argument had contained words that hinted at finality. He would never disturb Nicole usually. They both knew the severity of the situation. This was unlike him, to act on such a whim, and it sent a shiver down her spine. But if this was the way it was going to pan out, then so be it. Things weren't exactly going to plan with Claire Best showing up and trying to wreak havoc, and everything seemed to be slipping out of her control anyway. Why not add something else to the mix?

27

MARGO

Clarissa's number had been ringing out for over an hour now and Margo was starting to feel sick. Why was she not picking up? This was as serious as things could have got, and when Margo was out of town as well. But then it occurred to her. Of course it would have happened when she was out of town. She thought back to the car in the road, before she had left, the headless body. She didn't recognise the car of course, she had not seen the face of the driver. She had thought she was being paranoid at the time but now she realised she had been foolish to just walk away and pretend it wasn't happening.

Margo could hear the commotion of people getting seated for dinner from her bedroom where she was sitting with the door open. She wished she could just stay in the bedroom and listen to the subtle murmurs of socialisation without having to get too close but she knew she needed to be at the table this evening because it was what Nicole wanted. They had barely discussed any work business since they had been here and she knew her boss would want to make a start, as tomorrow, Saturday, was their last full day.

Margo began to pace the room – a sure sign that the stress was getting to her. She wished she had brought her trainers; she wasn't a runner, but she had been known to go for a speed walk from time to time when things really began to get to her. Margo paused by the window. It was cloudy and the sun was beginning to go down, but, wait, yes, she could just about make out the woman she had seen before. She was trying to walk along the path past the house that ran along the end of the driveway and then towards the cliff where they had walked earlier. But she was struggling because she was trying to pull another person along with her. The person looked to be a young woman; she was wearing a baseball cap and a coat, so she couldn't quite be sure, but she seemed to have a female look about her. The older woman had hold of her hand and was pulling her, almost yanking her to move but she wouldn't. Why would she be resisting? Margo shuddered at the way in which the girl seemed so adamant not to move and the way the older woman seemed intent on keeping her moving. There was no tenderness in the action and Margo could see the anger in the woman's face. Eventually, the younger woman started moving, and the older woman too, until they were finally past the house and away up the cliff.

Margo needed some fresh air and she had been intrigued by this woman since she had arrived, so she pulled on a cardigan and crept down the stairs. She got better phone connection at the top of the hill anyway, so she would try Clarissa once more.

She didn't fancy explaining her absence as she swept through the hallway and caught a glimpse of Nicole and Audrey and Oli gathered around the island. Paisley was sitting in the corner of the living area, unsurprisingly glaring at her phone. It seemed that Audrey had captured them all with one of her comments, so the ripple of laughter caused the perfect distraction as Margo crept from the house and along the driveway onto the path. She began the ascent up the hill and heard the voices ahead of her.

'I need to see,' came a young voice.

'There's nothing *to* see.'

'I'll decide for myself, thank you.'

Margo reached the top of the cliff. The two women had stopped just by the fence where the dead flowers were stuffed in at an angle. Margo smiled awkwardly as the women looked at her deadpan; Margo skirted round them but it was clear that they were trying to have some sort of moment and that Margo had interrupted it.

What with this being such a small community and the cliff walk being so off the beaten track, it was understandable that the women were cautious of walkers around them. Margo walked several paces ahead, then looked back. The older women definitely appeared to be the woman from the driveway who had been having a go at Oli. Now she had one hand on the rail next to the flowers. She was bent down, obviously crying. The younger woman had her hand on her back, soothing her. This, Margo thought, was someone who had been close to the person who had taken their own life on this cliff.

Margo took a breath and looked away, to give the pair of women some privacy, but as she did, her phone rang out loud, disturbing the women so they both glanced over at the same time.

Margo pulled her phone out of her pocket and hurried away, expecting to see Clarissa's name there, but instead it was another number, one she had never seen before. But somehow, she already knew who it would be. She answered the phone and spoke quietly.

'Hello.'

'Hello, Margo. I know where you are, and I am coming to find you.'

28

PAISLEY

She had three dresses laid out on the bed up in her room and as Oli talked about the menu for dinner, all Paisley could think about was which one she would be wearing tomorrow night. Now, as they were seated at the dinner table, Nicole seemed in fairly high spirits but Paisley had noted the way she was scrunching her fists tightly every now and again: a purely unconscious act but a sure sign she was anxious. Or angry maybe.

She watched as Oli rattled on; it was excruciating to see how much he was trying to impress Nicole. Perhaps a tinge of jealously on Paisley's part, she'd admit, because Paisley found it annoying how easily Nicole attracted the opposite sex. Paisley had made quite the connection with Oli, yes, but she wasn't able to tell anyone about that. Any envy would be short-lived though, because Paisley had something that she didn't. She had a baby growing inside her; she was going to be a mother. Nicole would never be able to say that, and now time was ticking on for her, it was unlikely that she would ever get to experience the joys of motherhood, and that thought sent a shiver of joy though Paisley. She hadn't realised she had actually shuddered until Nicole turned and looked at her curiously.

'Shall we have a drink?' Nicole quipped and headed to the fridge and pulled out a bottle of something fizzy-looking. Paisley felt her stomach tighten and saliva fill her mouth but she smiled regardless as Nicole popped the cork and filled three glasses.

'Woo-hoo!' Audrey said as she raised the glass to her lips.

Paisley smiled graciously again and took the smallest of sips. Even the bubbles popping on her tongue made her want to wretch.

'Shall we sit? Where's Margo? It's gone six. I said six for dinner, didn't I?' Nicole sounded jittery. Paisley watched as she downed her first glass of fizz in two gulps. Paisley looked at the bottle as Oli slid it into the ice bucket. Champagne. Nicole was going all out again tonight.

At that moment, Margo came through the front door. Her face was white, and she looked distressed.

'Margo?' Nicole looked around.

'Hi,' Margo said, and Paisley could hear the tension in her voice. What was she playing at? Had she come here to say something, to announce something? Paisley didn't want anyone stealing her thunder. She had been thinking about making the announcement tonight, whilst the mood seemed right. Tomorrow was the last full day and night after all.

'I just need to clean up.' Margo scuttled away and up the stairs to her bedroom.

'I'll pour you a glass of champagne,' Nicole called loudly up the stairs after Margo.

Audrey began digging into bread and olives and guzzling her champagne.

Oli brought the starter to the table, which was a salmon mousse accompanied by a caper and cucumber salad with melba toast.

Paisley spread a tiny amount onto a slice of toast and forced it down. The sickness had come on in spurts today; it was almost as if the validation of the positive test had spurred it on.

Oli then brought the champagne bucket to the table. It landed with a clang, the condensation on the bucket causing it to slip through his fingers. He was over-apologetic, and Paisley watched Nicole reassure him over and over. He seemed on edge. Paisley recognised the signs as ways she had dealt with her own anxieties. He touched his face a lot. He was also clearing his throat before he spoke. Paisley felt for him, because she too felt a little nervous. She glanced at him and he gave her the smallest of smiles. But Nicole was almost fawning over him like a puppy.

Margo hurried down the stairs to join them, apologising for being late, as though ten minutes was going to really piss Nicole off.

Once Margo was seated, Paisley clinked her champagne glass and found the words were out of her mouth before she could stop them. 'I have an announcement. I have an announcement.' There was something about the fork in hand and the tinkling on the glass and the power of the words which fizzled on her tongue much more so than the champagne ever had, that made Paisley feel fully in control for what she felt was one of the few times in her life.

The murmured conversation between Margo and Nicole when Margo finally sat down looking flustered abruptly stopped.

'Some of you may have noticed,' Paisley began, 'that I haven't been drinking so far on this trip, and that is because, I can confirm—'

There was a collective intake of breaths around the table. She even felt Oli stop in his tracks on the other side of the island.

'Oh my God, you're pregnant!' Audrey blurted out.

If Paisley wasn't feeling so joyous then she might have stood up and slapped Audrey for stealing the very lines from her mouth but she simply smiled and said, 'Yes, I am.'

Audrey cheered and stood up and walked around to Paisley and wrapped her arms tightly around her. Paisley took in the scent of her clothes and perfume and even though it was Audrey, she felt herself relax a little into the hug whilst revelling in the attention she was being given.

Paisley looked out across the table at the other two women. Margo looked her usual uncomfortable self, not knowing what to say or do but opting for a subtle 'Congratulations.'

Next, Paisley's gaze fell to Nicole. Her face didn't bear the look of someone who was happy for her. In fact, Paisley could easily go so far as to say Nicole's face looked grim, as if she might throw up any moment. As Audrey finally released her, Paisley could see that Nicole was standing up.

'Oh my God, I can't believe it. How far gone are you?' As Audrey shrieked with excitement, Nicole slipped away. She didn't even try and make any apology or excuse, she simply hurried out of the room.

Audrey appeared to clock Nicole's exit, and seemingly doubled-down on her positive energy, compensating for Nicole's departure, but Paisley didn't care. She had enough support with Audrey hanging on her every word. Besides Paisley always knew this news would hit Nicole hard. Paisley wasn't great at many things, but she dealt with people day in and day out, and having worked with Nicole for a year, she'd observed how her boss would turn away when conversations began about children and when clients brought their kids into The Studio. Paisley had even noted how cold she had been with the intern who was nineteen. It seemed her aversion to children stretched to young adults as well.

But within minutes, confusingly, Nicole was back in the room, and by Paisley's side, her hand on her shoulder.

'Sorry about that. Too much coffee today – my bladder was exploding. That's such great news, Paisley, you must be thrilled.'

Paisley looked up at her boss and grinned sweetly. 'I am so thrilled, Nicole, I really am.'

Nicole looked around, but Oli was already there with a bottle of champagne and handing it to her. 'Wow, thank you, Oli.' Nicole popped the champagne whilst Oli placed four glasses in front of her.

Nicole filled them all except one, which she simply added a splash to.

'You must toast, even if you don't want to drink.' Then she handed Audrey and Margo their glasses and everyone raised them in the air. 'To Paisley, and her new baby.'

Paisley took the glass to her lips and felt the effervescence liquid tickle her nose. She looked to Nicole, who was just to her right, and for that second, both of them with their lips to their glasses, Paisley could only see Nicole's eyes. In that look, she saw what she knew all along: the hatred that Nicole had for Paisley could no longer be hidden.

29

AUDREY

'I had no idea you were with someone?' Audrey asked once everyone was sitting back down at the table, gesturing to Oli to bring more champagne, having downed her own glass, and watched Nicole start on a second. 'Listen, I know you can't have any,' she said to Paisley, 'so I will drink your share.'

Oli popped another bottle and Audrey whooped. Paisley laughed loudly. Nicole was quiet next to her. Audrey could see she was trying her hardest, but it was obvious to Audrey now more than ever that Nicole was suffering with this news.

She felt a strong desire to reach out and hold Nicole's hand, but with it not being in the right context, it would appear weird, as if she were trying to connect with Nicole over Paisley's pregnancy, but that was not her intention. Audrey knew exactly how Nicole felt about Paisley because of her youth, her fertility, and now here she was, pregnant.

Nicole had tried to hide her feelings for so long, but Audrey had sensed it long ago, right at the very beginning. Nicole didn't get close to many people, and that was because she didn't allow herself to trust too easily, so Audrey knew Nicole granted herself much longer than anyone else would to assess any new acquaintances in her life. It took Nicole a fair while to warm to Audrey to start, and when she did, Audrey was so glad because it was worth the wait. Nicole had a lot of love to give. Love that should have been getting shared amongst children. So even though Nicole never made it public knowledge that she had an issue with Paisley – if anything she went above and beyond to praise her regularly – Audrey could see between the cracks, and now Paisley was announcing her pregnancy. That was bound to upset Nicole.

Audrey had always been proud of the way she could read people. And along with neediness, she often sensed there was a spitefulness to Paisley. She had seen it in the way she had spoken to Margo on many an occasion. Whereas Audrey was all about the banter, Paisley's comments bore an undertone of the authoritarian. Audrey had particularly noted it when she spoke with the customers. Seemingly Nicole hadn't clocked it, or, perhaps, she refused to because Paisley was the most loyal member of staff, never taking days off and always in early and happy to stay late. Which was why it was a mystery to Audrey how Paisley had managed to find herself a suitor amongst all that sucking up to Nicole that she did. She knew she wasn't able to monitor her twenty-four seven, but Audrey was almost one hundred per cent certain that there was no boyfriend on the scene.

'So who is he?' Audrey prompted again in her friendliest, most intrigued voice, leaning in a little closer across the table as though she were talking to one of her closest girlfriends; Audrey was good at pretending when she had to. 'You kept him quiet whoever he is. Does he have a name?' Audrey put an olive in her mouth and waited for Paisley to reply.

Paisley looked down at the table and moved her napkin two inches to the right along with her knife and fork. She rested her elbow on the table, it looked so casual, a kind of confidence that Audrey had never seen in her colleague before.

'That is quite a personal question,' Paisley said quietly and Audrey felt Nicole shifting uncomfortably in her seat next to her.

'Okay.' She held her hands up. 'I'm sorry. Not my place to ask.' She looked at Nicole and Margo for encouragement.

Audrey noted that the confidence in Paisley was growing by the second. It would have unnerved her more, but she decided to associate it with the baby that Paisley was carrying. Pregnancy changed so much about you, and not just physically.

'I think we should talk about The Studio,' Margo offered.

'So this nameless, faceless fertile Adonis, will we ever meet him?' Audrey continued, ignoring Margo.

'I think you're being a little rude now, Audrey.' Paisley's voice cut through the atmosphere like a knife and everyone looked at her.

'Sweetie, pregnancy is a very serious thing. We all wish you well. Don't we, girls?' Audrey looked around at the other two women. Audrey lowered her eyebrows in a questioning manner. 'We are just checking that you know, you're okay. This pregnancy has come about very quickly—'

'That's the funny thing about getting pregnant, it can be very quick,' Paisley snapped.

'Okay, well, what with you not having a boyfriend or anything, we just need to check that all is well.'

'I wasn't raped!' Paisley hissed.

Suddenly, Oli was next to the table with a colourful-looking drink.

'Congratulations! A mocktail for you.'

The table fell silent for a few seconds, enough for Oli to clear his throat and make his excuses.

'Oh, thank you, Oli – that's so sweet!' Paisley called after him half-heartedly. He nodded.

Audrey was a real woman's woman, news of any baby made her weep actual tears of joy, but a bad atmosphere had settled over the news that seemingly Paisley so wanted everyone to rejoice in otherwise, why would she have announced it, here; today?

Eventually, the conversation about the pregnancy faded, and they made it through the starters, with the focus finally moving to The Studio, but Audrey could tell Paisley's heart wasn't in it. She barely made any suggestions of ways to bring more clients in to use the pods and, in fact, didn't even engage as Margo pulled out a list and began to recite from it. Audrey was as enthusiastic as possible, but they were all subconsciously thinking about Paisley's rather vague news.

'I'm sorry,' Audrey said after a while, 'but can we all finish discussing the elephant in the womb?' Everyone looked at Audrey; Margo with horror, Paisley with anger whilst Audrey felt a smirk forming at her clever joke.

'I mean, we have questions, Paisley, I'm sorry. Like how far gone are you, where will you have the baby, and why are you being so damn cagey about the father?'

Audrey had been trying to rack her brains as to who it could possibly be, but The Studio had seen its fair share of men over the last year. And who knew, it could be the postman. It wasn't Audrey's business to keep badgering Paisley, but she needed to know. 'Just give us a name, for the love of god!' she said eventually.

Paisley was silent for another moment.

'I think you all need to just back off.' Paisley stood up.

Margo looked as though she was going to say something. Nicole let out a loud sigh. Oli hovered in the background, unsure whether to start removing the starter plates. Then Margo was standing up and excusing herself to use the toilet.

* * *

What the actual fuck? Audrey took a long swig of her champagne. What was going on here? Was it her imagination or was Margo acting completely weird?

Audrey excused herself and went to look for Margo. She found her outside the front door.

'What is going on? Why did you look like that when Paisley told us she was pregnant, and why are you acting so... well, more weird than usual?' Margo barely flinched at the remark. 'Why did you look so horrified when Paisley announced she was pregnant?'

Margo shook her head. 'I'm not great in those sorts of situations, Audrey, you must know that about me now. I'm not one to get thrilled about babies and stuff like that, am I?'

Audrey thought for a moment. Margo was right, this was not her domain at all. But still, there was something. She knew it. This wasn't just normal odd Margo.

'Right, well, fine. It's a bit weird, though, isn't it, her being up the duff and we having never even met the bloke? What do you know, Margo? Did she tell you? Was it even consensual?'

Margo looked terrified as she looked up at Audrey almost looming over her before she finally spoke.

'It happened at the party six weeks ago. And no, it wasn't consensual.'

30

THE PARTY

The studio party was now in what Margo would consider full swing. The noise level had increased to a level akin to a nightclub. The karaoke room was packed out; the door was constantly opening and closing, the blare of badly out-of-tune drunken singing slicing through the dance music coming through the speakers in the ceiling. Margo had felt her enthusiasm for health and safety dwindling. She was on her second glass of fizz of the evening after Nicole insisted she have a glass, and was now feeling at ease. Nicole seemed relaxed, if maybe a little *too* relaxed. Margo had helped her clear up after the broken-glass incident and then watched as Nicole began to drink. A lot. She knew Nicole liked a drink, but this was a lot, even for her. This, Margo thought, was her moment. No one else seemed to be aware of just how drunk Nicole was getting. Margo was now shadowing Nicole, her duties resumed.

As Margo followed Nicole around the party, unfortunately, it appeared that Nicole became aware of her growing presence and sidled up to her.

'Margo, Margo, lovely Margo. You're a— Hic... Good friend, aren't you?' Nicole was actually hiccupping. That was a sure sign she was drunk. And swaying. A lot. Margo looked around for Gram, but she couldn't see him in the foyer or any of the corridors.

It wasn't really a question, and Margo tried to work out what Nicole could mean. But now Nicole was leaning on her, so she took her to the end of the foyer, where the reception desk was and manoeuvred her boss towards the long sofa positioned opposite.

'Maybe you should sit here for a while. I'll get you some water.'

'You're a good girl, Margo,' Nicole slurred, and Margo went into the kitchenette to collect the glass of water. After she had given the water to Nicole, Margo said she would be back in a few minutes. It was past 11 p.m. Margo had thought the party would be winding down by now, but it only seemed to be getting louder. Margo weaved through the throngs, feeling her way, until she spotted Gram in the karaoke room as someone was leaving, the door swinging open for a moment or two.

Margo slid into the room and approached Gram, but just at the moment, he was swept away by a man in a green suede suit and hauled up onto the small stage where the karaoke was set up, complete with a screen with the lyrics and a selection of glittery garments to put on if the singer wished to try to emulate their favourite star. Margo then stood and watched as Gram and his green-suited companion murdered 'Don't Go Breaking My Heart' by Sonny and Cher. By the end, even Margo found she was smiling. There were whistles and whoops of applause, and Margo saw a very drunk Audrey throw herself at Gram as he exited the stage. Once she had peeled herself off him, he made a beeline for Margo.

'Hey!' he slurred at her and pulled her in for a hug.

Oh Christ, Gram was as wasted as Nicole was. He released Margo from the hug but held on to her hands. Someone was now singing 'Sweet Caroline' and the whole room was up on their feet, dancing and singing along, and now, it seemed Gram wanted to dance with Margo. He began to move his feet whilst still clinging to

Margo, not really looking at her and stumbling as he went. The room was beginning to close in around her. Someone had thought to open a window, Margo noticed, but she only felt heat from all the bodies surrounding her and the noise was making her brain feel as if it might implode.

Margo smiled at Gram and loosened herself from his grip. He barely seemed to notice and turned around and began dancing with a woman next to him.

Margo left the karaoke room and headed back to Nicole. Someone fell into her, and Margo gasped at the impact. She turned and Paisley was righting herself. She looked unsteady on her feet and Margo could see that Paisley too had probably had more booze than she should have done already. What was wrong with everyone? Did they really dislike themselves that much that they needed to drink to oblivion?

Paisley's eyes looked bloodshot and Margo decided she had either been smoking the wacky baccy or she had been crying. She put it down to the latter. She had seen and heard Paisley crying on quite a few occasions at work, but not being one to know how to handle other people's emotions, and the fact that Paisley's episodes had taken place where she would have presumed she was in privacy, Margo had never attempted to ask after her or soothe her before.

'Are you okay, Paisley?' Margo looked at Paisley, who stared back at her as though all of her soul had been extracted from her and she was a lifeless vessel. Paisley didn't reply and instead carried on walking into the karaoke room. Dear God, Margo thought. Everyone was a mess. At this point in the evening, anything could happen.

31

NICOLE

The news of Paisley's pregnancy had hurt more than Nicole had wished it would. She had friends from all around the world have babies and share the news with her. She had three nieces. She had cousins who were having babies. But it was because it was here, in The Beach House that the news hit her harder than it would have done had she been anywhere else. The trip down the road to Andrew Best's had knocked her slightly, and all she wanted to do was hold it together this weekend, for the sake of professionalism. So far, nothing seemed to be going to plan. They'd discussed next to nothing about The Studio, there was the ongoing drama with Gram, who was now on his way, and quite frankly Nicole felt sick. But she knew everything needed dealing with.

Margo and Nicole were both outside and Paisley was nowhere to be seen.

That left just Nicole and Oli. Nicole watched subtly as Oli moved about the kitchen with grace and dexterity. If she forced all the other thoughts from her mind, she could just concentrate on Oli and his presence in the room. She found her thoughts wandering to those moments she'd had alone with him and the effect he'd had on her. The way he had moved in close to her and her body had seemed to be drawn to his in a way she hadn't experienced in such a long time.

What would happen, she thought, if she made a move? Oli was clearly into her; she may not have felt anything towards another man for a long time, but she was well aware of the signs when someone was interested in her. Nicole took another sip of her champagne. It had slipped down too easily this evening.

She stood up and went over to Oli.

'Hey, sorry about all of that. You really didn't need to see or hear all the drama.'

'Hey, not my business.' He held up a hand.

'Oh, but it is.' Nicole fell into a chair at the island. 'I brought you here as a paid professional and you had to witness that... shitshow.' Even Nicole heard a slur to her voice. She hadn't realised how much she had been drinking during Paisley's announcement and the starter.

'Would it help if I said I've witnessed worse?'

Nicole felt a pang of something in her chest, some sort of instinctual draw to this man. Again, she was confused; she wasn't sure what it was.

Nicole smiled, enjoying how easily she could fall into conversation with him.

'How old are you?' The champagne loosened her lips.

Oli smiled and laughed. 'I'm thirty.'

Nicole nodded. She felt a stirring in the pit of her stomach, a desire that she had not felt for a long time.

'I suppose I must be able to ask your age now?' Oli smirked.

'Of course, I'm not going to get all lady like on you. I'm thirty-three.'

'You're so young, and you have all this.' He gestured to the room. 'And I obviously couldn't help overhearing the conversations about your business. Well done. You must be so proud. A massive achievement.'

Nicole felt the swell of warmth spread over her body and end in her cheeks. She hadn't heard that for a while. Gram would give her praise here and there, but hearing it from a total stranger was so much more gratifying.

Nicole took another long drink of champagne because she wanted to keep this feeling exactly where it was. She needed this high, because she knew once she was down, Oli's and anyone else's words would mean nothing. She wasn't a success. She was a failure.

She had just over twenty-four hours left at The Beach House with her colleagues. She looked out of the window at the sun going down on the horizon and for the first time in her life, she began to prepare herself to be swept out of her comfort zone. Now was the time to get focused. Now was the time for retribution.

32

MARGO

Margo bashed out a reply on her phone and then read it. Then she deleted it.

Peter was coming. To The Beach House. Her older brother was on his way and there was no way to stop him either. Margo had never been particularly strong around Peter. He had managed to make her feel small and incapable for most of her life but she wasn't about to let him do that to her any more.

And she certainly wasn't going to let him muscle his way in to her and Eric's life. Peter may be his son, but he had not been any sort of son to him the past ten years when he had really needed him.

The Beach House was not where Margo wished to air her dirty laundry.

She read the message again. It sounded pathetic. Her request to her brother to stay where he was and not come anywhere near her had been a first-class line from a blockbuster movie in her head, but written down it looked weak. Peter would just laugh at it. Margo had no control over what he was going to do. She would just have to deal with that once he arrived.

Margo could only think about how she was involved in something much more sinister than her brothers imminent and unwanted arrival. She had begun to explain to Audrey about what she had seen happen at The Studio party. Because if what she had seen was not consensual, then that night six weeks ago, Margo had witnessed a crime.

33

PAISLEY

I cannot believe that I am going to be a mother. It's not possible because I am so young, yet I feel so old. There are certain things in life that you are prepared for and this is definitely not one of them. I need my love, I need him here. But I cannot say his name, nor write it down because it is a crime. What happened was a crime. He would be sent to prison and then our baby will not have a father. I do want us to be a family, but I am also worried about what could be, how life will pan out. Please can someone just help me, who can help me?

Paisley slammed the diary shut and turned to her other source of comfort. Just one more play. Just once more. This could be the one, the making of her, then they could start again far away from here. He would never need to know anything about how much she had spent already. It could all be paid off, she would be able to show him that she was self-sufficient and that she could look after herself. It was love she was in it for, not just protection and security. She could hear Nicole downstairs laughing loudly at something, probably flirting with Oli. She heard another champagne bottle pop. How was it that two women could consume so much alcohol by themselves? Margo had barely touched a drop and Paisley was totally off it. It seemed that Nicole was on a mission to get drunk and no doubt she was sidling up to Oli again.

Paisley got comfortable on the bed with her phone in hand. She paused for a moment to think through what she was about to do. She had just over three hundred pounds left in her account. She could live off potatoes and rice for a few weeks if she had to. But she needed to conjure up some positivity, despite everyone prying into her personal life. She'd had a few lucky streaks in her time, but she had been too tame, she knew she had. She needed to go in bigger if she expected to win anything of any real value.

Tonight, she had shared the news for the first time with someone other than the father of her child, champagne was popping, downstairs. Surely this was all good luck?

She made the transfer and looked at the figure in her funds account on the app. She had heard about people making fifty or even a hundred times the amount from that one figure. All she needed was one spin with three hundred pounds and she would be off to a really good start with her and her little bump. She could set up a small repayment plan for the outstanding debt she had incurred over the last few months and have a nice lump sum of money to start off her new life as a mother.

Things could only keep getting better from here.

She pressed the spin button and closed her eyes. Images of a newly decorated front room, a Silver Cross pram and lovely outfits for the baby sprung into her mind and she focused on them for the few seconds the wheel did its thing. Finally, with all that positivity bubbling up inside her, she opened her eyes. Then she let out a guttural scream, as she threw her phone so hard she heard it hit the wall.

34

AUDREY

Audrey took the stairs two at a time. She was not Paisley's biggest fan, but she would not wish a miscarriage on anyone. The sort of scream they'd just heard would suggest Paisley could be upstairs losing the baby right now.

She burst through the door, not caring that she hadn't knocked or asked to come in. Her heart was thumping as the adrenaline shot through her, and she was ready to take action with her phone in hand. Therefore, she was somewhat perturbed to find Paisley sat on her bed, looking like a sulky teenager, her face red and tear-stained. She looked around the room for signs of blood or blood-soaked clothes. There was nothing.

'Paisley?' Audrey said from the doorway. She felt the other two women arrive behind her and the three of them stood there, waiting for an explanation. When nothing came, Nicole pushed her way through and went to the bottom of the bed where she knelt in prayer fashion in front of Paisley.

'What's happened, Paisley?' Nicole asked in her best-sounding soothing mother voice.

Paisley looked shocked to see everyone standing in the room

staring at her. Her face, which had been one of shock and horror, changed and she pushed her hair from her face and laughed. 'I stubbed my toe. That was all. I'm sorry for the noise. It's my worst thing. I always overreact.'

'Let me see,' Nicole said reaching for Paisley's foot, which was inside a satin slipper.

Paisley jerked her foot away and behind the other.

'Urgh, no. I can't. People touching my feet, gives me the heebie-jeebies. Hence why I screamed so loud. I can't.'

'I'll bring you some ice and you can hold it on yourself.' Nicole left the room and Paisley continued to sit on the bed, looking no more in pain than she had when Audrey arrived.

'If only you could have a drink?' Audrey said.

Paisleys eyes seemed to brighten. 'You know what, there are no rules – you can still have small amounts to drink when you're pregnant. Christ, some people are still drinking and don't even realise they are pregnant and the baby is absolutely fine.' Paisley sounded highly strung and strained.

'Okay, I'll bring the brandy. A small medicinal shot for the shock, yes?'

Paisley nodded; her eyes filled with tears. Perhaps at the kindness Audrey was offering, perhaps because Paisley was mad about something much more serious than her toe.

Audrey looked at Margo as she passed her on the landing. Their eyes met and between them they managed to convey a message. Something wasn't right. Margo had said Paisley was in trouble over this pregnancy, that she hadn't consented to it. If Audrey wasn't so close to the door, she would have said 'something is afoot' and laughed wildly with Margo. Of course, Audrey would have done the wild laughing and Margo would have nodded along. But they couldn't discuss it any further here and it seemed that Margo was rather reluctant to disclose any more information about the event without some legal advice. And Audrey knew just the person. She would call Julian later and ask him to have a chat with Margo, see if she would disclose to him what she felt she needed to keep to herself.

Audrey passed Nicole in the kitchen where Oli was helping her fix a tea towel with ice.

She found the brandy on the side in the kitchen and a nice brandy glass in one of the cupboards. She poured a generous shot and took it back upstairs. Paisley was still sitting with her foot tucked behind her but now holding the ice in her hand.

Audrey handed her the brandy.

'What are you doing?' Nicole said sternly.

'For the shock,' Audrey said. Paisley had already taken the glass and was sipping the liquor. Audrey looked to the doorway where Margo was hovering again, and they exchanged a glance. Something was not right, thought Audrey.

35

THE PARTY

The room seemed to divide like the parting of the Red Sea as Paisley marched into the karaoke room and headed straight for Matt. They had both been at the party for hours now but Matt seemed to be doing everything within his power to avoid her. When he arrived, he had greeted her politely and then moved away and joined a group by the fire exit. She had bumped into him at the bar and near the toilets and both times he had swiftly made his way past her. 'Treat them mean, keep them keen' was a saying she was familiar with but not one she would have ever associated with Matt. But the more the evening wore on, the more she was convinced he was playing some sick game with her. She was far too many drinks in now and so she marched up to him with such force that the small group that he had gathered with all took a few steps back so that it was just her and Matt, face to face.

'What the hell do you think you're playing at?' Paisley said with authority, a side to her she had never revealed to Matt nor anyone. She felt the rage come in a huge swell and there was nothing she could do to stop it. But already she was relishing the look of shock and then submission on his face.

'Paisley, I'm not sure—'

But Paisley wasn't finished. She was on a roll, and it felt good to let it all out. She had let Matt lead this relationship but now it was time for her to step up her game and demand that he acknowledge the kiss and the connection they'd had in the pub that night. She was aware that men sometimes found her a little too intense, but that was why she and Matt were perfect for one another; there would be no competition. All the men she'd dated in the past were incredibly masculine and their testosterone levels could be through the roof, but that was where Paisley was willing to change because Matt was not like the other men she'd dated in the past. He was a rare breed of a man that she had not come across before, he was so sure of himself yet not cocky and he was a gentleman. And she was ready to evolve. Matt just needed to know that she was serious.

'We spent time together, Matt. We had a connection that night and I'm sorry I haven't been forthcoming with my thoughts about it, but neither have you and I am used to men making the first move, and I am not accustomed to doing it—'

'Paisley, please, can we go somewhere, quieter, just the two of us?' Matt interrupted Paisley's rant and then looked around at the people around him staring. He then nodded a sort of apology to them and took hold of Paisley's hand. Paisley felt her heart quicken at the intimate gesture and then felt a warm glow rush through her as she felt the look of others upon her and Matt as he held her hand in his big soft palm and gently escorted her through the room and into the foyer.

The foyer was just as busy, a hub of excitement with people dancing wildly to the music pumping through the speakers, and Matt looked around, presumably for a quiet corner, but there were no spaces anywhere. Matt looked to the right, looked down at Paisley and then walked along the corridor to the far side of the building away from the party.

This was it, Paisley thought. She was finally going to have Matt on her own for enough time to make him see that they could be good together. And what a perfect place for her to get lost with the man she had fancied for what felt like an eternity. If she had known all this time that all she needed to do was take the bull by the horns, then she would have approached Matt weeks ago. He was a lot more reserved than even she had suspected.

They walked until they were passing rooms on their left and right, and then turned down a short corridor where Paisley knew there was a small room. It currently stored some beanbags and a small sofa whilst Nicole decided what she was going to do with it, but occasionally Paisley had used it for her break to get away from the hum of the reception, which could sometimes become over-crowded with people coming and going throughout the day, stopping to chat, sometimes for longer than Paisley thought necessary.

Matt opened the door to the room; Paisley regarded the condition, which was slightly unkempt since the last time she had been in here. The sofa had clearly been sat on and no one had thought to plump it up again after they had got up. There was also a pile of cushions behind the sofa that, at some point, would go on the brand-new corner suite when it arrived for the foyer. Paisley noted the large first aid kit open on the carpet that looked as though it had been raided, its contents spilling across the floor. Paisley stooped down and scooped up bandages, scissors and packaged syringes, putting them all back into the case. She was aware that her dress had ridden even further up as she knelt down and was now exposing the curve of her bottom cheeks.

She heard the click of the door being shut behind her and she remained where she was for another moment, conscious of her position and what Matt could see. She heard him let out a long sigh; from where she was, it sounded sensual. He was turned on, she was sure.

She raised herself to her feet slowly, a sort of reverse slut drop, and turned to face Matt. He was looking right at her, taking her in completely.

She took three slow steps, and she stood right in front of him. He was taller than her by a good couple of inches, but that wasn't unusual. Most men were.

'Hi,' she said, looking up at him.

'Hi.' His voice was raspy from where he had been shouting over the music or maybe he'd been singing karaoke. She could feel the heat from his body, the sweet smell of his skin.

She took his hand in hers and stroked it. Then she put her other hand on his waist and moved herself closer, so her breasts were pushing into his chest.

She tilted her head up further up and he dropped his head, so their lips were almost touching. He opened his mouth, sucked in air. 'Paisley—' But before he could say another word, Paisley stretched up, so her lips met his. She kissed him softly and he responded. She pushed herself in closer to him and felt up his back, letting her hand push its way up under his shirt where it had come loose. She felt his breathing ramp up and then the telling sign as his groin hardened and he pushed himself against her.

He began to move, her cue to walk backwards; they were heading for the sofa. She fell backwards onto the soft fabric, a small giggle escaped her lips. She looked up at him expectantly. He looked down at her, but then shook his head.

'I'm... I'm sorry, Paisley.'

Paisley felt the impact of his words hit her like a ton of bricks. Her entire body began to deflate.

'You're beautiful and I would be a lucky man to spend an evening with you, but I'm engaged. I'm sorry. As tempted as I am, I am not that kind of guy. I can't cheat on my fiancée.'

Paisley suddenly felt sick. She rearranged herself on the sofa, pulled her dress down as much as she could and tossed her hair across her shoulders. She tried to smile, but it felt painful. She wanted Matt gone. She *needed* Matt gone. So she could crumple into a heap, fold into herself, the way she had always done since she was a little girl. But for now, there was Matt, trying to let her down gently, but he had basically lifted her up and then dropped her from a great height. *He* had kissed her – twice now. He had a hard-on, for God's sake. Men were all the same. Paisley knew she was destined to be alone; it didn't matter what she did, she was never good enough. Her eyes stung with tears that she wouldn't let fall in front of Matt. Instead, she smiled. She wasn't going to make a scene. That wasn't her style. She had approached Matt earlier in front of his friends because she deserved an answer and the alcohol had given her the confidence. Now she felt all the joy and energy seeping out of her.

'I'm really sorry,' Matt said again, and Paisley wanted to punch his face.

'What's her name?' Paisley said, the pain in her voice only slight.

Matt looked confused for a second, obviously not expecting Paisley to be interested.

'Oh, um, Freya.'

Of course she is, thought Paisley.

'Beautiful name.'

Matt looked coy.

'She's a very lucky girl,' Paisley said, echoing the sentiment that Matt had made to her moments ago, although she knew he didn't mean it. He was just saying it, like they all said those things. It was their way of letting her down, but disguising it with a compliment.

'Thanks,' Matt said, and now he looked uncomfortable, restless, as though he wanted to leave. Paisley looked at his trousers for any sign of where he had been turned on moments ago, but there was nothing. Had she imagined it?

'Okay, you're dismissed,' Paisley said with a chuckle that could easily have been mistaken for a cry.

Matt laughed, so beautifully, and Paisley felt sick at what she was losing out on. Again.

He scuffed his feet and then he stepped forward as though he were going to kiss her. Paisley felt herself recoil; she wouldn't be able to bear the sympathy.

Maybe he sensed her energy because he stepped back and turned to the door.

'Still mates, yeah?' he said as he reached the door.

'Obviously,' Paisley said with a roll of her eyes, trying to imply that she was already over him.

She felt the door close because she couldn't bear to look at Matt leaving. Then she felt the wave hit her. Fear, grief and a big helping of sadness. Paisley took herself from the sofa, she wanted to be in the most enclosed space possible. She climbed over the beanbags and lay down on the cushions behind the sofa. She closed around herself as tightly as she could, so she was almost ball-shaped. No one would even know she was here if they came in. She felt as safe as she could in that moment.

36

NICOLE

Outside seemed to be the only place where Nicole could manage to bring her breathing back to normal. She had to get away from it all and had left Audrey to tend to Paisley. She felt so much frustration she wanted to rip her insides out. She had been angry a long time, and she had held it all in, but Paisley's pregnancy was hurting her. A lot. Gram had been living with a woman for five years with so much pent-up anger and she had never been able to express her feelings; she had been a terrible partner to him all these years. But here they were, these emotions, finally rising to the surface, the ones she had been pressing down for so long. Everything about being here was triggering so many things within her. She walked up and down the garden, trying to burn off some of the adrenaline when she heard the back door open. She swung around and saw Oli illuminated in the doorway.

'I thought you might need this.' He was holding a glass of brandy. She walked to the back door and took the glass from him.

'And one of these.' He was holding two cigarettes in the other hand. 'I smoke when I am stressed sometimes. Seems like there is a lot of tension in the air tonight.'

'Thank you.' Nicole took one cigarette from Oli, and he held out a lighter. She lit the cigarette and took a long inhale. When Audrey had been out here smoking yesterday, the smell had brought back so many memories, and now being here with Oli and actually inhaling, the nostalgia was overwhelming. She downed the brandy in one go, placed the glass on the floor and then returned to her cigarette.

'Oh my God, that is good. I haven't smoked for so long. I smell it all the time and now people have those ridiculous vape things. I would choose a real cigarette every time.'

Oli was quiet. He was observing her, but this time he had a small smile on his face. 'I'll hold off the mains for another half an hour until everyone has settled down,' he said eventually.

'Thanks, Oli. You're such a bloody nice guy, how is it that you are so nice? And why haven't you been snapped up?' Nicole felt the heat of the alcohol surge through her body. She was already well on the way with the few glasses of champagne, but the brandy had just elevated her to officially inebriated. The hit of the nicotine meant she felt high on top of it.

She edged closer to Oli. 'Unless I am mistaken' – she bent to look at his hand – 'you're not married?'

'I'm not married,' he said, his voice catching in his throat slightly. 'And you're not married?'

Nicole held up her ring hand. 'I'm not married.'

Thoughts of Gram entered her mind. The lack of a wedding ring. Who was that down to? It had been so long since either of them had discussed it that she had forgotten. And soon he would be here; he was coming. Suddenly, the reality of her life felt so over-bearing that she no longer wished to be in it and that to step outside of it even for just one minute felt like the lifeline she needed right then.

She took one tentative step forwards, assessing Oli's body

language, which remained open. She could kiss him, and he would probably kiss her back.

'Oh my God, there you are! We're all famished in here now after that dra—' Audrey had appeared at the back door, but suddenly stopped speaking. She must have been assessing the situation, the closeness between Oli and Nicole. Nicole didn't step away from Oli, even thought there was only about twelve inches between them, but she spoke hurriedly.

'We're sharing a cigarette.'

Audrey looked at them for a moment. 'Well, I say that's very risky for you, Nicole!' Audrey said and walked back inside.

Nicole took a final drag of the cigarette and stubbed it out on a brick. She could still hear Audrey's words and the tone of her voice. Had she been referring to the cigarette or how close she had been to Oli just then?

She glanced at Oli as she skirted past him to head back inside. He looked at her longingly.

Shit, Nicole thought to herself. What had she just almost done?

37

MARGO

Margo hung around outside Paisley's room wondering whether she should go in or just head downstairs. She knew that Oli was keen on keeping the dinner going, but now might be the perfect opportunity to speak with Paisley alone, tell her what she knew and give her time to confess. But Margo had watched too many crime series to know she was not a detective, nor an interviewer. She wouldn't know how to start a conversation like that.

It was awkward and embarrassing for Margo, she would have to talk about sex, and say words out loud that would make her squirm.

If she could just get Paisley to open and admit what had happened, then she wouldn't have to be the bearer of this terrible secret any longer.

Margo took a deep breath and then a step towards the door.

'Ah, Margo,' Audrey said quietly. Margo hadn't even heard her coming up the stairs. 'I think we're ready to continue with the dinner, what do you say.'

'Sure.' Margo said, half relieved that he didn't have to go through with speaking to Paisley, but she was also now left frustrated as she continued to hold on to what she knew and unable to find the words to tell anyone.

38

PAISLEY

Deep breaths. Deep breaths. That's what people said, that's what she had heard time and time again from so many people, whether it was on a TV show or from overhearing others' conversations.

This was the first time Paisley had lost herself in the company of others. She had not thought about the possibility that the girls would come and see what had happened. She had thought fast with the toe thing, and she was pretty squeamish about her feet to be fair. But she was beginning to feel as though she were toppling over the edge, as if all her emotions from the last few years had built up and were finally ready to blow. Perhaps it was the hormones, didn't the book say that she would start to feel a little less like her usual self?

But why did she always go and get so frustrated? Goddammit. She had what she wanted and yet she'd still decided to take once last gamble, and now she had lost the rest of this month's money, which meant she would have to live on whatever was in the cupboard: Pot Noodles, potatoes and beans. Unless she would be supported immediately. But what if he wouldn't? She could hardly make him if he really didn't want to.

'Right, we're going to try and wrap this dinner up, if you're okay to come downstairs, Paisley?'

Audrey was in the doorway and Paisley wished they would all just go away. She could quite happily be here all alone.

'Can I help you at all? You'll probably have a limp. Lean on my arm if you like.' Audrey held her arm out and Paisley stood up, remembering to put barely any weight on her right foot; she'd done a little amateur dramatics in her teens so she should be able to wing a sore foot for a few hours. But Paisley felt her rage still simmering, which was further fuelled by Audrey's patronising tone. She was sure Nicole believed her, but Audrey had a suspicious look on her face and was now making blatant comments about limping, as though anything less would give her away.

She was ready to tell them all to fuck off, but she needed to see this weekend out for the sake of her dignity, of making everything perfect. Until then she would limp and do whatever she needed to get through the dinner because tomorrow would illustrate exactly how far she would go to get what she wanted, even if that meant trampling over another woman to get it. But for now, she reached out and took Audrey's arm and smiled.

39

AUDREY

Christ, Paisley made Audrey sick. She held on to Paisley's arm, but just as easily she could have twisted it and broken it with one sweep. Audrey was a black belt in karate and in jiujitsu, so manoeuvring herself out of situations was surely as easy as manoeuvring someone into them. If it wasn't for the fact Paisley was growing a human, Audrey could have easily seen herself instigating a fight with her this weekend and she couldn't quite put her finger on why. Going away with people always brought to the forefront elements of their personality that you wouldn't see or sense ordinarily, but this was something else; there was a feeling, an aura about Paisley that felt off-kilter and Audrey wished she could fathom it out. Sure, Paisley had obviously got herself into some sort of trouble, but what was it and why couldn't Audrey just feel sorry for her? She was usually so good at sussing this sort of stuff out, but then she had also missed Nicole's overall mood and it had been Margo who had brought it to her attention. Maybe it had something to do with the house, it seemed to distract Audrey from things she would normally pick up on She had however noticed that moment outside between Nicole and Oli, who wouldn't have! Nicole hadn't been very swift in defusing what was obviously a pretty close and intimate moment – or an almost moment, had Audrey not stepped outside when she did.

Audrey and Paisley reached downstairs and Audrey escorted Paisley back to her seat.

Oli was back behind the island in the kitchen, as though he hadn't almost had his tongue down Nicole's throat ten minutes ago.

'Hey, we need to crack on with this champers, don't we? Margo, what do you say?'

Audrey turned to her, but Margo was staring at her phone, her mouth agog.

She went to speak, as though she were about to tell Audrey what she was looking at, then there was a loud bang. Everyone stared at the door because of the loud urgency to it, and out here, in this fairly remote house with the sky black outside, even Audrey felt her blood run cold and braced herself ready to fight.

40

THE PARTY

Another glass of champagne was in Audrey's hand as she swayed to the music in the karaoke room. She was feeling slightly disoriented. She didn't know what time it was, but the alcohol had numbed the pain in her foot. Nicole had been very attentive with the plaster but it hadn't left her and Gram with much time to talk to one another. Was that Paisley she had seen march in here a moment ago, looking like a woman on a mission? She looked over at Gram, she couldn't be that drunk because she recognised that he was slouching over and stumbling around. She hadn't seen Nicole for a while. This was a good opportunity to get Gram to herself before he went completely comatose.

She walked over to him, and he looked up at her. She raised one eyebrow, a skill that had served her well over the years. He automatically walked towards her, and she took his hand and they headed for the door. Audrey looked over her shoulder at Gram and giggled. He laughed back at her. There was a sudden impact on her shoulder. She swung around to face the front. Margo.

Margo, who she had just collided with, looked at her and then she moved her head to look at Gram behind her. Audrey smiled at her.

Margo held eye contact with Audrey for a few seconds, and it was Audrey who broke eye contact because she was drunk and she needed to get somewhere quiet so she could sit down.

She held tightly to Gram's hand as she turned left out of the karaoke room, taking him through the corridor, turning left and then right again, before finally arriving at a small room that had been commandeered by a couple of staff members as a sneaky break room. There were a few spare rooms like this on. Had Nicole been aware of how much space she was taking on and how that space might be filled and by whom? No, was the simple answer.

Audrey stumbled into the room, kicking her shoes off as she did. Audrey laughed long and loud. It felt good to hear her own voice after shouting over everyone all night; she was looking forward to having some one-on-one time. She fell onto the sofa and let out a loud groan.

'Ooh my God, it feels so good to be away from the madness.' She flicked her hair from her eyes. 'Do we have drinks?'

Audrey looked at Gram as he produced two miniature bottles of champagne from the back pockets of his jeans.

He held them up triumphantly and Audrey felt her heart swell.

'Oh my gosh, you're amazing. When did you pilfer them?'

'From that table on the way here.'

'I didn't even see it.' Audrey took a bottle and then Gram produced two straws. 'Oh, you're good.'

They both slid the straws into the drinks and took a long sip. Audrey patted the sofa next to her.

'Take a pew. Tell me all about it.'

That was Audrey's signature sentence to Gram. She knew he had things he needed to get off his chest and that he would share with her. He always did.

'How's Nic tonight?' Audrey asked.

'I think she's finally kicked back and relaxed. Last time I saw her, she looked pretty gone.'

Gram sat down on the sofa next to Audrey, his head was pressed against the fabric. He turned to Audrey and their eyes met. She smiled.

'I suppose that's good, in a way. For us I mean.'

'Yes, 'tis.' He sounded slurry. 'But I feel bad.'

'You shouldn't. She brought it all on herself. She'll thank us, you know she will.'

Gram laughed. 'She'll kill us is what she will do.'

'Ha, I'd like to see her try.'

Gram's laugh stopped suddenly, and sensing the change in atmosphere, Audrey placed her hand on his. Gram took in a deep breath that sounded shuddery, as though he might cry but was trying not to.

'Has there been more talk about it?'

Gram shook his head. 'I try. She deflects. Always deflects. It was never meant to be, Aud. Any of it.'

'I'm sorry, Gram. Is it still something that you want?'

He looked very drunk now to Audrey, and she felt bad for asking, but it was obvious he wanted to talk about it. Gram always wanted to talk about it.

Gram let out a noise, which Audrey recognised immediately. She grabbed him and pulled him towards her, so his head pressed into her ample chest. She let him cry for as long as he needed because this wasn't new to Audrey. Gram cried a lot, especially when he was drunk. It had become a sort of pattern that they followed these days, especially when they found themselves drunk alone, which was quite often as Nicole would drink so quickly that she would pass out somewhere or she avoided them when she could see they were getting too squiffy together. Why she never just joined in with them was beyond Audrey. So now it had come to this. Again.

'Shh, it's okay, Gram, I'm here.' Audrey didn't want to tell Gram that things were going to be okay, because she wasn't entirely sure they would be. He and Nicole were on completely different trajectories when it came to their life plans.

Gram lifted his head up and looked at Audrey.

'I'm sorry,' he said through bleary eyes. Audrey could see how much more drunk he was than her; they weren't going to get any quality time together today.

'It's fine. I get it.'

'I... I just want a baby more than anything, Audrey. I want to be a father. I want kids. I'm thirty-seven. I've been with Nicole for five years. Why does she keep refusing to talk about it? If it was because she couldn't have them, I would understand, but she won't come off the damn pill.'

Gram moved back from Audrey and leant his head against the back of the sofa.

'I've even tried to sabotage her taking them. I've moved them from her bedside table in the hope she'll forget, and then we might... we might have a child.'

Audrey was not shocked by the outpouring from Gram. She was used to it, because he had been devastated by Nicole's refusal to have children ever since she had known him. It was one of the first things they had ever discussed, and it continued to come up in conversation a lot.

'I think I just need to accept it and move on. Don't I?'

Audrey wasn't going to be the one to tell Gram that he should leave his long-term girlfriend if she refused to discuss having a baby with him. But it was making him so desperately unhappy, she wasn't sure what to tell him any more.

'I just want to be with someone who loves kids. I just want to be a dad so badly.'

Gram leant his head back. The bottle he was holding was now empty. He closed his eyes, and it was a few minutes before Audrey realised that he was asleep. The bottle was tilted and sliding from his hand. Audrey grabbed it just before it fell and held it along with hers for a few minutes. Gram looked so peaceful, and Audrey felt her heart fill with sorrow for the predicament he found himself in.

The best thing he could do was sleep it off for an hour or so.

Audrey stood up and crept from the room.

41

NICOLE

Nicole knew what she almost did with Oli was bad, very bad. She was still very much with Gram, and it had been her who had been refusing to discuss children for the five years they'd been together. She didn't want them was what she had told Gram, but what she had meant to say was she was scared of having them. The last few years of their relationship had been based on Gram's resentment for Nicole and Nicole's inability to tune into her real feelings and convey them to her boyfriend.

This was what she needed to tell Gram when he came. Just thinking about it made Nicole feel lighter. The sound of the front door being thumped thrust her back into reality. Nicole looked around the room, as though someone might be able to tell her who was at the door, but they all looked as dumbstruck as she felt. Well, all except Paisley, who had an air of excited puppy about her, as though whoever was on the other side was there for her.

'Should I get it for you?' Oli asked in a way that Nicole thought was pretty chivalrous.

'Er, no. Thank you.' Nicole didn't need to be scared in her own home. The Beach House held some pretty messy memories and a hefty collection of its own ghosts but she was familiar with all of them, and surely there couldn't be anything that could surprise her at this junction.

Nicole thought that out of everyone, it was Margo who looked like she had seen a ghost, but then she had been acting weird since they arrived.

Nicole felt herself float back to the past for a few seconds as she approached the door. The loud bang had triggered a memory that was fierce and wild. Her stepfather walking to this door late at night as Nicole cowered in the corner. A distraught woman on the other side of the door, words peppered through wails and screams. Her fault, it was all her fault.

She pulled open the door, almost ready to be faced with the past again, but the face of a strange man greeted her.

'Hello, can I help you?' Nicole felt her nerves spike. Her skin prickled as the hairs on her arms raised with the cold air outside.

'Is Margo here?' the man said. As Nicole assessed him, she could see he looked nervous. His eyes shot between Nicole and the car that was parked at the end of the drive, then he looked fleetingly past Nicole.

His face softened. 'There you are,' he said, and suddenly Nicole could see the similarity: this was a relative of Margo's.

'Don't.' Margo approached the door. 'Don't let him in,' she said to Nicole. 'You shouldn't be here,' she hissed at him. 'Please, ask him to leave. This is your house and he was not invited,' Margo said firmly to Nicole.

Nicole looked to the man. 'What can I help you with?'

'I am here to see Margo – it's a family matter. Not urgent.' He held his hands up to emphasise the point. 'But please, I am only asking for five minutes, Margo. You owe me that. We can sit in the car?' He turned to the car sitting at the end of the driveway. The one she had seen outside her house before she had left to come here.

Nicole looked at Margo, who was often torn between what she should and shouldn't be doing, and decided to intervene.

'We have a study, just through there.' Nicole pointed to a door off the hallway. 'No one uses it any more, you two are welcome to have it to yourselves for your chat.' She turned to Margo. 'And we're all here, if you need us. Just shout. Oli has sharp knives.' Nicole laughed, and Margo almost smiled, but still looked unsure.

Nicole turned back to the stranger and stood back to let him in. 'Seriously though, Audrey is a black belt in various martial arts and Oli has some serious knife skills.'

The man stepped inside and stood awkwardly and looked around.

'May we have your name?' Nicole asked.

'Oh, yes, sorry, Peter. Pete. Call me Pete.'

'Well, Peter, Pete, would you care for a beverage?'

'Um.' Pete looked at Margo and she nodded softly.

'Sure, a soft drink would be great.'

Nicole turned to Oli, who was standing behind the island with one knife poised in his hand, and Nicole almost laughed.

'Oli, would you make our guest one of those delicious mocktails?'

'On it,' Oli said, and Nicole's stomach flipped at the sincerity.

Pete was ushered to the study by Margo, their hushed tones disappearing as they closed the door. Paisley and Audrey were chatting animatedly about the mystery guest and Oli was already mixing the mocktail, so Nicole turned to the door to close it but stopped.

There, at the end of the driveway, a figure loomed, staring up at the house and at Nicole. After glancing behind to see check everyone was keeping busy, she silently slipped out into the night and down the driveway to meet them.

42

MARGO

'You didn't have to come here!' Margo said through clenched teeth. 'This is work. This is my work family.'

'Doesn't look much like work to me.' Pete laughed and then stopped when Margo glared at him.

'Margo, stop taking everything so seriously. You know why I am here – I should be really mad with you, not the other way around.'

Margo looked down at her hands sheepishly. Pete was leaning against the desk in the study. He took a long slurp of the mocktail. 'This is good. Your own chef and everything. Check you out.'

'Pete, you need to leave. You can't stay here.'

Pete took another long sip of his drink and then put the glass on the table.

'I'm not going anywhere, Margo. I'm home now and you need to accept that. You can't keep Dad away from me.'

'I'm not keeping him away from you, am I now, Pete?' Margo felt a surge of annoyance that manifested as some sort of gumption. Pete was taken a back.

'You went away, you left us remember. And now I'm not sure I can trust you any more.'

43

PAISLEY

If only that had been him, thought Paisley, she could have ended this pointless endeavour early and be getting on with her life. She was quite happy to just walk away into the sunset, never to see any of these losers again.

Paisley had tapped out a few more messages in the hope that he had changed his mind but he didn't seem as forward with his emotions via text message as she would have liked but she knew that she could be a little overbearing at times, but it was only because she was too passionate, and surely that wasn't a bad thing. She knew he had passion; she had seen it in him, felt it from him. So she would accept his one-word replies for now. Things were already getting better. She would file the loss of all of her money under a one-off mistake in her brain. She was a mother now, and she was going to make only good decisions from here on in.

44

AUDREY

The window from the hallway was not the best view for Audrey to see what Nicole was doing. Nicole must have thought that no one had noticed when she slipped out of the front door after Pete arrived, but Audrey clocked it straight away. And now she could just about make out the silhouette of Nicole at the bottom of the drive next to someone else. It was too dark to tell if they were male or female, and Nicole was standing in front of the person and blocking them from Audrey's view.

Audrey was suddenly keen for a cigarette, and poor Oli had been trying to serve the main course for some time. Should she risk popping out and trying to overhear? If she went out the back door, she could creep to the front of the house without being spotted or heard and she should be able to hear everything that was being said.

'Just popping for a quick fag whilst we wait for Margo,' Audrey said and slipped out of the back door before Oli could protest. Not that he had protested at any of the goings-on so far; he had been very patient and understanding, considering he had four women under the roof all with varying levels of hormones and emotions and dramas.

Audrey lit the cigarette outside and then walked slowly around the house. She could faintly hear voices and as she finally arrived at the front corner of the house, she heard Nicole's voice.

'You can't be here. You need to leave immediately, or I will call the police, do you understand?'

There was no reply, just the sound of footsteps on the path as someone walked away into the night. *Dammit*, Audrey thought. She had been too late. If only she had thought to come straight outside instead of trying to look out of the window. She retreated – whilst still smoking – to the back door and leant against the wall, finishing off her cigarette. She heard the front door slam and Nicole's voice declaring they all needed to eat. Audrey stubbed out the fag and went back inside. Margo and Pete had emerged from the study. Paisley was sitting frantically texting again, not looking like someone who had screamed in agony not half an hour ago.

Nicole brought the champagne to the table, topped up her glass and then Audrey's. Audrey watched as she took a large gulp then looked anxiously around the kitchen. Who the hell had that been outside with her moments ago that was making her so agitated? Audrey picked up her glass of champagne. It was very good champagne; the best she'd had in a while. *Better make this the last*, Audrey thought to herself. She really ought not to be getting so drunk, not when there appeared to be so much going on; somehow she felt she needed to keep her eye on the ball. She watched Nicole downing another gulp of champers. Audrey leant over the island, watching Oli finish plating up the mains.

'What a total drama of a night! Paisley's pregnancy, then her stubbed toe, some stranger arriving and now Nicole is outside talking to someone in hushed tones, something about calling the police. I mean there has been some funny goings-on around here.'

Audrey wobbled as she spoke. She usually held her drink pretty well, but she'd had a lot of champagne in a short amount of time and it was still flowing.

Oli simply glanced up at her, acknowledging her for a second, before returning his focus back on the task at hand. Audrey walked back to the table and took her seat opposite Nicole hoping the second course was a bit more successful.

45

THE PARTY

The vomit hit the toilet pan and Nicole clambered up from the floor whilst wiping her mouth. She unlocked the cubicle door, stood at the sink and washed her hands; she felt almost sober again. Now all she needed to do was drink a lot of water. She looked at her watch. How was it almost midnight? She left the bathroom and the sound of the party hit her. She could barely remember the last hour of the night. Who had she left in charge of the punch? It must have been lethal.

She would do one round of the floor, look for Gram and then she would need to head home.

She stuck her head around the door to the karaoke room and that was enough to send her head spinning again. Just as she was about to turn to leave, she caught sight of Audrey dancing in the corner of the room. No sign of Gram. That was something, at least. Her head hurt. She bumped into Margo.

'Oh, Margo. Was it you who helped me, earlier?' Nicole pointed awkwardly to the sofa.

Margo nodded just as awkwardly.

'Okay, well thanks for that. I, erm, wondered if you could do me another favour?'

'Sure.' Margo nodded enthusiastically.

'I need to go home. Are you staying around at all?'

'I can do,' Margo said, always eager to please.

'Would you mind locking up, once everyone has gone? Rick is here, he can make sure everyone gets out.' Nicole pointed at her friend Rick who she had paid to be security for the evening. She knew most of her guests, but she also knew what they could get up to if there was enough alcohol in their systems. Rick had stood in position just inside the foyer for most of the night.

Knowing her business would be safe, Nicole stepped into the Uber and she felt her gut begin to gurgle. She tried to focus on the fact that she would be home in twenty minutes – she was never good on too much alcohol, and she had certainly overdone it this evening.

She could not deny that things had got bad between her and Gram these last few weeks; he needed a blow out and she could do with getting home early. Nicole had completely given up talking about the one thing that had consumed their relationship for the last year: babies. That, it seemed, had affected Gram more than the actual discussion of children. There was nowhere else for them to go with the conversation; they were trapped. Or rather Nicole had trapped herself.

As Nicole sat in the back of the cab, she had a sudden realisation that she had forgotten her keys. She could see them in her mind's eye in her office. She asked the driver to turn around, and she headed back to the party.

46

NICOLE

Nicole's mind was a flurry of images and sounds and sights. She tried to suppress the memories that she was now processing here at the dinner table with three colleagues, a chef and now Pete, the brother of Margo, who she had invited to stay for dinner, but they were overtaking her. The only way to mute them was to drink. She gulped back the champagne and poured another glass. She went to top up Audrey's glass, but it was still half full. Oli was very attentive this evening, she hadn't seen an empty glass all night. Christ, she had even overtaken Audrey this evening. She needed to slow down. She shouldn't be in a bad way for Gram's arrival tomorrow; she wanted to be clear-headed, she wanted to be in control, have her say.

Her mind transported her back to the party from six weeks ago. She had lost so much of the evening to that damn punch, thinking back, Nicole was the one who had insisted there was punch; she had been responsible for the inebriation of half her colleagues and friends.

She thought about the moment she made the decision to go back for her keys; it was almost as if she had a sixth sense that night. She had seen how drunk everyone was, how close Audrey and Gram had been getting again and that had made her anxious. Paranoid. And so she had returned to The Studio. And now she had to live with what she saw. But first she had to confront her colleague and make her pay.

47

MARGO

Margo knew she had done a bad thing. She had practically disowned her brother when he went away. It wasn't that she was trying to hide her father but more that she was trying to keep him safe from Pete. From the day he had gone down, she had been ignoring all contact from the prison. Pete hadn't always been a good brother. Margo had convinced herself that when Pete did finally come home, that he would take all the money and leave her with nothing once he was out of prison, the way he had swindled all of that money out of that couple and their business. It had been all over the news and Margo had tried to follow it but it had been far too distressing for her at the time. Also Peter was older and cleverer than her. He had to be clever to be able to get all of that money out of someone and for them not to notice for a very long time. Margo had never considered herself to be on par with her brother, and she had always seen him as the one with all the power. Margo couldn't face being left with nothing. Margo reluctantly accepted she was never going to make much of herself, nor settle down with a significant other, she realised the inheritance was all she would ever have. She would have happily have shared it with Pete but he had never been good at sharing as a child. But it wasn't as though she could hide from Pete for long, once he was out, the first place he would come was home. He had explained to Margo that she would never need to worry about money. And now here was Pete, trying to convince Margo that he was a changed man. Prison had done its job for once. And he was sitting at the dinner table with them and they were about to tuck into steaks and delicious veg and sauces and all sorts, and it should have felt like home and Margo should have allowed herself to feel a little of something that felt like acceptance and living in the moment.

But she couldn't.

'Hey.' Pete squeezed Margo's leg.

'Hey.' Margo smiled.

'Relax. Everything is going to be okay now.' Pete uncurled Margo's fingers, which were in tight fists, the way she would unconsciously keep them when she felt stressed. Margo's palms were sweaty as she unclenched them to appease her brother.

Margo faked a smile at Pete as something began brewing in the pit of her stomach. Something much worse than all of this business with her father and Pete. Now she had been relieved of the nightmare that had been hiding from her own brother, she realised the pain and the terror was still there. It had been hiding beneath her anxiety over her dad and Peter. Now she didn't have to think about that, she realised just what a mess she was in the middle of. She needed to tell someone about Paisley; she had almost managed to tell Audrey and had been seconds away from entering Paisley's room to have it out with her but it was still stuck in her. This was something she felt solely responsible for, something she should have brought to Nicole's attention weeks ago. And maybe Pete's presence had just added a whole new level because something seriously bad was brewing in The Beach House this weekend, and in the next few hours things were only going to get worse.

48

AUDREY

Maybe a little more of a top-up in Nicole's glass and then Audrey could just ask her out right who she had been talking to outside. Who did Nicole not want the rest of the house to know was here? And now, Christ, Margo's brother was here, it was turning into quite the event. And they had barely touched on the bashing out any solutions for The Studio.

But Audrey wasn't going to push that either because there was a lot at stake, and she didn't want to rock the boat. Not yet. Not here. Not when Nicole seemed so damn vulnerable. Not now she knew so much about Nicole. The 'slut' comment had brought a lot of attention to the private messages on their Insta account but the messages from Jess were nothing like she could have ever imagined. And she had almost missed it amongst the masses. Amongst the madness. And Nicole would need to hear it from Audrey. But again, not here, not this weekend. Everything balanced on Nicole remaining as calm as possible until tomorrow night. Then she and Gram could speak with her.

'Well, isn't this jolly nice?' Nicole sounded the most relaxed she had been so far. Had she taken something? She certainly looked more laid back than she had been an hour ago, Audrey thought, and she allowed herself a smile at her friend's happiness.

'Here we are, Pete, our guest for this evening. Once Gram gets here, it will be quite the party!' Nicole scoffed; a small amount of champagne spilled from her glass on the table as she lifted her glass in a sort of semi-cheers to herself action.

Audrey wasn't sure she had caught that last part right. Had she just said Gram was coming tomorrow?

'Gram?' Paisley piped up.

'He'll be up tomorrow afternoon – I guess he misses me.' She laughed and hiccupped at the same time. Pete laughed loudly.

'Did he say why he's coming?'

Nicole glanced at Paisley, as though she were an annoying fly; Nicole was quite drunk and even Audrey guessed that it was an unnecessary question.

Then Nicole's gaze swerved over to Audrey. 'So that will be nice, won't it? *Our* Gram coming to visit.' Audrey detected the high pitch to her voice and the way she held her gaze for longer than necessary. Was it the alcohol or was Nicole, in fact, acting a bit weird? But then, everything about this trip seemed to be taking a strange turn and even Audrey, who was used to landing in some of the most unusual situations and powering through, was struggling to get on board with everything that was happening. But Audrey wasn't drunk enough to miss Nicole's clear intention of making reference to Audrey and Gram. Nicole knew what they had been up to behind her back, and that was why Gram was coming here. Why ask her to keep schtum for a few more days if was going to ruin everything by intercepting them here at The Beach House?

What could Audrey do now? She had no choice but to sit and wait until Gram arrived tomorrow.

49

THE PARTY

The set of keys to The Studio were inside Margo's jeans pocket and she kept touching them to make sure they were still there even though she could feel them pressed against her leg. But being tasked with locking up the studio was a big responsibility and one that she hoped she would execute well enough that Nicole would start to see her as more than just head of marketing and her PA. Margo enjoyed her job, but she saw herself as more of an operations manager. She had so many ideas of ways to utilise the remaining space here and bring in extra revenue throughout the day and evening from the current rooms.

Right now, though she was going to do exactly what Nicole had asked of her and make sure everyone left safely and that the building was secure. Everything would fall to her.

As she began to do the rounds, Margo found she was smiling in an authoritative manner that might suggest she was the one in charge here, even though everyone was far too gone to even acknowledge her. She was now the eyes and ears of this place – although she had already been so, if unofficially, before she had been tasked with the job.

The karaoke room was still in full swing, and Margo thought of her dad back home, who would be fast asleep by now, the way he was every night. She'd called in the agency and the usual lady had been over to sit with him until ten when he was in bed. She had received a text to say that she had left and so she knew he would be fine until about two or three in the morning when he'd wake up to use the toilet and she needed to be home for that. Time to start shutting this party down. The first thing to do was to bring everyone into the main foyer and karaoke room areas so between her and Rick they could begin to herd them out like sheep.

There were doors open and people sat on floors, leaning on tables and even a few people laid out on the floor.

'Hi there, everyone. I'm going to be shutting these rooms up in the next few minutes, so can you all please make your way into the foyer?' Margo tried on her best authoritative voice with each room she came to. She quite liked the sound of it, even if the response was lacklustre: a few people looked up at and she received the occasional nod and even a small 'no worries'.

When she reached the last few rooms, she couldn't see anyone in them. The doors were closed, and the lights were off but she peered into them to double-check. As she walked past the room that had been commandeered as a slouchy staff area, she saw a flash of light through the small glass pane at the top of the door. She stopped by it and peered through the window. Margo gasped and stumbled backwards. Then she moved back to the pane of glass again and stayed there for several more minutes. So many thoughts were running though her head, but mostly that she knew what was happening was wrong. Margo thought of her father back home and how her brother had committed that terrible crime against that couple. There was only a short amount of time left until his release date. If she called the police, she would be a part of this and then they might start asking questions, questions about her home life, about Pete, they would surely know him and what he did and so why would they believe someone who was related to a criminal. Margo knew that what she had just witnessed had to stay behind in that locked room. She couldn't be a part of it. She could never tell Nicole.

50

NICOLE

When Pete had arrived earlier this evening she had slipped away into the driveway, and before she knew it Nicole was shouting at Claire Best. It had been years since she had seen Claire. She had been a child when it had all happened, and now after all these years had passed, why was she here?

Nicole looked around at the table, at the dinner that had dragged out. She felt as though she had been eating for hours. So much had happened.

Here were all the women she had invited and she wasn't even sure why she was here any more. Claire's presence was pushing everything else to the background. Nicole felt as though she were having an out-of-body experience. She had drunk, but had it been that much? Nicole tried to think back to the words she had just exchanged outside on the driveway.

Nicole had ruined Claire's life eighteen years ago. Was Claire now about to try to ruin hers?

51

MARGO

Margo felt like a fish; her mouth had opened several times to speak to Nicole, but nothing had come out. When there was a spare moment in between courses, she felt she could just say, 'Can I have a minute?' or 'Can we speak outside quietly, Nicole?', all the things she had seen people do on TV shows and films over the years but she had never quite been able to summon the confidence to speak in such a way. Which was why, even with alcohol loosening her tongue slightly, she still couldn't find the strength to say what she needed to even though she knew time was running out.

Margo knew why Gram was coming here and it all made such terrifying sense to her. Margo had no legal understanding, but she knew it was all about to kick off. And it was only Margo's word and who was going to believe her? Paisley was pregnant and she was not telling the truth about how it had happened. Margo knew how people saw her, and it was unlikely that anyone would believe her. Before long, Gram would be here. Nicole was completely unaware of what had gone on at the party and now the consequences would be catastrophic.

52

PAISLEY

'So tell us something about yourself, Pete,' Paisley said, trying to keep her hands still even though all she wanted to do was pick at skin around her nails, or click her knuckles. Anything to distract her from what she really wanted to do, which was run to her room and have another flutter on the app.

'I love eighties and nineties thrillers. They are just the best. The amount of jump scares – I mean I just don't think you get the kind of kicks out of a movie now as you did back then. There was always someone creeping about, hiding round a corner, ready to just leap out on someone. They were awesome.'

Pete laughed at himself as he monologued, and Margo's own light titter showed just how uncomfortable she was at her brother's sudden and impromptu presence.

'And then there were the slasher movies, and it was always someone you would least expect, like the most inconspicuous character that everyone barely paid attention to.'

Oli arrived at the table carrying the beef joint, which he laid down on the table, ready for carving. Pete looked at Oli and continued. 'Like if this was a slasher movie, this dude would one hundred per cent be the slasher. He's just hanging around here all day, not saying much, and then' – Oli raised his knife, ready to share out the succulent meat – '*boom!*' – and stabbed it into the flesh.

Everyone froze. Pete's mouth was agape. Oli stayed, still looking directly at Pete. Eventually, Pete's mouth morphed from agape to an expression of joy.

'Oh. My. God. Talk about timing.' He stood up and bowed down to Oli. Then he held his hand out to shake it. 'That, my friend, was absolutely bloody brilliant. Hands down that will be my best anecdote all week. There I am talking about slasher, and then your chef does that. Amazing.'

Paisley looked at Pete, her eyes squinting with contempt. Why were some people so intent on bigging someone up only to expose themselves so blatantly as the one who required all the attention? Pete was one of those really loud friends on a night out who insisted on a running commentary purely for the benefit of having an audience for themselves. Paisley detested people like him. They were the absolute epitome of the kind of man that Paisley had steered clear of for so long. But her situation was still far from perfect. And, in fact, she was in more of a mess than she had been a few weeks ago. She had been in a few situations with men like Pete, who were so aggressively confident that they bordered on abusive and bullish. Men in clubs, pubs, sometimes just walking along the street. Now she was shacked up in a remote holiday home with one. The only saving grace was the chef had a very sharp knife. But even Oli would be leaving soon, and what if Pete stayed? Paisley had been watching how much champagne he'd consumed already in the short time he had been here. It was so strange to think he was related to Margo, who was so timid in comparison.

Oli had given her a fright when he pulled that knife, but she felt her heart rate return to normal now as he confidently carved the meat in front of them. But she still wasn't hungry. She watched the meat juices oozing out of the beef and she thought she could throw up. The atmosphere had changed in the last few hours. Was it time to just go? She could feel the walls of the house closing in around her. She couldn't breathe.

Paisley's stomach churned, and her mouth began to fill with saliva. It must be the pregnancy. But she was still in the early stages; too early to have serious bouts of nausea, surely? Paisley had felt strange since they all sat down for dinner. The arrival of Pete had thrown her, and with the imminent arrival of Gram, there was too much going on. Even the damn roulette app was creeping around in her subconscious, willing her to make a move. She looked around at everyone at the table and then her eyes fell upon Nicole, who was staring at her. She glanced away, hoping that when she looked back, Nicole would have dropped her gaze. But when she looked back, she saw Nicole's mouth form into two words.

'I know.'

53

AUDREY

Audrey was stuck behind Paisley, waiting to move past the table where Oli was bent over, carving so brilliantly and neatly that she didn't want to disturb him. She had, for a moment, thought it might be fun to try to squeeze past him through the tiny space and offer him crotch or bum, but she'd looked up and seen Nicole's face and now was definitely not the time. But then, Nicole turned and stared at her, and Audrey's blood ran cold as her friend and colleague mouthed those words. 'I know.'

Frozen in time, for what felt like an eternity but must have been half a second, Audrey pulled herself together and surprised herself with the almost-relief she felt for a few seconds. There was no point trying to pretend any more. Gram would be here tomorrow, so they could all have it out in the open. She felt a slight sickening in her gut at how the words had finally been spoken between them. It was a pretty sneaky and downright villainous delivery from Nicole. Not her usual way at all. But she had a lot more to be angry about. There wasn't just the issue between her and Gram, but the message on the Insta to deal with. She may as well just go full pelt and lay it all out on the table tomorrow with her. Audrey was certain that

Nicole would be comatose by pudding. That way, Audrey thought, she could pack Paisley off to bed and get some alone time with Margo. If her irritating brother pissed off, that was. Unless he was planning to blag a bed for the night as well as dinner; he seemed like a bit of a freeloader and Margo appeared scared by him. Even Audrey was not at all comfortable with the idea of a strange man in the house. There was a time when she was quite happy to sleep in a room/bed with many men she was unfamiliar with, but those days had been and gone. She was happy with Julian, and quite often would retreat to one of the spare rooms, which she had begun to make her own space over the years.

Pete was giving off a vibe, something which reminded her of her early days in modelling. A sort of desperation. She had seen him look at her in 'that way' a few times, but she was not worried about him trying anything with her. She had her own back, but she didn't like to feel uncomfortable in her own surroundings. Sure, she and Nicole would have words tomorrow and then Nicole would see that everything that had happened was for the greater good. It had been a hard secret to keep but this time tomorrow, Audrey would be able to breathe a sigh of relief; she would no longer have to lie to her friend.

54

THE PARTY

It was an unusual situation, even for Paisley, and one that she'd never expected to find herself in, but suddenly, it all became obvious and in a split second, all the pieces of the puzzle just fit into place.

She had lain behind that sofa and listened to the entire conversation that had been happening between Gram and Audrey, and to be honest, at some point she thought they were going to start shagging right there on the sofa, which would have been entertaining on some level but excruciating to listen to on another. Yet it wouldn't have surprised her that Audrey would do something like that to her friend and colleague Nicole. She had seen the way Audrey and Gram were together, like a pair of love-struck teenagers sometimes with their hushed conversations and how they were always giggling over something that no one else could ever seem to understand. Yet Nicole seemed to ignore it. She often, Paisley had decided, pretended it wasn't happening.

But lying there, listening to the conversation from behind the sofa where neither Audrey nor Gram knew she was there, she had heard a piece of information that had become like gold to her. She had been so sad after Matt had rejected her. She had felt so mad, so angry. She had experienced so many emotions in such a short period, that by the time Audrey had left and the words that Gram had spoken were still ringing in her ears, she knew the plan that she had set out for her and Matt was still on the table. Yes, this had been all about her and Matt in the beginning. The short dress at the last minute, this particular night when she knew he would be drunk, the quiet rooms where she knew she would be able to get him alone. And, of course, the perfectly timed ovulation. When she had done the test, she could hardly believe her luck. Matt was not the sort of guy who would have turned his back on a pregnant woman, even it had only turned out to be a one-night stand. But as it turned out, Matt did not want her. Had never wanted her. Even when he had kissed her that night after work, he had never wanted her. He had been with someone else all along and now he was engaged to be married. It had made Paisley feel sick. The thoughts in her mind had been dark as she lay behind the sofa. But upon hearing Gram declare that all he wanted was a baby, a child he could call his own, then it all became so very clear.

Here she was, a woman literally lying in wait for him, her body ripe, having recently deposited a fresh egg that was all ready to fertilise.

And here he was, a man, who was in trouble in his relationship with Nicole, which was obviously more than ever now that he had finally admitted it. He was drunk, he was needy. He would do anything to have what he wanted.

Paisley slipped out from behind the sofa, and he grabbed hold of her leg. Paisley froze.

55

NICOLE

Oli brought out the dessert, but Nicole could barely face it. She had drunk too much champagne, she knew that, and would suffer terribly in the morning. She needed to get some sleep, she needed to... Oli was topping up her champagne glass. Had he been doing that all night? She glanced around the kitchen and saw several empty champagne bottles. Pete was here and he had been drinking. He'd outstayed his welcome somewhat now, if Nicole was being honest, but Margo would never see that, and even if she did, she wouldn't do anything about it.

'Fill her up!' Nicole called as Oli held her gaze.

Oh, Nicole, what are you getting yourself into? she thought as her insides fizzled and then melted at the prospect of something happening between her and Oli tonight. Part of her longed for it, because why not? She had been clinging on to her relationship with Gram with her fingertips these last few months. And she had messed things up good and proper between them. Nothing was going to be the same from here on in anyway, so why not take a chance with Oli? Gram could barely look at her some days. He had put on a good show at The Studio party because that was what couples in trouble did: They showed the word that all was well.

'And then the ball went straight over his head, missing him by a millimetre, straight into the hole. I mean, you couldn't have predicted that, and I'd never played a round of golf in my life. So I guess I must have a secret skill for it.' Pete lorded on, and Nicole felt her skin prickle at the level of his voice. Why had she allowed him in and offered that he stay for dinner? She had offered that, hadn't she? Or had he presumed he was invited? Was it too late to ask if he was heading home tonight? Margo did not look comfortable, but Nicole could only feel the swell of her veins as the alcohol rushed through. She couldn't consider the feelings of others. She didn't want to have to think, she just wanted to feel something, lose her thoughts in the moment, and as the evening drew on, she was sure that the only way to do that was with Oli, somewhere alone and just the two of them.

As Pete kept talking loudly, Nicole looked at him with contempt.

She could see more food on the table: pink macarons an array of fruit, and was that a crème brûlée?

'I'm going for a fag before I even think about any of that.' Audrey stood up and headed to the back door.

Margo excused herself to go to the toilet.

Nicole waved her hand. 'No more!' she said, her head drooping.

'I think someone needs some fresh air,' came someone's voice and Nicole wasn't entirely sure whose it was. Then there was a hand on her shoulder, and Oli was behind her. She allowed him to walk her unsteadily to the hallway and help her on with her coat.

'I just wanted to say thanks for having me over this evening, you know, at such short notice.' It was Pete, drunk on her champagne, invading her weekend, throwing all her plans out of sync.

'No notice, you mean?' Nicole said, and Pete laughed loudly. Oli said nothing.

'Oh yeah, right. Yeah, sorry. I did tell Margo I was on my way, but she's always been a bit slow and—'

'Slow?' Suddenly all Nicole's senses were on high alert.

Pete looked shocked; he took a step back.

'Yeah, well you know Margo – she's not quite as normal as the rest of us, is she?'

'Margo? Margo is the most normal person I know.'

'Oh, right,' Pete said.

'I presume you're too drunk to drive anywhere this evening. There's a spare room down the hallway.'

Pete looked at both of them for a long time.

'All right, mate – see you in a bit,' Oli said and walked outside with Nicole.

56

MARGO

'Where is Pete?' Margo sounded tense. She looked at Audrey with pleading eyes because Audrey was a proper grown-up and she would know how to solve a problem. She looked at Oli next, but he only glanced at her briefly from the counter where he was clearing down. Dinner was finally finished and only Margo, Nicole and Paisley remained at the table.

'Have you seen him? You did the jokey thing with the knife earlier; I know he is annoying, but I only really have him, see and—'

'Margo, take a breath already,' Audrey said in that American twang that Margo had noticed often came out when Audrey'd had a drink.

Margo looked at Audrey and remained silent.

'Does he smoke?' Audrey asked.

'Yes, sometimes, when he's had a drink.'

'Right then, we presume he has had a bit too much to drink and that he needs to just walk off some of that alcohol with a cigarette.'

'But the cliff. Someone died up there.'

Audrey put her hand on Margo's shoulder. 'Someone threw

themselves off there a long time ago is what happened. Now, your Pete, who seems to have quite the personality, would not think about doing anything like that, would he?' Audrey said it as though the matter were settled, but Margo shifted uncomfortably and opened her mouth to speak, emitting only a slight sound.

Audrey let out a sigh. 'What is it, Margo?'

'My brother, he… he only just got out of… prison.'

'For fuck's sake,' Audrey said. 'For what?'

'Fraud.'

'Double for fuck's sake. Margo, you know you don't just invite an ex-convict into your employer's house and then neglect to tell them he has just got out of prison. This was a girls' weekend, no men invited! I did wonder why he was guzzling back that champagne – he must have had a bottle and a half to himself.'

'That's what I mean, he hasn't drunk for years, and now he's had that much. He might…'

'Might what?'

'I don't know!' Margo shouted and Audrey looked surprised.

'I just don't know what to think, he's my brother, but I haven't seen him for over ten years, and I don't know what he is capable of, or what his state of mind is.'

'Great. Well, I didn't fancy a great big hunt for your brother but needs must. Coats on, everyone.'

Audrey looked around as Paisley was arriving back from downstairs.

'You coming?' Audrey asked her.

'I don't think so, that man gave me the creeps. I knew it, Margo, when I saw him. I'm totally triggered, Margo. Like totally.'

Margo saw Audrey raise her eyes to the ceiling. Margo then turned to Oli imploringly.

'Sorry, girls, I'm homebound. Early start tomorrow. Final day and all that.'

'Yes, yes, of course,' Audrey said, but Margo had seen the way Oli had looked at Pete; the way he had slipped that knife out so suddenly, it was such a coincidence.

'Nicole? Where's Nicole?' Audrey looked around the living space as though she might just see Nicole draped over a sofa.

'Bed,' came Oli's voice. Margo looked at him.

'How do you know?'

'Because after I brought her in from her fresh air, she went straight upstairs. Paisley saw her,' Oli said and walked past Margo, giving her a sympathetic smile. He went to the hallway where he pulled on his coat.

Paisley nodded and gestured upstairs. 'Out like a light.'

'Thanks so much, Oli. It was so delicious as always. See you in the morning.' Audrey followed him into the hallway and picked up her coat.

Margo watched as Oli walked out of the door. Little bits about the way he walked and the colours on his coat were still running through her mind long after he had closed the door.

'Come on, Margo, what are you waiting for?' Audrey said authoritatively.

Margo stopped staring and came to. But she couldn't stop seeing the one thing she had locked onto as Oli walked out of the door. And that was the slight glint of a small knife gripped in his hand.

57

PAISLEY

The disappointment was real when the door opened seconds after Oli left and Pete was standing there, looking slightly dishevelled and embarrassed.

'I'm sorry, sis,' he said and proceeded to have what appeared to Paisley as some sort of breakdown. His shoulders began shaking uncontrollably and he was stumbling forwards as though he might fall to his knees, but Margo was there, and she reached and grabbed him and he fell into her arms instead. Margo stood as stiffly as she could manage.

'Oh Christ, he's gone, he's actually gone. Let's get him to his bedroom, shall we, Margo? Between us we can manage that,' Audrey said and moved confidently over to Pete. Audrey was of typical supermodel stature and Paisley was sure she had heard her refer to her black belts in several forms of martial arts before. Pete was smaller than Audrey, so Paisley was not too worried on that front, but as Audrey navigated Pete to towards the stairs, she turned and mouthed at Paisley.

'Lock your door.'

Paisley stood up and went first to the front door and locked it, then she checked the back door and locked that too. Then she headed upstairs, and when she was on the landing, she heard the pitiful wails of Pete.

'I'll be gone in the morning. Nicole told me to be gone. I'll be gone, don't you worry, sis. And I'm sorry, I'll be better. You were right, I've been a terrible brother...' On and on he went, and Paisley felt her back prickle with irritation. But she supposed she ought to get used to repetitive crying, as there would be lots of that to come soon.

Audrey came out of the spare room where Margo was with a still wailing and crying Pete.

'What a night,' Audrey said.

'What a prick.' Paisley indicated to the room.

'Prison life will do that to you. It will take him some time to acclimatise to the outside world again. We shouldn't judge.'

'Prison?' Paisley screeched, and Audrey shushed her. 'I'm sorry, but he shouldn't be here. And I'm judging. I'm judging hard.'

'Oh, do pipe down, Paisley. I'm going to check on Nicole.' Audrey headed upstairs followed closely by Paisley. The door to Nicole's room was not locked and ajar. Audrey peeped her head in and then stood back to show Paisley.

'Fast asleep, by the looks of it.'

Paisley nodded at Audrey.

'Best let her sleep it off,' Paisley said, and Audrey agreed.

'Yes, she went heavy on it tonight. Night.' Audrey stepped past Paisley and headed for her bedroom, and then, a few moments later, Paisley heard her door close and then lock after her. Paisley stood by Nicole's room for just a few seconds more, looking in at the heap under the blankets. Then she smiled softly to herself until that smile became something much more: Paisley was grinning from ear to ear.

'Sleep tight, Nicole,' she said and closed the door.

58

AUDREY

The bed was firm enough, but Audrey missed her super-sized bed at home. She tossed and turned, not sure if it was the alcohol, the stranger in the house, or the imminent arrival of Gram.

She bashed out a message to him. Even though it was late, it was likely he was still awake, unable to sleep as well. She needed to know what his intentions were when he came here.

Everything okay? I hear you're beach-house bound.

Audrey waited a few seconds and saw that Gram was typing.

Yes. Not what I wanted, but something has cropped up. Something big.

Shit, thought Audrey. All their months of being careful. All the planning, all the lying to Nicole. For nothing.

Has the business deal fallen through?

Audrey typed quickly, her heart racing.

No, funnily enough, it's all gone through fine just this morning. I have the funds to become an investor in The Studio. The business my girlfriend loves more than life is saved. For now.

Well, that was something. Audrey felt the relief wash through her. All the work they had been doing to help Gram move his assets and equity around, all the secrecy, all the lies. With help from Julian and his solicitor friends, they had done it. Gram knew how much Nicole loved The Studio. This was his one last attempt to win her back. The gap between them had widened so much and Gram was certain that she would never want to discuss having babies, and it was unlikely that at this point she would ever agree to having any – this Audrey now understood better than she ever had. So when The Studio started showing signs that it was in trouble and might not survive another year with just Nicole on board, Gram began working behind the scenes to get himself involved as a silent partner. Nicole would still run the business as she had been doing, except now she would have a proper amount of money to play with to invest and do all the things they needed to do to make the business not just a success but something bigger than either of them had envisioned. There might not ever be a baby, but this was something that they could nurture together.

That's amazing, Gram. I'm so proud of you. No more lying, no more sneaking around. Are you going to surprise her with the news tomorrow?

Did you not read the first text properly? Something has gone terribly wrong.

There wasn't even a sad emoji face, which meant that Gram was being perfectly serious. Whatever had happened was indeed bad.

Audrey hit the call button, at first it went to answerphone.

Gram's voice sang out at the other end. '*Hey, tell me something awesome.*'

'Call me back, you twit,' Audrey spat down the phone.

Two minutes later, Audrey's phone rang.

Gram was on the other end, crying.

'Help me, Audrey, I don't know what to do.'

59

NICOLE

Her head hurt like she'd whacked it against something; she knew she should have stopped drinking earlier than she had, but she couldn't even remember going to bed or closing the curtains. The room was very dark, but it must have been morning, as she could hear the seagulls screeching outside the window. She opened her eyes a fraction and her body seized up. Where was the window? And why was she lying on this side of the room? She sat up, trying to take in her surroundings, her heart pumping, her body filling with adrenaline. She was not in The Beach House, but she couldn't be too far away from home, surely, because of the seagulls. So where the hell was she? Then Nicole looked across to where the window was on her right and then glanced down at the floor. At the bare floorboards and the long crack that ran from the bed to just under the window.

'No,' Nicole whispered quietly. How could it be? she thought. How could she be here? In this house?

She managed to sit up more so she her bum was at the head of the bed. It was a double. A different double. Not the double she had known before. Her head was fuzzy, everything ached and hurt.

She heard a creaking on the stairs and then a rattle of a key in the lock. She turned to see the door opening and then someone standing in the doorway.

'Good morning.'

Relief and confusion swept through her all at once.

Oli.

She cast her mind back to last night and what had happened. Lots to drink, feeling angry, lost, sorry for herself, ready to throw herself into the arms of another man, into the arms of Oli.

'What the hell happened last night?' Nicole laughed but the nervous waver must have given her away. She was unsure, she was vulnerable, she was scared. She had heard the door being unlocked. Why was she locked in? Nicole looked around the room and laughed again, but this time very aware that Oli wasn't laughing. He wasn't doing much actually except staring at her in that way he had been looking at her since Thursday. Nicole felt her stomach jolt as if she were on a ride at a theme park and she had just been dropped, stomach left behind. Why was it only clear to her now that the way Oli was looking at her had never been with sexual intent. He was and had only been observing her. He was fascinated with her, *obsessed* with her.

'This house,' Nicole said quickly, realising she might be running out of time, maybe she had an opportunity to turn things around to get Oli on her side. To let her out of this room. But there was already too much desperation in her voice.

Oli seemed to change his expression slightly, it wasn't a smile as such. Just an acknowledgement of what she was saying. 'Of course, you recognise it?'

'Yes, I—' Nicole wanted to go on, but she stopped. She didn't need to say any more, did she? As her gut began to sink further, she thought about all that had happened and understood that, for whatever reason, Oli knew what this room was and what it meant to her.

Oli brought himself closer to Nicole until he was almost at the bed. Nicole went to push herself away to the edge of the bed with her feet, but one of her feet wouldn't move. She looked down; there was some sort of leather strap around her ankle that was attached to a chain secured to the end of the bed.

'It's funny, because I never actually spent any time here. This was my father's house, the house I was never invited to after he left me and my mum. For her.'

Nicole gulped. His father. This house. Nicole's head spun as she tried to piece Oli into this scenario, this house. But he just didn't fit.

She was thirsty, her head hurt, she needed water. Why didn't she drink more water with her meal last night instead of guzzling champagne like it was fizzy pop? If she was a little more hydrated, she was sure she would be able to think clearer, would be able to get herself out of this situation.

Nicole prided herself on being assertive and having great people skills. It was what had got her where she was today. Except the last few months she had let herself go; she had been distracted with the past. With the year. The year she had been focusing on for so long, when it had been far enough away that's she didn't need to worry about it. But 2022 had hit and she knew she was going to be a wreck. And things had slowly started to go wrong. She had taken the eye off the ball big time and basically given Gram a free licence to find love elsewhere with the lack of love and attention she had given him. He would be coming to The Beach House to see her today. What would he do when he couldn't find her? Nicole knew her phone was not anywhere in the vicinity. She had put it in her coat when she went out last night and… The final moments of what she could remember from last night came rushing back to her all at once. The meal, the endless champagne, refilling her glass. She'd needed fresh air, and Oli had helped her. A little walk before bed, just the two of them. And she had put on a coat and she had bloody well gone, hadn't she? But then she didn't remember anything after that, it was a big fat black void in her mind. Again, Nicole's mind was drawn back to the champagne and just how much there had been and why had Oli been so keen to keep refilling her. She had been drugged.

Nicole took her mind back to the comment Oli had just made about his father.

'Your father's?' she asked, even though it sounded naïve, because there was only one reason she was in this house, one reason she had been brought here, one person who connected her to this house and that was Andrew Best.

'Yes, Nicole, my father. We all have one, whether we know it or not, and that's what you and I have in common, I guess. I was initially drawn to you and the story, I even felt sorry for you, but my mother told me not to be. She told me you were a desperate little whore who cared about no one but herself.'

'Oli, I—' Nicole began.

'No, please, Nicole, let me speak. I think you've had long enough to speak up, it's been over eighteen years, hasn't it? You've seen Claire about the place, haven't you? You even thought she had moved back in here, didn't you, Claire, Andrew's wife— Oops, sorry, his *widow*.'

'So, you... you live here?'

'I bought this house years ago, couldn't bring myself to live in the place though, I mean, why would I? It's crawling with memories, sad and depressing memories, and I was never even a part of them! I believe you met my cleaner? She's here more than I am. You were quite the celebrity in her eyes. So why buy the house you must be thinking?' Oli asked as Nicole opened her mouth to ask the very same question. 'Because it's all I have left of him. I was too young to buy it the first few times it came on the market, but once I was an established chef earning a pretty decent wage, I had a big fat deposit. I've been saving for over ten years, Nicole, in the hope that one day it would come on the market and then it did! You see my dad left me and my mum for that witch Claire and then you come along, all young and fertile and turning his eye again! And the next thing, the pair of you are at it, sometimes here, aren't I right?' Oli looked around the room. 'She was a nurse, his other wife, worked nights didn't she? So you were safe here, weren't you, until safety was the very operative word. Forgot to take the pill or did the condom split?'

Nicole was thrust back to the very night in question, when she lay here in Andrew's arms, when she realised she had forgotten to take the pill. She went back to school and was behind on her exam revision, then Claire came home, and Andrew said she was suspicious. Days went by and she suddenly remembered, she hadn't taken the damn pill again. She went to the doctor, but it was too late. And so she prayed and prayed even though she was not religious, but weeks went by, and she just knew. She took the test with Andrew by her side. She was pregnant. He said he would stay with her, that he would support her no matter what. But he didn't. He took his own life a month later.

60

MARGO

There was a quietness to the house that didn't feel right to Margo. A quietness she had been used to all her life, when she would wake up and her brother had gone missing again and she would come downstairs to find both of her parents sitting in silence in the sitting room, unable to speak to one another, not knowing what to do. They had been considered geriatric parents – almost sixty when Margo and Peter were in their early to mid teens – and they had no friends who had children the same age. Their friends' children had grown up, and some were already grandparents. They never knew what to do and so they would just sit, quietly until he came home, often accompanied by the police, invariably with a black eye or split lip.

Today, The Beach House was that sort of eerily quiet, and Margo wasn't sure why. It was nearly eight and she was certain that Oli ought to be in the kitchen, getting ready for their Saturday brunch, so she had expected to be hearing clanging pans. He must be running late, for whatever reason. Margo got up and dressed, brushed her teeth and hair. She stepped outside onto the landing and waited to hear any noises from the other three rooms. Paisley's door was shut fast, as was Audrey's, but Nicole's was ajar. Margo stood outside and listened for any noise, any breathing. They were all advised to lock their doors last night by Audrey, but Nicole's wasn't. Margo's chest started to heave. What if Pete had been up in the night and done something terrible? Margo had always been a worrier, but after what she had witnessed on the night of the first anniversary party, she was never going to doubt anything ever again. Stranger things had happened.

But for now she needed to check that Nicole was okay. She stepped into the room and listened again for the sounds of breathing. Nothing. She stepped closer to the bed and leant down to the mound on the mattress. Nothing. No movement. And there was no smell in here. Margo was sensitive to smells and usually, the scents of other people in the morning after a full night's sleep were very potent to Margo. Whereas, it smelt quite fresh in here.

'Nicole,' Margo whispered. 'Nicole,' she whispered louder.

There was no stirring, and so she gently and tentatively reached out her hand and rested it on top of Nicole.

She pressed down, but was met with no resistance. Hovering her hand above the linen, she hesitated before pulling the duvet from the top to reveal a pillow placed on top another pillow. As she pulled the duvet back further, she could see there were a total of four large pillows arranged to look as if there were a person in the bed.

'What?' Margo couldn't fathom why Nicole would try to fool them that she had gone to sleep when she hadn't. Then a memory, a glint of a knife as Oli left last night. He had been making eyes at Nicole since they arrived. Margo was almost certain that Nicole was with Oli. But she had no idea where he lived. Gram would soon be here, and Nicole needed to be back and ready to receive him. And

Margo would be there to help with the blow, which would be hard for Nicole. But Margo had no choice; it was all out of her hands. She was just sorry she had kept everything to herself all this time and she hoped that Nicole would forgive her.

61

PAISLEY

The smile was still on Paisley's face when she woke. Today was the day her life could truly begin. She thought briefly about Nicole and where she was right now and how she was feeling. Paisley felt a little bad for her, but what Nicole had done was unforgivable.

Did the others think she was so stupid that she didn't know the log-ins of the social accounts? They had been left on a piece of a paper after one of the first meetings when The Studio opened. Since then, Paisley had viewed the social media every day. Margo and Audrey were the ones who dealt with all the social stuff and so neither one of them would bat an eyelid if a message had been read before they got to it; they would just assume it was the other.

When Paisley first arrived, she had hours before anyone else was there, and so she and Oli had spent a little time getting to know one another. Before long she knew all about Oli, who he was and how he was connected to Nicole's past. Oli had convinced her that he could get Nicole out of the house after dinner and over to Crest Wave, the home of his late father, Andrew Best. Once Nicole was out of the picture, Gram would be able to appreciate Paisley in all her pregnant glory. Once he arrived, he would see her against the backdrop of the wonderful house and then they would talk about the future, and everything would be how it should be. Because a baby is a gift, and not something to be given away.

It was fortunate that Paisley had found the diary in Nicole's room the day she arrived at The Beach House. There was a reason she enjoyed being the first to arrive somewhere. She liked to get her bearings, she liked to know what she was dealing with, and usually this involved a bit of a poke around. She never really needed to look far. A knicker drawer or under the bed were the usual places. And that was where Nicole had left her diary, slipped in between the divan and the mattress. At first, reading Nicole's words, Paisley felt as if she could have been reading her own diary. Paisley opened up the diary and read the final entry.

28 October 2004

I think today is the day. I feel different. I think the baby is coming. Once he or she is here, then they will take them straight away. I have said I never want to see them. It will be easier. Mum said I will be sad, but I don't think I can be any sadder than I am about losing you. You were the love of my life. I will never love anyone as much as I love you. If only we could have been together. Why did you have to do it? Why did you have to leave me? We could have been a family. We could have raised the baby together. I would never have been able to look at the baby without thinking of you and the loss I feel inside. I am sorry for what I did. For being the reason you took your life. Everyone told me you were very ill in your mind, but the upset we caused was what made you do it. But it was me getting pregnant that made you do it. So I know it is my fault. I promise you one thing: I will never have another baby. I will be childless because I now know I don't deserve one after what I did.

Wherever you are, I hope you can forgive me. I am yours forever.

Nic x

62

AUDREY

Eyes wide open, heart pounding. Shit, was it the menopause or was something really bad about to happen? Audrey jumped out of bed, panic high in her chest. What had she been thinking, just going to bed and leaving Nicole last night? Why hadn't she slept in the same room as her. She had been having nightmares all night about locks and keys and now she realised that they had all gone to bed, locked their doors and left Nicole's wide open. Audrey raced to Nicole's room, but the door was open and the pillows were in the middle of the bed. That was odd, Audrey thought. She raced downstairs, not caring she was only in a revealing nightdress.

Margo was in the kitchen when Audrey arrived downstairs. She looked stressed.

'Oh crap, what's going on?' Audrey was almost weeping. After her last conversation with Gram before bed, she was going nuts thinking of everything she wanted to do to Paisley and how she needed to be there for Nicole today.

'I can't find Nicole. Her car is gone, her phone is not connecting, and I don't know where she is. She can't have just driven off.' Margo sounded panicked.

'She might have,' Audrey said and looked at Margo. 'We need to speak about the email that we both read.'

'Email?'

'On the social site. I knew there was something bigger on your mind than the "slut" comment. I read the mail, but they had already been read, so it must have been you right. So let's discuss.'

'I haven't read any mail.'

Audrey frowned. 'Are you sure?'

'Positive.'

'Then what have you been hiding all this time?'

Margo took a deep breath.

'I saw something on the night of the party six weeks ago. Nicole left me in charge, and I was trying to get people out of rooms, and I looked into the room with the sofa in it and there was Gram with Paisley and—'

'I know,' Audrey said.

'You know?'

'I know. Gram told me. Last night.'

'So he knows what happened. He's not blind to what went on?'

'Oh, he knew what went on. He doesn't remember much, but he knows it was not good.'

'He doesn't remember much? What does he remember?'

'Oh my God, that was the best night's sleep I have had in like, forever.' Pete wandered into the kitchen, looking better than he did last night. At least he wasn't crying.

'Sis, we need to buy a place like this. The sea air, the amazing mattresses. My back didn't know what had hit it.'

'Pete, Nicole is missing,' Margo said.

'Margo, she's not missing. She...' Audrey looked at Pete. 'But I specifically remember her asking you to be gone before breakfast, and I'd like to have a private conversation with my friend, so whilst

I'm thrilled you had a good night's sleep, I really must speak with Margo in private.'

Pete held his hands out. 'Look, I've had a great time and I don't need to hang around, not unless there's a bacon butty going?' Pete looked past Audrey at the kitchen counter.

'No, chef's not here yet,' Margo said.

'Where is Oli?' Audrey asked.

'That's another thing I need to speak to you about,' Margo said, and they both looked expectantly at Pete.

'All right, all right, I'm going. Unless, like, you need some help here, it sounds like there's a few people missing. It was pretty messy last night. I could hang about, help you search or whatever. I know Margo must have filled you in on me being inside and all that. Some say I'm a bit handy to have around, so—'

'No, thank you, Pete. This really is a private matter now, so if you wouldn't mind...' Audrey used her most professional voice with a hint of faux cheer in it.

'Sure, I'm gone. Sis, I had a blast. I'll call you. We can all have a catch up. Me, you and Dad?'

Margo nodded. Pete grabbed his coat in the hallway, waved and then shut the door.

'The thing is, Audrey, I saw Oli leave here with a knife last night.'

'He is a chef, Margo.'

'I know, but...'

'Chefs carry knives, especially expensive ones that they don't want other people to steal.'

Margo furrowed her brow.

'We have more important things to worry about.'

'Like what?' Margo said, but Audrey already had her phone open on the Instagram message.

Audrey gave Margo a minute to read it.

'What the...?' Margo furrowed her brow, the closest she would probably ever come to crying or showing any emotion. Audrey had never seen her even close to tears.

'Mind blowing, isn't it? Now if you didn't read the message, then that only leaves one other person who did.'

They both looked up towards the ceiling and then began walking up the stairs together.

63

NICOLE

Tears were falling silently down Nicole's cheeks. Oli had taken a seat on a small chair in the corner of the room.

'I have another sibling. Somewhere out there, I have a sister or a brother. You know, my mum had even come around to the idea of us all just being one big happy family. She was going to bring me to see the baby. We all knew Dad had mental health issues. We knew he was never going to be totally well, but we, Nicole, his family, knew how to look after him. He loved me. But you, you may as well have got up on that cliff face and pushed him over the edge because of what you did by getting pregnant... He didn't want to live. He knew he had done wrong by starting the damn affair with you, but when you told him you were pregnant, that another life was now involved in this horrible mess, he didn't know how to process that emotion. But you did, Nicole, didn't you? You gave away a baby, my dad's child, my sister, to a complete stranger and then you just carried on with your life.'

Nicole felt the heave of tears come on and it took her breath away.

'I... I... I can't.'

Oli looked on, unfazed. 'I listen to your podcast, you know. I know you still visit regularly. I knew you would be here this weekend. But I figured you wouldn't be here alone. And I figured you would need a chef, like you always do. So a while ago, I put my card through the door so your mum and stepdad would see it, so they would think of me when the time came and recommend me to you. I use my mum's surname, always have done. No one would associate me with Andrew Best.'

'It's... a... girl,' Nicole spluttered.

Oli leant closer in his chair 'What?'

'You said... sister. The baby was a girl?' Nicole fought out the words through the tears.

'Yes,' Oli said thoughtfully.

'M-m-maybe I could help you find her.' Nicole spluttered, realising she had a slither of hope of getting out of this situation. 'I have resources, I am sure I could very easily—'

'You stupid woman. I don't need your help! I know exactly how my sister is. Her name is Jessica.'

Nicole gasped at the words and felt her heart swell. She was transported back to the night in the hospital when she went into labour. A swift seven hours and the baby was out. She hadn't looked. She had shut her eyes tightly and then only opened them when she saw the back of the midwife closing the door behind her, with a tiny, wailing bundle in her arms.

Oli stood up, and for the first time, Nicole noticed that he was holding a knife. Had he been holding a knife the whole time?

'I think you and I need to go for a little walk, don't you? Why don't we pop over and pay our respects to my dad? What do you say?'

64

MARGO

'This is ridiculous,' Margo hissed as the pair of them stood outside Paisley's door.

'It's not,' Audrey shouted, lifted her leg and gave the door one almighty kick. It swung open, the door semi-off its hinges. 'I mean, the place looks nice, but they really scrimped on these doors.'

Audrey walked through and Margo followed very closely behind Audrey.

Paisley was sitting up in her bed, her duvet pulled right up to her chest.

'What the hell is going on?' she whimpered.

'We need to get you out of this room immediately, for your own safety,' Audrey said and approached the bed. She held her hand out to Paisley. Tentatively, Paisley took it and stepped out of bed. Margo noted the jogging bottoms she was wearing, which looked tired and tatty, and there was a smell about the room that Margo didn't like.

'What the hell is going on, Audrey?'

'We all need to get to my room now. Let's just go.'

Paisley left the room. They crossed the landing to Audrey's bedroom. Paisley walked in first and Margo tried to step through after her and Audrey put her foot out to stop her. Margo looked confused. Once Paisley was inside and looking around the room, Audrey slammed it shut and produced a key from what seemed to be between her breasts and locked the door.

Suddenly, there were screams and cries from the other side of the room as Paisley banged on it very loudly. 'What the hell are you doing?' came the words through the door.

'We can't leave her in there?' Margo said.

'She is perfectly safe. No sharp objects and I locked all the windows and took the keys out. There's a small window in the bathroom I left open plus plenty of bottles of water. She is good for a couple of hours. Now, if Nicole has just popped out or something, then we need madam here safely in that room. It's for her own safety, Nicole could try and kill her.' Audrey turned to the door. 'Did you hear that? She will probably want to kill you.'

Audrey began walking down the stairs. 'Now first things first, chef is absent, and I, for one, am starving. Gram will be here soon, and the shit is going to well and truly hit the fan, so I suggest we fuel up.' They reached the kitchen. 'Margo, put the kettle on.'

65

PAISLEY

After fifteen minutes of shouting herself hoarse and crying her tear ducts dry, Paisley gave up. She went to the en suite bathroom, sat down and pulled her joggers and knickers down. She hadn't imagined it. There were several very obvious spots of blood in her pants. She stuffed some tissue in there and stood up. She had felt it last night when she had got into bed and went to the toilet in the dark because she couldn't bear to look. But she was sure this was it. Some sort of mini miscarriage, a period? Was she ever pregnant? Had she imagined it? It didn't matter now because it was all over for her. This was supposed to be her happy ending; she was supposed to get the guy and walk off into the bloody sunset, but, as usual, the universe had other ideas.

She had heard Audrey say that she had locked all the windows, so she hadn't even bothered trying. Audrey had one of the larger rooms and there were three windows in here altogether. Paisley tried the first two, which were very obviously locked. Then she tried the final one. Also locked. In the bathroom, there was one main window and one small window, which Audrey had left open. But when Paisley tried the main window, she was shocked to see it was not locked. She swung it open and inhaled the salty sea air. She would have to climb onto the sink to get out and then she wasn't sure how she would get down when she got up there, but she was going to take a chance because she had nothing left to lose.

66

AUDREY

Audrey pushed her plate away. 'My God that was one fine bacon sandwich. When your brother mentioned bacon, I got a real hankering for it.' Audrey sipped her coffee and then looked at Margo. 'You've barely touched yours, what's up?'

'Everything. My brother showing up last night, Paisley locked in that room, that email you have just shown me, Gram arriving, Nicole missing and Oli is still not here. Do you not think that is weird?' Margo asked Audrey.

Audrey thought for a moment. 'It is a little weird, but I just figured he'd had enough of us mental lot.' Audrey waited for Margo to agree, but when she didn't and gave her that look of panic and bewilderment, Audrey stood up and groaned.

'All right, I'll find some of Nicole's clothes, and we'll go and try and find his place, it must be round here somewhere, right?'

Margo nodded and looked instantly brighter. 'Right!'

* * *

Ten minutes later, Audrey was in a pair of slouchy trousers that would have reached Nicole's feet but came to Audrey's shins. The T-shirt and the jumper fitted better.

She pulled on her Doc Martens in the hallway and then her coat. 'Let's go.'

'Oh, should we leave a note for Gram?' Audrey asked herself. 'I'll text him.' She bashed out a short text explaining they had all popped out, and to ignore any banging from upstairs and to wait for their return at The Beach House.

Margo already had her coat and boots on and a bottle of water in hand.

'Good girl, the hangover is fierce today,' Audrey said.

They left the house and walked down the drive.

'I think we should try the village bit first, then we can always come and get the car if we need to go further.'

'Fine,' Audrey said, already regretting not finding something better to wear as the wind made its way up her too-short trousers.

The women walked in silence, and Audrey wondered what Margo was thinking, and what the hell Gram would say when he arrived, and what Nicole was going to make of all of this when she arrived.

They trudged for ten minutes down a steep hill that seemed to go on forever before reaching a row of terraced houses on the left. On the other side of the road was a road that led off with plenty of houses and then there was another road on their right, on the corner of which was a small house with the sign *Crest Wave* on it.

'Hold on a minute,' Margo said, pointing along the road at a parked car. 'That's my brother's car. That's the car he arrived in last night,' Margo said.

'Well, why is he parked down here? I thought he was going home?'

'Maybe he is lost or broke down?' Audrey said. They both

approached the car, but it was empty. They looked to the only house along this road, after which the path then continued down to the sea.

'Do you think he is down there?' Margo pointed.

'I don't know your bro that well, Margo, but he did not strike me as the outdoorsy, let's-go-for-a-sea-cliff-walk-at-nine-in-the-morning kind of guy.'

Margo nodded. 'That is true. Before prison, he was not like that.'

'So I doubt prison instilled that in him either.'

They both looked up at the house. 'Well, he must be in there then. Come on.' Audrey marched to the front door and banged loudly.

There was no reply. Audrey banged again, this time Margo squinted and put her hand out to Audrey.

'Wait.' Margo squinted again. 'Can you hear that?' Margo asked.

'No, Margo, I'm not a bat. What is it?'

'I can hear a voice, like really tinny, like really far away.'

Audrey banged again and then stood back so Margo could do her listening thing again.

A few seconds later, Margo turned to Audrey.

'I'm almost certain it's him. It's Pete. Audrey, do you mind—'

'Not at all, Margo, step aside.'

Margo stepped back as Audrey lifted her leg high in the air once more.

67

NICOLE

It was windy on the cliff and Oli had put a large duffel coat on Nicole. Oli had hold of Nicole's arm with one hand, but underneath, inside his own coat, his other pressed the knife close to her ribs. To any passing walker, the two of them looked like a couple of lovebirds on a morning stroll. How funny that Nicole had thought about Oli in those ways for the last few days and now here they were acting out that role.

They arrived at the part of the fence with the dead bouquet.

'Now, would you look at that!' Oli said. 'Claire's little offering to my dad. She tried to tell me off for coming back here, said I shouldn't be here, messing about. I told her to mind her own business, and that people needed to earn a living.' They stopped and leant on the fence. 'There's a cost-of-living crisis, didn't you know!' Oli shouted across the fence and down to the beach below, where one dog walker looked up. Nicole thought about gesturing for help, but she was too far away from anyone, and she didn't know what he was going to do with that knife. 'And you pay very well, Nicole.'

He turned to face her, and then with his free hand, took her face in his hand and pushed his lips against hers. He tasted of sweat, and it was nothing like the kiss she had fantasised about over the weekend. But before she could make it longer so she could try to arouse him, perhaps distract him enough to release her, he had pulled away.

'Yep, just like I imagined it would be. Shit,' he said and sounded so truly disgusted it was hard for Nicole not to feel hurt despite her current predicament.

'So, do you have a girlfriend then?' Nicole tried another tactic.

'Why are you so interested? Are you just gutted things didn't work out for you and Gram in the end? Did someone manage to get in the way of that?'

'What the fuck do you know about my life?' she growled.

'Showing some spirit now, girl.' Oli grabbed the back of her hair and shoved her head forwards, so it was pressed against the fence.

'What do you suppose his last thoughts were before he threw himself off here, hmm? Do you suppose he thought about you, about me, about his unborn daughter?' Oli's voice was getting louder, and his grip was getting tighter, Nicole could feel the burn from the fence on her forehead but she stayed still; she didn't want to rile him up, or make any sudden movements which could send them both off the edge.

'Oh my God, what is that woman doing?'

A voice came from the left of Oli and Nicole. Oli suddenly released the grip on Nicole's hair and they both looked up. Two women with dogs were looking out over the cliff, staring at something. They both followed their gaze, and there was Paisley. Dressed in scruffy tracksuit bottoms and a T-shirt, hair flying free in the wind. She had climbed over the fence about twenty feet away from them and was balancing on the rocks.

68

MARGO

'Pete?' Margo called tentatively as they stepped inside the house.

'Up here!' Audrey and Margo climbed the stairs, following the voice of Margo's brother. 'I'm in here. He locked me in.'

The voice was coming from a room further along the corridor. The women paused before Audrey opened it with the key that was still in the door. When the door swung wide, Pete strode out, looking dishevelled and rubbing his hands through his hair over and over.

'I don't even know what happened. But he had a knife, it was on her neck, Nicole's, and he told me to get in here or he would slit her throat. I fucking knew he was a no-gooder! I saw it in his eyes yesterday when all you lot were drunk. I had a few sips, I haven't drunk for a decade, have I? And then I took this turning by mistake, thinking there was a road that would take me along the seafront, bit of scenery on the way home, you know, and I saw them in the bedroom window. He was hurting her, pushing her around, and she was crying. I knocked on the door, and next thing, I find myself trapped in here.'

'So they must be at the beach? Come on!' Margo ran back down the stairs, followed by Audrey and Pete.

'Listen, thanks for trying to save our Nicole. I'm sorry I turfed you out this morning and was rude to you.' Margo heard Audrey saying to Pete as they made it through the front door and took the path to the cliffs.

'Ah, don't worry – I've been treated worse.'

They continued a sort of breathless chit-chat whilst Margo marched ahead, her mind focused on what they needed to do. They reached the cliff path and Margo pointed up. 'We need to be up there,' she pointed to the cliff. She looked at Audrey and Pete. 'And someone should call the police.'

'Christ, yes.' Audrey pulled out her phone and did the honours. A few dramatic minutes later, as Audrey got off the phone, she said, 'I finally got to use my What3words. I never thought I would see the day—'

'There they are!' Margo shouted breathlessly after the steep uphill climb.

'Shit!' Audrey said and began running. Pete did too and within a few seconds they were all metres away from Oli and Nicole. But now they could see there was a small crowd of about five or six people forming. But they weren't looking at Oli and Nicole. Margo looked over the fence to the dangerous rocks that were the balcony to a sheer drop to more rocks below. And on them stood Paisley.

Audrey turned and grabbed the other two by their arms, so they were in some sort of half rugby huddle. 'We get Nicole away from that mad man first. Pete, you grab him from behind, drag him back and I'll pull Nicole away. Then we'll worry about madam.'

Pete nodded. He was clearly ready and raring to go, keen to help out and was behind Oli in a second. He yanked him back and as he did, Nicole fell backwards.

'Get the hell away from her! The police are on their way. You're not going anywhere but straight to prison,' Audrey said.

'And let me tell you, sunshine,' Pete said into Oli's ear in a voice that sounded much more cockney than Margo had ever heard him, 'a pretty boy like you won't last five minutes in th—'

But before Pete could finish, Oli was already off and running. They didn't give chase though because they had Nicole and Paisley to think about.

'You'd better run, pretty boy!' Pete shouted after him.

Some of the crowd turned to look at the commotion behind.

'We've called the police,' one woman called in a posh accent. 'Do any of you people know this young lady?'

Audrey had her arms around Nicole. They all slowly walked to the spot where Paisley was teetering on the edge.

'Yes,' Audrey said. 'We all know her.'

69

PAISLEY

The edge looked so pretty from where Paisley stood; the crevices in the rocks looked like flowers in bloom. It would be so quick; it would all be over in a flash. There was nothing left for her now: no partner, no financial stability. No baby. But there had been. Just for a few days.

It was so peaceful up here. Paisley began to think back over the last six weeks, how it had all been such a terrible mistake.

'Hey,' a voice behind her. 'Remember me? I was that annoying prick at dinner last night.'

Paisley turned her head slightly and saw Pete standing on the other side of the fence.

'Why are you here?' Paisley said in a monotone voice.

'Well, that's the funny thing. It's a long story and quite an interesting one, I can tell it you if you have time?'

Paisley didn't say anything. She wasn't interested in why Pete was or wasn't here. She didn't want to speak to anyone.

'I know how you're feeling,' Pete said.

Paisley snorted.

'I do, Paisley, I've been where you are now. Not this exact cliff, but something similar. I have had feelings exactly like yours. I thought my world was over, not worth living. But I came through it, and I am trying to make a difference. You see, there is hope for you, Paisley. You are loved and liked and needed on this earth, and if you come over this side of the fence, we can have a chat about some of the ways I and so many other people can help you.'

Paisley stood still. The prospect of jumping was inching away from the forefront of her mind. She had been so focused and now Pete was throwing her off course. It had been the only thing she could think of today, but not the first time she had thought about doing this. There had been plenty of other moments when things weren't going quite right and she thought there would be no more chances for someone like her. Too many mistakes, too many bad choices. No matter how hard she tried, she always seemed to come back to this point.

'So what do you say? I saw a nice café on the way here yesterday, just a few streets away. We could go and check that out. I fancy a hot chocolate with marshmallows – I bet that's just the sort of thing they do.'

Chocolate, Paisley thought. She had barely touched the food last night and she felt her stomach rumble. Her body was aching for nourishment; it was trying to live. To fall off this cliff now would be a sorry end to an already sorry tale. What if Pete was right? What if he had overcome things and she could too? She shuddered as the cold began to penetrate through her thin sweater.

'I can give you my coat. I'm feeling pretty warm myself, but I reckon you could do with it – it looks chilly up there.'

Paisley turned and looked at him and her eyes pooled with tears. She didn't know this man, but it felt like the kindest thing anyone had said to her for a long time. That was all she wanted, was for someone to offer her their coat, put an arm around her, check she was okay. She wasn't desperate for a man, although to have a partner would be nice, she just wanted to feel a connection. People came and went all day at The Studio, but she rarely felt as though she had any meaningful exchanges. People were settling down and getting married and having children. Where did she fit in with all of this? she wondered.

She heard the sound of police sirens in the distance.

Paisley turned and took one careful step towards the fence. Pete was there, his body stretched far across the fence so both hands were held out to her. She put one hand out, felt it grabbed by his and then the other.

70

AUDREY

'Is your brother some sort of suicide-negotiation expert?' Audrey said to Margo as they watched him help Paisley over the fence and then place his coat around her.

'We'll be in the café if the police need us,' he called to Margo as they passed them.

'What the actual?' Audrey said. 'I wasn't convinced, you know, when he showed up yesterday but he has turned out to be quite the hero. You should tell him that's the line of work he should be going into, not the fraud business.'

Margo tried an attempt at a laugh, but it sounded wrong under the circumstances.

Nicole was sitting on the bench opposite the bunch of dead flowers. Audrey and Margo went over and joined her.

'Quite the weekend. Not what we had in mind at all.' Audrey put an arm around her friend.

'Nicole, I need to tell you what I know about what happened, at the party,' Margo said.

Nicole looked up at Margo.

'You know I always thought I could trust you the most out of everyone,' Nicole said, and Margo looked as if she might cry. 'It's not your fault, Margo. I know you saw what happened. I don't blame you, it's a hard thing to have to tell me.'

'Wait, what, you know?' Margo ran her hands through her hair.

'I know. I was there. I saw it all happen.'

71

THE PARTY

The Uber pulled up at The Studio and Nicole left the driver with strict instructions not to drive away. She stumbled back up the stairs, the effort of doing so leaving her light-headed. She opened the door to the foyer and the sound of the party hit her; it was still in full flow, but she didn't care. She had asked Margo to sort it and she knew she could trust her. She had always been able to trust Margo.

She bobbed her way along to her office keeping her head down, not wanting to engage anyone in conversation. She just wanted to grab her key and go home to sleep, to forget about how the business was failing, how her boyfriend was slowly slipping away from her, slowly giving up on them. On her.

She pushed her key into her office door, the only door that she had kept locked this evening, and fell into her soft spinning chair, another expensive investment because Nicole had envisaged herself spending hours in this room, having meetings, processing endless paperwork and admin and executing marketing strategies. But in the last year, the room had barely been used. Nicole would only ever really come here to escape the madness of The Studio, or to balance herself out after recording *Laying It Bare*, often with tears pooling in her eyes, needing to have a small cry in order to release the pent-up stress and tension, the thoughts of her past mistakes that haunted her daily and followed her around no matter what.

Nicole's office was where the security system had been installed. It ran all day and night overseeing the front entrance, the foyer, the three main corridors and every one of the rooms on the floor.

Nicole picked up her set of house keys from where she had left them on the desk and went to leave. As she did so, she glanced at the monitor on the wall that showed twenty-one little squares of pixelated live feeds, a few with a lot of action, others with barely anything happening. And it was one of those images that Nicole was drawn to and made her stop in her tracks. There was so much going on in the foyer reception and the room she had assigned to karaoke but there was one video playing that had caught her attention. It was showing her the third corridor, the one that led to some of the less-used rooms, and in that live stream, she could see Margo. Margo was standing on her tiptoes and peering through the glass pane at the top of the door. She then dropped to her heels, put her hand over her mouth and then leant in again to look into the room. Nicole swung back around and slid back into the chair at her desk. She nudged her desktop to life and clicked into the security system, navigating to the room where Margo was standing outside and clicked into it. She expanded the image so it filled the whole page and there she saw, in the informal staff room, Gram and Paisley. And then, for the next three minutes, she witnessed the entire sordid act.

72

THE PARTY

Margo peered through the gap in the pane of the door. The room was illuminated by a small amount of light. It looked to be the screen from a phone which was lighting up the face of Paisley, who was crouching over a man who was laid flat out on the sofa. His trousers were around his ankles and oh, Margo gasped, as she finally realised what was going on. Paisley's hand was grasping the erect penis of... She looked up towards the man's face, which was barely visible in the low light that was coming from Paisley's phone. Was she recording this? Why was her phone lit up?

When it finally hit her that the man lying almost comatose yet happily accepting this act from his wife's employee was Gram, she almost stumbled backwards, overcome with fear and dread for what she was going to do with this information. Of course, she would have to speak out, tell Nicole. Find her now. She rested her weight on her heels for a second, then she was back on her toes peering through. Something was happening, something she had never witnessed before in her life in any capacity. But she was unable to move or breathe as she watched and took it all in, and

knew that what she was seeing was going to affect the lives of so
many people.

73

THE PARTY

Paisley held Gram's erect penis and watched as he reached climax, still partially unconscious, still unaware of what was going on, and who was actually in the room with him. Without having to think very hard she grappled for the empty cup that was close to her foot and held it adjacent to Gram as she emptied him into it. Paisley dropped his manhood and looked into the cup with the light from the torch of the phone.

Wow, she thought. That was a lot. Someone had not been seeing much action for a while. Had Nicole been starving him of affection, not tending to his very basic needs? No wonder he had succumbed to her so quickly; he had no idea which way was up but he needed that release. Paisley knew she had seconds to spare and the first aid box that she had seen lying with its contents spread everywhere was just under the sofa. She emptied the contents onto the floor again and picked up the plastic syringe. She heard Gram make a small sound and he moved slightly on the sofa but whatever semi-conscious state he had just been in, he was now lightly snoring. She plunged the syringe into the cup, sucked up the contents and then lay on her back. She carefully inserted the syringe inside her as far in as she could get in and then pushed down the plunger. She could instantly feel the surge of life; she was sure she had managed to do it in enough time without all the sperm dying. She remained on the floor with her knees raised up still; she wanted to stay here for a while, let gravity and nature do its thing. She was sure she would be pregnant any minute now.

The faces of both women were sullen. Margo was apologising over and over.

'For the love of God, Margo, it's not your fault. You didn't do anything,' Audrey snapped.

'But I could have told Nicole.' Margo was frantic, unable to stand still.

'It wouldn't have made any difference. I always knew,' Nicole said. 'I was just trying to decide what to do with that information. I thought… I thought if I brought her here, I could confront her, have it out with her.'

'Is that why you organised this?' Audrey asked. 'It didn't seem like your bag, the whole brainstorming, marketing thing.'

Nicole was shaking, the adrenaline was wearing off. 'It's not. Let's face it, I'm pretty rubbish at running a business.'

'You occasionally say the wrong things,' Audrey sniped, clearly referring to the slut comment.

'Yeah well, that was obviously aimed at Paisley. It just sort of slipped out. I knew Paisley would never know it was a direct insult to her, but I also didn't think far ahead enough to the backlash it might cause. And did cause.' Nicole dropped her head.

Audrey placed a hand on her friend's leg. 'It doesn't matter now. It was all too much for you, you just needed to ask for help. Gram and I, we... I helped him to find a way. He wants to invest, Nicole. He loves you so much, he wants to do whatever he can to help you.'

Audrey's phone rang and she pulled it out of her pocket. 'It's Gram,' she said. 'He's probably looking for you.'

Nicole took Audrey's phone and answered it.

'Hi.' Both women were quiet as they tried to listen to Gram on the other end. 'Okay,' Nicole said after a few seconds. 'We're just at the beach, we're coming back now. See you in ten.'

Nicole handed the phone back to Audrey. 'I don't know about you, but I'm ready for a coffee.'

Gram was waiting at the front door when the Nicole, Audrey and Margo walked up the driveway. The walk back had been hard, but when Nicole saw Gram, she started to run. He started towards her, and then they were both wrapped in one another's arms. Gram was crying and whispering into her hair words about how he loved her, how he was sorry, how he didn't know, and more apologies.

Eventually, when they both pulled back and looked at one another, both red-eyed and tear-stained, Nicole spoke. 'I'm sorry, Gram. I've been— I don't know where I've been, but I've not been here for you. I've not been good enough. I want kids so much, but I'm scared,' Nicole cried. 'I'm scared I'll do it wrong, that something will go wrong because of what I did, because I already gave up my child.'

'Nicole, for Christ's sake.' He took Nicole's face in his hands.

'Listen to me, you were just a kid yourself, and that man, as much as you thought you loved him, he shouldn't have pursued you, he shouldn't have laid a finger on you. You can't keep carrying this guilt, okay? No girl is ready to be a mother at fifteen.' He pulled her into his chest and held her.

'It was a girl.'

'What?'

'The baby. She was a girl. The chef, Oli, who was here, he told me. He is Andrew Best's son. He drugged me last night. He was trying to get some sort of revenge on me.' Nicole broke down again and Gram took her in his arms. She knew there was so much that they needed to say to one another about the baby she had given up, her fear of never wanting children, the years of pushing Gram away, turning her focus to a business that was failing because she had tried to do it all alone. How she had known about Gram and Paisley but did nothing because she didn't think she had the right to when she had not been the girlfriend he had needed her to be. Nicole didn't know what category the act that Paisley performed would fall into; she hadn't really considered it a crime before, as she had been too focused on her own failings.

'Umm, guys,' Margo's soft voice came behind them. Nicole stretched around to look, still clinging to Gram as if she never wanted to let him go. 'I think there's someone here to see you.'

Margo was pointing down the drive as several things appeared to be happening at once. One, a police car had just pulled up at the end of the drive, and two, Claire Best was walking up the drive.

'Who's that?' Gram whispered.

'It's Andrew Best's widow,' Nicole hushed back at him. She released herself from his grip and stood up straight, ready to greet her guests. This was going to be a long morning.

'I'll go and make coffee.' Margo headed back into the house.

Gram inched back but took hold of Nicole's hand. Claire approached them with an uncomfortable look on her face.

'I'll be fine.' Nicole released herself from Gram's hand. 'Go and bring the police in the house, and help Margo make the coffee.'

Gram eyed Claire warily, but then he walked past her and down the drive towards the squad car. 'Hi there, officers,' Gram's voice rang out. 'We've had quite the morning.'

'Nicole,' Claire had stopped a few feet away. 'I can see you're busy here, but after last night, well you were obviously too drunk to be making any sense. I'm not sure what I told you went in.'

Claire was wrapped up in the yellow cagoule she had been spotted in a few times and looked cold.

'Would you like to come in?' Nicole gestured to The Beach House.

'No, I won't, thanks. I can see the police are here, so I guess that's about Oli.'

Nicole nodded.

'I tried to warn him off, but he wouldn't listen. I knew why he was here, but he insisted it was just work. But he had been here as a kid, so I knew he held a grudge.'

Nicole's brow furrowed.

'He was the one who did all the stuff back then: the dog mess, the cow pats, the letting down your car tyres. He did similar things to my house after Andrew died. It was all the angry emotions of a thirteen-year-old boy, but I didn't grass him up – it wasn't his fault. His mum had to send him away to London in the end. We were the bad ones in his eyes, the ones who took his dad away from him.'

'Me more so than you.' Nicole looked down at her feet, ashamed of her former self, even though she was just a child.

'I never blamed you, Nicole.' Claire's voice broke. 'You were a child. And Andrew wasn't a very well man.'

'He never hurt me, or forced me.'

'Well, I don't know, do I? You don't know, really. He shouldn't have been with you though. Surely you understand that now as an adult?'

Nicole heard Gram's words again and how they echoed what Claire was saying. But she had blamed herself. She had felt as though she was in control of the situation. Andrew Best was obsessed with her. But Andrew Best was a man and she had been a child. She knew all this, but why did it suddenly feel like a weight was being lifted? Like she felt there might be some redemption for what she had done, for the guilt she had cradled close to her chest, as though it were the very baby she had given up all those years ago. Then the horror slipped through, because even though she had been shielded and shaded from the media and helped to live a normal life, she didn't ever remember the two people she was closest to telling her what she had just heard from both Gram and Claire. She should have been told over and over again until it she was sick of hearing it, until someone looked at her and said, 'Do you understand?' and she was able to say yes.

She wasn't to blame for what Andrew did to her or to himself, but she did make the choice to give away her baby to a stranger. Nicole had shed a tear about it every day of her life. There wasn't a day that went by when she didn't relive the scene of that midwife leaving the room with her child, whom she now knew to be a daughter, wrapped in a blanket, never to be seen again.

Nicole tried to nod, but she felt as if the world around her was coming apart. She hadn't drunk anything in hours; she was weak and needed to sit down. As if he had sensed her fragility, Gram was there, his arm around her. 'I think you should come in now, Nic, get some rest. The police have some questions, obviously.'

Claire nodded at them both, and Nicole and Gram turned to walk into the house.

'There's just one more thing,' Claire called after her. They both stopped and looked back at Claire.

'She came here this weekend, she has been in contact with me for a while now. Your daughter. If you want to see her. She wants to see you.'

75

ONE MONTH LATER

Nicole twisted the ring on her finger. It was a nervous act. It would take some time to get used to wearing one on her second finger. Gram said, 'Don't think of it as an engagement ring – think of it as a significant-other ring or whatever,' but she was going to take some time to think about what she wanted from the relationship now. Were children now one hundred per cent out of the question? She wasn't sure. Nicole supposed that was a good thing, as she had spent eighteen years telling herself and then Gram that she would never be a mother. Gram said he would be happy to foster or adopt, and Nicole had so many feelings and emotions to deal with that she needed a little time to get her head around the fact that a very special person was about to come into both of their lives.

It was a quiet morning in the coffee shop around the corner from their house. Both of their cups were empty in front of them. She wasn't late; they had been early, like two very excited teenagers.

'Are you okay?' Gram asked and grabbed her hand.

'I think so,' Nicole said. 'No, I feel sick. What if she doesn't like me? What if we're too boring for her?'

'Stop,' Gram said. 'Let's just take each day at a time.'

Nicole's head was full of *what-if*s and *but*s but before she had a chance to speak again, the door to the café now opened, and there in the doorway was the most beautiful young lady Nicole had ever set eyes upon.

'Oh my God,' Nicole whispered. She was, Nicole thought, even more amazing in real life, despite Nicole spending hours poring over photo after photo of Jess over the last few weeks. Nicole felt herself choke up as she stood up, but Gram was there by her side. She took a step forward towards the girl, her daughter, and Jess's eyes lit up, and then after eighteen years, Nicole could finally break the video that had been playing over and over in her head. The midwife walking away and her never seeing her daughter again would now be replaced with this moment, of her taking her baby in her arms again and holding on to her so very tightly.

ACKNOWLEDGMENTS

It's been over a year since I have had a thriller out in the world, so I am excited to be back and sharing this story with you all. Thanks to the readers and everyone who has supported my journey so far. Thanks for your patience!

Thank you to Boldwood. To Amanda and Nia for your patience and understanding and kind words of support always.

I love working with my editor Emily Ruston, she is such a lovely human and always on the same page as me, literally and metaphorically.

I moved to the Highlands during the editing process of this book and I have been so inspired by the landscape. I am now looking forward to an exciting chapter in my life with my husband, kids and Missy the dog. I can feel a few ideas brewing already. Watch this space for a highland based psychological thriller soon.

BOOK CLUB QUESTIONS

1. A house can often be seen as a supporting character in a book. Did you feel The Beach House was a character with all the secrets it was holding on to? What other books can you recall where the house is very central to the story?
2. Who was your favourite character out of the four women and why?
3. What was your reaction to the way Paisley became pregnant? Was this what you were expecting? How does it compare to a man taking advantage of a woman?
4. Can you understand why Nicole was attracted to an older man as a teenager based on her own childhood experiences and why she blamed herself for the death of Andrew?
5. Did The Studio seem like a real place to you? Could you imagine it as a functioning work environment?
6. Why was it important for Audrey to hold on to her role at The Studio, even though she'd already had such a long and successful career in the modelling world?

7. Did Margo's neurodiversity seem apparent, and do you think these are traits we recognise and accept the more we see them?

8. It is a difficult situation when one person in a couple wants a baby and the other doesn't. How does a man wanting children and a woman not, compare or contrast with a woman wanting a baby and the man not wanting them?

ABOUT THE AUTHOR

Nina Manning studied psychology and was a restaurant-owner and private chef (including to members of the royal family). She is the founder and co-host of Sniffing The Pages, a book review podcast.

Sign up to Nina Manning's mailing list here for news, competitions and updates on future books.

Visit Nina's website: https://www.ninamanningauthor.com/

Follow Nina on social media:

 twitter.com/ninamanning78

instagram.com/ninamanning_author

facebook.com/ninamanningauthor1

bookbub.com/authors/nina-manning

ALSO BY NINA MANNING

Psychological Thrillers

The Daughter In Law

The Guilty Wife

The House Mate

The Bridesmaid

Queen Bee

The Waitress

The Beach House

Women's Fiction

The 3am Shattered Mums' Club

The 6pm Frazzled Mums' Club

THE

Murder

LIST

**THE MURDER LIST IS A NEWSLETTER
DEDICATED TO SPINE-CHILLING FICTION
AND GRIPPING PAGE-TURNERS!**

**SIGN UP TO MAKE SURE YOU'RE ON OUR
HIT LIST FOR EXCLUSIVE DEALS, AUTHOR
CONTENT, AND COMPETITIONS.**

SIGN UP TO OUR NEWSLETTER

BIT.LY/THEMURDERLISTNEWS

Boldwood

Find out more at
www.boldwoodbooks.com

**Follow us
#BoldBookClub**

https://bit.ly/BoldwoodBNewsletter

Printed in Great Britain
by Amazon